Before Him Comes Me

Alexandria Sure

Before Him Comes Me

Alexandria Sure

ISBN 978-0692352366

To my mother,
For all the love and support, and for the blue.

Every day, I walk the walk
One step
Two step
Forward momentum
My world in black and white
Then today,
You.
An energy shift
Your color runs through me
My world vibrates
My world glows
You move away
Taking your color
My world in black and white
ONE STEP … STUMBLE.

CHAPTER 1

Zara opens her eyes, her bedroom already filled with morning sunlight. Closing her eyes, she lays perfectly still taking inventory of her body, her feelings and her overall state of mind. Turning eighteen has not made Zara feel any different, yet today will be the first day of her new life.

Looking up at Audrey Hepburn in her *My Fair Lady* poster, Zara takes a deep breath and begins to memorize her belongings that she will never see again. Zara shifts her gaze to the two framed pictures on the nightstand. The first is a picture of her and her best friend Sloane from the first time they went horseback riding. Both of them got the giggles so badly that Sloane's mother threatened to bring them home if they didn't pay attention to the lesson.

The second picture, taken eight years ago on Zara's tenth birthday, is of Fredrik giving Zara a bouquet of daisies. Ever since then, he has given her daisies on her birthday and they have become her favorite flower. This neither pleases nor displeases their father; therefore it continues to occur.

Zara begins to take mental pictures of each object surrounding the frames. The mini stuffed PINK dog from Victoria's Secret was something she and Sloane each had to have. Convincing both mothers of the need for the PINK dogs was no easy task and the effort alone required the prominent display of their victory. This neither pleases nor displeases her father; therefore it continues to occur.

Next she notices a pink and green polka dotted hair tie. There is nothing special about it, but it was the first of many she and Sloane made over the summer. Their mothers had been looking through craft idea cards in a store when they found one for making easy hair ties. They had spent the longest time picking out fabric for their new project. Zara picks up the hair tie and slips it around her wrist like a rubber band.

Funny... the things I'll miss.

On the back of Zara's nightstand is a bottle of cucumber melon lotion that she won in a drawing at the mall. Never believing for a second that she would win, Zara filled out the entry form. Sloane had cautioned, "The Community exists on the fringe of society, Zara. The less direct interaction that we have with outsiders, the better."

Zara giggles recalling their mixed surprise when she won.

Of course I would win.

Picking up the lotion and popping the top open, Zara takes a big whiff. She quickly closes it and places it back in its home on the nightstand. A chill travels the length of her back as the details of the only night she wore the lotion comes into focus. Zara's father promptly sent her back to shower off the odor he found offensive and she was forced to listen to a lecture on how it is up to her Dom to pick the scents that please him. Until the time comes for Zara to be handed over to her Dom, there would be no scents worn in this house that were disagreeable to her father. Vanilla... for her father, it is vanilla on her mother and because Zara's father does not like the smell of cucumber melon, it is not used in his home.

Propping herself up against the headboard, two items stand out. A massive bouquet of daisies from Fredrik sits on her dresser and an equally massive wedding dress for the ceremony is hung on her closet door. She smiles at the flowers. He had given them to her a day early so she could enjoy them one last full day. Zara aches at the reality of not seeing Fredrik or getting her birthday daisies after today.

Concentrating on her breathing to keep the tears from falling, Zara looks up at the ceiling and takes a deep breath. When she regains control, she looks once more at her lovely flowers sitting on a dresser in a bedroom in a house with a family that she will say goodbye to forever, for she follows traditions that go back generation upon generation. Very soon Zara will walk out the door and that will be that.

While most brides pack suitcases of new clothes and take old belongings into their new life, there will be no packing for Zara. It is customary for the father to transfer his daughter into her new life with nothing from her old life. Once she is in the care of her Dom, her family steps away and the Dom is responsible for every aspect of his new submissive's wellbeing. This includes integrating her into the Dom's family at every level.

The wedding dress hanging in the corner demands Zara embrace the fact that today is her wedding day. Glancing back at the daisies, she wipes the single tear that escapes down her cheek. There will be no daisies for Zara at her wedding. The dress is not of her choosing. The ceremony will be the beginning of a life of no voice and no opinion. The dress is exquisite and the ceremony will be perfect. Zara's father will be pleased.

Zara begins to move through her normal morning routine, knowing there is nothing normal about this particular morning. Her damp chestnut hair feels healthy and full after its recent cut. Pausing to look at herself in the mirror after her shower, the first signs of cracks in her well-trained armor begin to appear. Her green eyes are a tad puffy and have a hint of red. Raising her hand to her bare neck, she realizes it is only a matter of hours before there is a collar. And a Dom attached to it.

Zara, no thinking about it yet. It is what it is!

Zara walks into her bedroom, sits on the corner of her bed and begins to focus. Using a technique her mother taught her to get through stressful moments like this one, she closes her eyes, inhales deeply… holds her breath… and slowly exhales. So as not to give any indication that the focus is on anything but the here and now, she concentrates straight ahead on a spot on the wall. As she has been trained, deep concentration shifts her away from the overwhelming feelings that are trying to take hold of her.

Zara chooses a memory of riding her horse, Gentlemen, crossing the field at a full gallop, with no one else around… just the two of them. She remembers the feeling of control as she sits deeper in the saddle, her legs wrapped tight around him, pushing him just a bit faster. The air whips through her hair as they cross the open field. The sun beats down making the colors of the sky and field more vivid. It is a feeling of complete, unadulterated freedom.

Three swift, hard knocks on the door jar Zara back to the present.

"Come on in, Fredrik."

"Ready!" Fredrik throws the door open with a loud clap. "I am taking you to a few of your favorite places to say a final farewell. NOT THE MALL, so do not even ask. We have two hours on our own if we hurry. Mother and the other ladies are going to transport the dress and other wedding stuff for you. But, Zara... this is it."

Standing slowly, Zara walks around the room that she has lived in for the last eighteen years. It is a room that is down the hallway from the brother that she adores. She touches her dresser and runs her hand over the footboard. It is a relatively simple room, but she loves it. Standing in front of her Monet print, she smiles and then glances at the Hepburn poster.

Stepping over to the chair by the window, she picks up her current read, *Little Women*, and removes the bookmark. Zara rests it on top of the book and puts the book on the chair. While Fredrik patiently waits, Zara moves the curtain and takes in what a lovely sunny day her last birthday in Chattanooga is turning out to be.

"I guess this is it," Zara whispers as she walks towards the door. Fredrik steps out of the room to allow his sister one final moment alone with her thoughts. Reaching back in, Zara grabs the cucumber melon lotion and squirts one last pea-size amount into the palm of her hand and replaces the bottle. Then she closes the door of her bedroom and her childhood.

Zara walks quickly past Fredrik and out of the house she can no longer claim as "hers" to Fredrik's car. Once inside, she rubs the lotion into her hands with a small kernel of satisfaction. Leaning back against the seat, all that is left for Zara to do in this moment is breathe, so she does. Deeply.

After a moment, the driver side door opens and Fredrik slides in. He hands her the travel mug she has used since she began drinking coffee.

"Where are we off to?" Fredrik asks in a surprisingly cheerful voice. Without direction from his sister, he starts the car and begins to drive.

Zara takes a sip of her mother's blended coffee and stares silently out the window. The taste of home is all she can think of as she tries to stomach another sip. The coffee is perfect, but the vast memories of what she is leaving behind swirl around inside the mug. She pops the top closed and puts it in the drink holder between them.

After a short drive, Frederik pulls the car into a familiar

wooded area and turns off the engine. They both open their doors at the same time and start walking in silence up a trail that is barely visible. Zara takes off at a slow jog with her brother following behind, yelling at her.

"ZARA FAITH, if you fall and hurt yourself, we will both be dead! You know that. Father will kill me first and make you watch." His last statement stops Zara in her tracks.

Fredrik runs into the back of his sister. "Zara!"

They walk the last few yards slowly and cautiously in silence. At the clearing, Zara rushes to the creek's edge to listen to the sounds of the water rushing by. Sitting upon a boulder, she stares into the churning bubbles. Fredrik sits on the ground next to her and offers her a handful of smooth stones to toss in.

With a light toss, the stones hit the water in a series of lyrical plops. Zara brushes her hand off on her jeans. Not accustomed to wearing anything but shorts or shirts in the southern summer heat, she wanted to wear her favorite jeans on her last day in her home and had dug them out days ago in preparation.

"Hello?" Zara hears Fredrik say as if repeating himself. "Did you hear anything I just said?"

Zara shakes her head and shrugs.

"I asked if you remember the stories Mother used to tell us about Aunt Laura. Do you ever think about that?"

Fredrik realizes Zara is not going to answer so he gets up to gather more stones. "I wonder why she stopped telling us about Aunt Laura. Those were great stories."

Zara pulls her knees up to her chest and wraps her arms around them, making herself as small as possible. She lays her cheek on her knee. Taking a deep breath and speaking very slowly to control her words, Zara explains to her younger brother, "After one of your doctor visits, I made a comment that I wanted to be a doctor."

"What?"

Zara turns and looks at Fredrik. "Mother stopped telling us stories about Aunt Laura because she broke from the Community. She left because she wanted a different life. She secretly took college entrance exams and scored high enough for scholarships. Then one night, she snuck out to start a new life for herself. She got her education and now she has a career doing who knows what or where.

"As soon as I was old enough to connect the dots, Mother sat me down to explain that my future was already decided for me. I was not going to become a doctor. I was not going to get an education. And I was definitely not going to sneak out in the middle of the night."

Zara turns her head back toward the creek when she finishes speaking.

Fredrik is quiet for a moment. He walks closer and kneels next to her. "Zara, do you wish it was different?"

"It is not different, Fredrik. Not for me. I have known for years that this day was coming. It does not make it any easier. Thank you for bringing me here. This was the perfect place to bring me, my temporary escape. The one place on earth where I can forget who I have to be and can just be. Would you do something for me?"

"I will try. You know that."

"Would you just talk… about anything? I will miss the sound of your voice and I want to lock it in my memory before we have to go." Zara forces the words out around the large lump in her throat.

"WOW! Am I on the spot or what? Okay! This is my last opportunity to tell you how much I am in awe of you. You are the strongest person I know. The training that you have had to endure to get you ready for today… learning different positions, serving lessons, mental lessons to deal with whatever situation you have to deal with. I know that I only know portions of what your training entailed because Father did his best to see that I stayed as far away from that as possible.

"But mostly I am sorry that you had to grow up thinking that your opinions and thoughts were not valid or even considered," Fredrik exclaims firmly as he kicks at something on the ground in front of him.

Zara jumps off the rock and throws her arms around her brother. He wraps his arms around her waist and takes two steps back to prevent them from toppling over into the creek together.

"You have always listened to me, Fredrik. You made me feel heard. All the time we spent talking in my room will be memories that I will keep with me forever."

Releasing her brother, Zara is surprised to see his eyes are filled with tears.

"Sorry, I know we are not the most affectionate family, but..."
Fredrik pulls Zara into another bear hug. He whispers into her hair,
"I think you would make a great doctor."

"That was just a child's comment. I wanted to be a policeman,
banker and jockey that same year. Dreaming is dangerous for the
daughters of King Council members. I stopped a while ago."

After a moment, he releases her and the siblings stand at the
edge of the creek in silence. It is Fredrik who bends down and
picks up a stone to throw in the creek with a loud plop.

"I remember when we were younger, you would take care of
me for hours. You are only two years older... just a kid yourself.
You never seemed to mind that I followed you everywhere. You
have been the best sister. I am going to miss you like crazy."

Fredrik turns and walks down the path toward the car. Slowly
Zara scans the area creating more mental pictures of a place she
will never visit again. She notices the shade of the green leaves on
the tall skinny tree growing in from the hills, the clarity and level
of the water. Closing her eyes, Zara listens to the sounds the water
makes, and the sound of each step on the gravel underfoot as she
begins to back away from her favorite spot for the last time.

As they walk back to the car, Zara tells Frederik, "Thank you
for today... I will never forget it. Promise."

Fredrik nods somberly and starts the car.

The drive to the Center is short and silent. As they arrive at the
front door, Zara's mother darts out of the building and up to the
car. "You are ten minutes late! We have a schedule to keep.
Fredrik, please take care of what I have asked you to. Zara,
move... move!"

"Yes, Mother," Fredrik responds respectfully.

Zara follows one step behind her mother into the Center. The
pair walks up the steps and head directly to the Peach Suite. The
mothers traditionally use this suite to prepare their daughters for
the Circle Ceremony. Front and center, the wedding dress, with its
huge princess skirt and layers upon layers of tulle, is the first thing
Zara sees as she enters the suite.

The top layer, covered in carefully spaced crystals, adds an
extra element to capture the light with every step. The corset
bodice is made to fit so tightly that Zara takes a deep breath just
looking at it. Once the dress is on, deep breaths will be out of the

question.

Zara notices a shoebox on the chair next to the dress and slowly walks over. She reaches to pick it up.

"ZARA FAITH!" Zara's mother shrieks.

Startled, she places the shoebox back on the chair and rushes to her mother's side.

"We are in a hurry. Please sit!"

Zara sits immediately and several women descend on her in a flurry to make her Circle Ceremony ready.

Zara holds perfectly still in every position she is placed in as she is processed for her pending walk down the aisle. As the last button is secured on her dress, her mother circles around her to get a full visual. Instructed to get into her presentation position, Zara lowers to her knees, careful to not catch any portion of her dress. Sitting back on her heels, she rests her hands in her lap, one crossed over the other. The ladies apply the final layer of hairspray and insert the last of the hairpins before leaving Zara and her mother alone in the suite.

Back on her feet, Zara struggles to regulate her breathing within the confines of the dress. She gazes into a full-length mirror, alone with her thoughts. A few hours ago, she woke up in her own bed and now she has been prepared for a short walk that will change her life forever.

Her mother steps into the reflection behind her. "You look lovely, Zara Faith. I am very proud of you today. You have taken everything I have taught you and made it your own. You are ready for whatever is placed in front of you."

"Thank you, Mother," Zara replies in a hushed whisper.

There is a knock at the door as mother and daughter look at each other one last time. Zara's gaze returns to her own eyes in the mirror. She squares her shoulders and takes as deep a shallow breath as she can. Her mother turns and takes a couple of steps toward the door leading out of the suite.

"Zara Faith, there is one thing I want you to know before your ceremony. You may not understand, but I love and cherish your father with all of my heart. It will be difficult today. The traditions work. Trust in them."

Harder knocks at the door end the mother-daughter moment. Zara reaches the door first, but knows not to open it. Stepping aside, she waits as her mother opens it and lowers her gaze. Zara's father stands on the other side waiting to gather his daughter for the ceremony.

"It is time!"

CHAPTER 2

The march to the Center Circle is long, each step taking Zara closer to her unknown future. The weight of the dress presses upon her like a reminder that her life is not her own and in a very short time, that ownership will be given to a man who was chosen not just by her father, but by the council of the Community. Once this man, this stranger, enters the Circle and places the collar around Zara's neck, he will become not only her Dom, but her husband as well.

One step behind her father, Zara carefully places one foot in front of the other. She passes children dressed in their very best, always in training and sitting still under the watchful eyes of her Community. Their eyes are lowered to the white carpet laid specifically for tonight's ceremony, but Zara knows from experience that quick peeks are being sneaked as she strides by.

Zara catches a glimpse of Sloane in a pale blue dress sitting with all of the other single females of the Community. Zara catches her wink and sees her cross her fingers in a silent signal of solidarity.

Sloane and Zara had talked about this day for months. With Sloane's ceremony only four months after Zara's, it had been a hot topic. While both were nervous, Sloane had an air of excitement when she had talked about her life-changing event while Zara had rued her loss of freedom. Only Sloane knows Zara would rather be walking down a different path tonight and she would always keep that secret safe.

Once inside the center of the ceremonial Circle, Zara's father turns and places a kiss on each of her cheeks. He does not see the tears being held at bay. Years of training allow Zara to maintain her line of vision straight down to the floor in front of her.

He gives the command to take her presentation position. Zara is well-versed in the steps of the Circle Ceremony. Her position as daughter of a King Council member has required her attendance at all ceremonies since the age of five.

Her mother rushes to adjust the gown. There is nothing left to do but wait for the inevitable. Zara concentrates on breathing. Years of training have prepared her to maintain her position motionless for as long as necessary.

In outsiders' weddings, the attention is on the bride, but in the Circle Ceremony, it is squarely placed on the Dom and his family. The Dom and his family are the unknown in the ceremony. While the submissive and her family are from the local Community, the distance the Dom travels can vary from across the state to across the country.

Sloane had attempted to figure out the criteria once. She quizzed Fredrik when he returned from one of his 'Pre-Dom' retreats, as Sloane liked to refer to them. All he would say is, it depended on the strength of the King Council network in the region and the reputation of the candidate's family.

A rustling in the hall alerts Zara to the entrance of her future family. The whispers amongst the guests follow him as he walks down the white carpet.

Exploring the surroundings within her peripheral vision, Zara is careful not to stir from her statuesque position. Her eyes lift to the table where the collar rests, waiting to be placed around her neck.

The collar is clasped. Zara sees no key. Her heart skips a beat.

Something is wrong.

Her eyes frantically scan the table. Her mother clears her throat and she knows she has been caught in the slightest change in orientation.

Breathe. Just breathe.

Her mind is racing.

Why is the collar locked? Where is the key? Think.

In all the past ceremonies Zara had attended, the collar lay open. The open collar is the symbol of the Council's approval of the match between the first-born daughter of a Council member and the son of a Council member from a different sect. The key to the collar is the symbol of ownership for the first-born's daughter by her Dom. The history of this ceremony requires the collar to be unlocked, the key ready to be presented to the Dom.

When one's life has been filled with inevitability, processing surprises becomes difficult. Zara's mind sifts through all of the ceremonies that she has attended, fast-forwarding to the point when the open collar is picked up and placed around the "birthday girl's" neck. In every memory, the collar is lying open before it is picked up.

Zara's breathing becomes labored. All thoughts of the collar evaporate as someone steps into the center of the circle.

Shoes.

What can be determined about a man, a Dom-to-be, by his polished, square-toed black shoes?

Nothing.

The dress restricts any attempts at taking a deep cleansing breath, so Zara tries employing a technique taught during years of training to settle her thoughts. The curiosity to sneak a peek at the man now standing next to her becomes an overwhelming challenge destroying her control.

The need to look at his face begins to vibrate through her entire body. Moving would bring her mother's throat clearing and a definite lecture the moment they are alone later at the celebration. Zara tries another deep breath in an attempt to settle. It doesn't work.

Discovering what he looks like will not change my future.

The hall quiets as the Master of Ceremonies steps into the circle. Zara's shoulders fall. This is her final moment of freedom.

A hand comes to rest on Zara's shoulder and a moment later she hears her mother suck in all of the oxygen in the hall. With all the strength she can summon, Zara keeps her eyes locked on the floor directly in front of her, ignoring the weight of the fingers pressing down on her.

"Please. Open it. Read it." The quiet plea in his voice mesmerizes her.

Wait! What am I supposed to be doing? This is not how I remember any of the other Ceremonies.

"Zara, please read the letter."

He lightly taps her shoulder. The envelope is at eye level and there is no mistaking what he wants. Slowly, she reaches for the envelope and brings it down to read without raising her eyes.

Dear Zara Faith Evans:

Congratulations on your admission to Michigan State University and welcome to the Spartan Family.

Confused, Zara rereads the first sentence of the letter.

Michigan State University? My name is clearly on the letter. But… how?

"I don't understand," she says in a whisper more to herself than to him or anyone around.

"Zara."

For the very first time, Zara raises her eyes to look at the man who is to become her inevitable future. Before she can stop herself, Zara gasps at seeing his face.

He is more attractive than expected with his large brown eyes, high round cheeks and strong square chin. There is a sense of warmth behind his eyes as Zara's eyes meet his. Even the sound of her mother's threatening throat clearing cannot break their eye contact.

"ZARA FAITH!"

There is no mistaking her Mother's harsh tone and her streak of disobedience is broken. Returning her gaze to the spot on the floor, Zara's hands tremble making the paper shake. She tries to take another deep breath. Gently the letter is removed from her hand, is refolded and slid out of sight.

The magnitude of Zara's disobedience has far exceeded a mild lecture at the celebration. She begins to feel lightheaded. The responsibility which her position demands within her family is clear. She closes her eyes and tucks her chin into proper submission.

"Mr. Evans, I would like to speak to your daughter privately for a few minutes. After this display, I am sure you will give me a bit of latitude."

Without hesitation, Zara's father takes a couple of steps back allowing the two strangers to speak privately.

The entire hall gasps in unison and Zara's eyes fly open wide to find her Dom-to-be kneeling in front of her. In a voice only Zara can hear, he begins to speak.

"I am not your Dom. I am not your husband. I have an offer for you. We can walk out of this Circle as a collared couple and begin our lives like both of our parents before us and their parents before them. Or, we can leave this Circle in a new way. I will be here every step of the way to take care of all your needs while you attend college.

"You can use this time to discover who you are and what you want. It is my sincere hope that four years from tonight you will again be waiting for me within the Center Circle, that at such time, you will be ready to complete the ceremony freely. Whether or not you are in the Circle waiting for me in four years will be your choice and only your choice. I know this is not as you were trained, but we have a very tight window to make this work. I need you to nod… if you wish for me to take you away to college."

Though too shocked to process everything that is happening, Zara understands this is the only way out of a life she has had no design in choosing for herself.

She nods.

Straightening to his full height, he extends his large hand and helps her to her feet. Zara is shaky and realizes again, she does not know what to expect. She finds her mother's eyes and stares into them attempting to convey love and her need to take this unexpected opportunity.

"Aubrey."

Zara's father ends the silent communication between them, the tone making it clear what is expected of her. Zara's mother's eyes drop to the ground directly in front of her and she slowly lowers herself into the kneeling position that her father's tone demands. There would be no point in hoping for more eye contact with her mother. She is no longer Zara's mother. She is now her father's slave.

Addressing Zara's father, the man at Zara's side says, "I would like for my mother to have five minutes with this submissive before we make this official. Protocols are important where I come from. I am sure you understand."

"Of course," her father replies. "I am confident that you will find Zara Faith's training satisfactory. We would be happy to give you five minutes to ensure you are getting the best possible submissive."

Thankful she had followed her instinct on not eating earlier, Zara swallows hard at being addressed as if she is livestock to be traded at auction. With his hand still clasping hers, he leads Zara out of the Circle, passing the collar that Zara had been prepared her entire life to wear. With her eyes still cast down, Zara passes her mother in her kneeling position with her arms crossed behind her back, her eyes affixed to the floor in front of her.

They quickly walk past everyone: the King Council members, Doms with their subs, Masters with their slaves and the section of unattached males and females that are whispering fiercely as they pass. Together, they are walking away from everyone and everything that Zara knows.

"Son?"

Pausing to address the soft-spoken query, a beautiful dress steps to join them and form a small circle of three. Zara never lifts her eyes to look at anyone's face.

"This is it. Do not stop until you are on the plane. Zara, this is a big decision. Are you positive about this?"

Zara gives the slightest nod and with that unspoken signal, everyone parts ways. Pulled to an exit at a near run, they reach the door to the outside of the building in record time. Zara notes how unusual it is not to have staff present to open the door for them at a formal event, that the abrupt change in schedule has altered the routine.

He reaches to open the door and releases her hand. The absence of his hand unsettles her just as his first contact only minutes earlier had. Not knowing what to do with her hand, Zara lifts the dress and steps through the opening he provides.

His hand finds the small of her back and rests there, his warmth seeping through the dress. Tingles shoot to every part of her body as he guides her towards a limo parked just a few feet from the door.

An older gentlemen steps out of the driver's side and quickly opens the back door. With a friendly smile, they work together to tuck all the layers of the dress into the car. Once inside, the two men stand outside the car and speak together briefly.

Before Zara's mind gets an opportunity to start processing the events inside the building, he climbs onto the seat beside her, lifting the wayward layers of the dress to avoid sitting on them. Without fanfare, the car pulls away from the curb. The man beside her takes out a cellphone and makes a call.

"Yes. Fine. Hopefully, the beach, but if not, in town. No. No. I understand. Peter has already notified them. There won't be any delays. I will. Okay. Okay."

Hanging up, he sighs. His head rests against the back of the seat as he tucks the phone back into his jacket pocket. Not knowing where they are going or what tomorrow will bring, Zara sits silently waiting to be addressed. It is how she watched her mother live her life and how she had been prepared to live her own as well.

The boning in the dress is making breathing difficult at her angle. The night's plan had not included a car ride. The dress was only meant to be worn for the Circle Ceremony. Once the collar was secured and the vows exchanged, Zara would have walked through the Dom's door having removed all the clothing of her past life, including her wedding dress. Zara would have been redressed in clothing of his choosing and assisted by his mother, then finally, she would have exited out of the ceremony hall through his door.

"Zara, it's going to be okay."

Startled, Zara jumps when his words break the silence. She nods and keeps her face schooled with the same half smile that she has worn since arriving at the Center several hours ago.

When the car stops, Zara carefully surveys her surroundings. Surprised to find they are parked a few feet away from a plane, she stiffens. The car door opens from the outside and the man sitting next to her exits. Once out of the car, he extends his hand back in to assist Zara and her dress out. Her exit is far less graceful.

A light mist makes the air feel cooler and she trembles, eyes still on the ground in front of her. She sees him remove his suit coat then feels it put over her shoulders. Her years of training betray her and her gaze wanders towards his face. With all of her strength, Zara slowly drags her eyes back down his body until they find their way to where they belong on the steps ahead of her.

"Zara, this is the first step of you experiencing life on your own terms. Please… trust me."

CHAPTER 3

Inside the plane, it is impossible for Zara to continue looking at the ground. When her heels hit the plush carpet, he wraps his arms around her to prevent her from falling. She leans into his chest taking in the interior of the plane.

"Wow," Zara exclaims in awe, stiffening as the word comes out.

"I was wondering what it would take to get you to start talking. Unfortunately, the plane is my dad's corporate plane but now you have given me a goal."

He chuckles as he walks her past four seats grouped together. Through a doorway, he points to the first set of seats on the right-hand side. They are nothing like the group of seats located at the plane's entrance. In this section, they are three times wider and covered in caramel colored leather. There is also a long couch of the same caramel leather accented with a coffee table. Opposite the couch are two more deluxe seats. Beyond the couch is a closed door.

Zara slips into the closest of the plush seats. She watches in wonder as he gathers her dress and tucks it around her as much as he can. Inhaling his scent, she is reminded of sun-touched water just as a summer breeze blows by. It is the smell of happiness playing in water.

A seatbelt is snapped in place and pulled to a snug fit. Zara feels him staring at her before he steps back.

Although there is a seat next to hers, he sits in one directly across from her. With a sigh, Zara returns her eyes to the carpet in front of her. Now is not the time for her to continue her exploration of the plane. With him seated across from her, Zara must remember her training and keep her eyes cast down.

Zara tenses at a small jolt as the plane begins to move. She can feel him watching her and senses her best efforts to mask her fear may not be enough.

"Little One, is this the first time you have flown?"

Keeping her eyes on the puffiness of her dress, Zara nods with the slightest response.

"Zara, please look at me."

Zara's body stiffens at the request. Slowly raising her eyes off her dress, they move up his body. Her gaze travels up his stomach to his chest. Without his suit coat, she gets to examine the body that she was just leaning against as they entered the plane. Her heart begins racing with the anticipation of looking into his eyes once more as she catalogs every inch of him for future analysis.

In the ceremonial hall, his eyes were light brown, but in this light they appear brown with flecks of green. His brown hair is still slicked back but she sees evidence that he has run his hands through it since they stood in the circle together.

Finding him smiling at her has an unexpected effect on her body. The shivers that she felt when he touched her hand to help her stand and when his hand found its way to the small of her back are small compared to the body shivers she gets looking into his eyes now.

He leans forward, resting his hands on his knees. He is close enough to touch her dress if he extended his fingers. She keeps staring into his eyes, becoming lost for the first time in her entire life.

A blush infuses her cheeks as Zara rips her eyes from his and returns them to her dress. Taking a steadying breath, she allows her eyes to take the journey once more up his body to his face. As she reaches his smile, the plane lifts off the ground and with a gasp, Zara grips the seat's armrests.

"Zara, breathe. Little One, this is the beginning of a wonderful adventure for you. I told you in the Circle that I am going to take care of you, and that includes ensuring that you arrive at our destination safely."

The further the plane gets off the ground, the tighter Zara's hold becomes. Thoughts of her mother's extreme fear of flying flood Zara's mind.

Calmly, he begins to speak at a volume she has to strain to hear.

"John. John Garrett."

The brilliant smile that spreads across his face makes Zara instantly forget the fact that she could crash to the ground and die at any second. The smile is not the tight-lipped one he flashed at her earlier. It is a smile that would make his cheeks hurt if it went on too long. It is a smile that Zara feels all the way to her toes.

"If the ceremony would have been completed tonight, you would be wearing my collar. I would be your Dom. Your husband. But you are not wearing my collar. Therefore, the tradition of calling me Dom or Sir does not fit our situation. My name is John Garrett Dawson. In the world, I am known as John but my family and very close friends all call me Garrett. I would like you to call me Garrett."

Focusing on the crystals in the skirt of her dress, Zara gives the slightest nod.

"Little One, I would like you to look at me. You have beautiful eyes and I would like to spend some time looking in them. Please."

Wide-eyed, Zara looks in his eyes. Tilting his head, he watches her eyes move from his eyes to his lips. Zara blushes again as she sees his knowing smile spread wider across his face. Not wanting to disappoint him, she locks onto his stare.

"That is so much better. We need to–"

A loud bell interrupts his sentence and startles Zara. Looking around, it hits her again that she is in an airplane. Once more, panic hits and Zara white knuckles the arms of her seat.

Garrett unbuckles his seatbelt and moves to the seat next to her, speaking softly. "That is the all clear sound from the pilot. No need to worry. It notifies us that we are able to move around the plane."

Lifting his hand to cover hers, he gently works to loosen her grip on the arms of the seat. "Zara, I need for you to trust me. I take your safety very seriously and I would not put you in any danger. I have flown hundreds of times and have never had one problem. Please, trust me."

He releases her hand to unbuckle her seatbelt. Standing, he extends his hand and waits for Zara to accept it. Hesitantly, she slides her hand into his and allows him to assist her up. Trembling, she cautiously steps to the back of the plane.

He opens the door to reveal a full-sized bedroom. Walking through the threshold, he gently tugs Zara inside. The trembling becomes full-body shaking. With eyes the size of saucers, Zara stares at the bed.

"Zara, take a deep breath," he says with a firmness that she had not yet experienced. "Do. It. Now."

Looking at the ground directly in front of her, Zara takes a deep breath. The command re-centers her, bringing back all the years of training. Two more deep breaths and Zara feels a calm settle inside.

"Yes, breathe, Little One. No need to worry, this is not our time," he says in a much softer tone.

Taking Zara's other hand into his, he watches as she again attempts a deep breath. With her hands squeezed lightly, Zara looks up to find warmth in his eyes.

A small smile crosses his face as his eyes slowly travel the length of her body. Casually, his eyes rejoin hers and Zara feels a new type of heat come up from her belly to spread over her entire body. A tremble reveals the calm she felt a moment ago has been replaced with an entirely different nervousness.

"Although you look lovely, I would like for you to get out of this dress," he states while maintaining the hold on both of Zara's hands as she tries to pull away.

"Through that door is a bathroom with a shower. I am sorry there is no bathtub. I would very much like for you to take a relaxing shower. You will find an outfit has been placed in the bottom drawer of the cabinet for you. I will be out on the couch if you need anything. If you wish to lie down following your shower, please do so. I will wake you before we land so that I can get you safely buckled. If you would rather come back out and talk, that is fine too."

As he finishes speaking, he releases her hands and walks toward the door. He begins to close the door and pauses.

"I am very glad you decided to come with me tonight."

Then he shuts the door... leaving her alone. Zara sits on one of the two chairs facing the bed, her mind racing.

What have I done? What is going to happen to me?

She touches her neck.

No collar.

Her entire life had been in preparation for this night. There was never a question as to what her life would hold. Zara was to be a collared married woman tonight.

As her hands return to her lap, she contemplates how her father intended to hand her over to the Dom whom he and the King Council had selected to be her mate. Zara's responsibility, her only expected contribution, was to produce the next line to ensure the continuation of the community. Every hour of preparation, all the years of training, now seemed useless.

Once again, uncertainty and self-doubt find their way into Zara's thoughts. Questions begin bouncing around inside her head.

Why didn't he want to complete the Ceremony and become my Dom? Why is he taking me to college? Where will I live? Will I be able to do this?

Tears gather in her eyes for the second time tonight.

A knock on the door brings Zara back. Unable to push anything out of her mouth that resembled words, she sits in silence staring at the door.

"Zara?"

Opening the door, Garrett finds Zara sitting in the chair looking at him. He takes two steps and kneels in front of her. The brilliant smile falters as he stares at her and sees a tear escape from each eye. Ashamed, she lowers her gaze but she feels his thumbs brush her eyelashes as he wipes them away. Sliding his hands on top of hers and gently forcing them apart, he moves his thumbs slowly over the tops of hers.

"Little One, I know there is a lot going on inside your brain right now. I am confident you have questions about your future, and I want to help you by answering anything I can. We will discuss everything, but first I want you out of your pretty dress. I want you to shower and change into some comfortable clothes."

The motion over Zara's skin soothes her in a way that disrupts her balance. She starts to pull her hands from his but he tightens his hold.

"No, Little One, don't pull away. Allow me to comfort you. Allow me to show you that everything will work out."

"Thank you." Zara finds her voice.

With a quick nod, Garrett stands in front of her and takes a step back. "You have twenty minutes to shower and join me on the couch."

Standing, Zara finds her balance and walks to the bathroom

without hesitation in her stride.

Wow!

An overwhelming smell of roses conjoins with the beauty of the room and accosts Zara's senses. Standing just inside the doorway, she takes a moment to admire it. Behind the curve of glass doors, she sees shelves have been stocked with products. A glass sink with a cabinet below is right next to the shower. A small table with several small drawers stands to the right of the sink and hosts a glass vase brimming with elegant white roses.

Remembering her instructions, Zara begins unbuttoning each of the little buttons along the side of her dress. Taking a deep breath, she bends over in relief when the last button is undone. Her fingers brush over the area that has just been freed and feel indentions in her skin. Fighting the layers of the skirt, Zara slowly lifts it over her head and carefully hangs it by its hidden loops on the inside of the bodice.

Closing her eyes, Zara bunches up her toes in relief after removing her shoes. She slowly slides her bra off and works her panties down her legs. Naked, she reaches into the shower and turns it on to warm up. Closing the door, she steps in front of the mirror above the sink.

She quickly removes the hairpins that have held her hair in place since early afternoon. Zara runs her fingers through the heavily sprayed hair to do a final check for hairpins. She pauses to take in the moment. As her hair cascades down her back, her eyes rest on her bare neck.

No collar.

Remembering the time limit for her use of the bathroom, she opens the shower door and steps inside. The spray of warm water on her skin sends the tension gripping Zara's shoulders down the drain with the water.

Once Zara's hair becomes saturated, she reaches for the products on the shelf. With surprised delight, she reaches for the same brand of shampoo she uses at home. Her smile wilts as she remembers that was her parents' home and no longer a place for her to call home.

Closing her eyes, Zara begins lathering shampoo into her hair. Rinsing the suds from her hair, she grabs the conditioner, shaking her head in wonder at the fact that both the shampoo and conditioner are the same brands she favors. The smell of peppermint and roses engulfs her as she rinses the conditioner out of her hair and soaps her body. With a final quick rinse, Zara turns off the shower and wraps herself in a warm, fluffy towel.

Stepping to the table of roses she opens a drawer and finds a toothbrush, toothpaste and dental floss. In the next drawer, Zara finds a comb designed for long wet hair. Beside the comb, she finds the leave-in conditioner her mother always instructed her to use.

Curiously, she picks up the toothbrush and toothpaste. Like the Dr. Bronner's Peppermint Soap, both are brands she uses. She lays them on the edge of the sink. Bending to open the bottom drawer, she covers her mouth to silence the gasp. Zara pulls out her favorite pink fleece pullover and her old black yoga pants. Squeezing her eyes tight, she hugs them to her towel-covered chest.

After a couple deep breaths, Zara reaches for the other items in the cabinet. She discovers her pink bra and matching panties, her warm fuzzy socks and her old pink running shoes. Excitement courses through her as she dresses.

Finishing with the toothbrush, Zara places it into a travel holder also found in the drawer and returns it and the toothpaste to the first drawer. With a last hug of appreciation of being dressed in her own clothes, Zara neatly hangs the wet towel, grabs her comb and leave-in conditioner and heads back to the bedroom.

On the nightstand, Zara notices a large bottle of water covered with condensation. Drawing near, she sees raspberries at the bottom and a slice of lemon near the top. She removes the cap and relishes the cold fruit-infused water. Taking three long pulls, she returns the bottle to the nightstand.

Unsure of the time, she works the comb through her hair as fast as possible and walks to the closed door leading to the main room of the plane. As she reaches for the door handle, she pauses.

I am on an airplane.

Smiling to herself and grabbing the door handle, she has intense feeling that she has forgotten something. Shaking her head, she opens the door.

Zara sees him sitting on the couch with a drink in his hand. He looks up slowly, letting his eyes wander down Zara's body, nodding once as his eyes spy her feet in tennis shoes.

She closes the door behind her and he smiles.

"Ah. Much better. Am I correct?"

The corners of her mouth turn upward and her eyes stay fixed on his lips.

"Yes, Sir."

"Yes, Garrett," he corrects her with a hint of persuasion in his voice. "Come and sit with me."

Taking the last four steps more confidently in her sneakers than in the heels she was wearing before her shower, she lowers herself onto the couch a couple of cushions down from Garrett. Gathering her damp hair in both hands, she releases it in the middle of her back.

"Here. You might need this."

Looking at his extended hand, Zara gasps when she sees her pink and green polka dot hair tie. Slowly reaching for the hair tie, tears well up in Zara's eyes.

"I… I thought I would never see this…" The words had come out more of a whisper as if speaking to herself.

"Garrett. Zara, I would like for you to call me Garrett." Reaching behind him, he pulled a tissue from a box and raised it to her cheek. "Say it for me, Zara."

Swallowing at the gentle touch of the tissue, Zara's eyes remain fixed on her hair tie now crumpled in her hands.

Quietly with the first hint of the southern accent from her home, Zara whispers, "Garrett."

"I would have never known you are from the South until you said my name. Yes, I would like you to call me Garrett and say it often." Not pausing to make mention of the blush spreading over Zara's face and neck, Garrett continues. "Our traditions have their place and some would never think to break them, but removing all of your previous belongings once you became my sub was one that I felt comfortable bending. Also, we did not complete the ceremony, therefore you do not belong to me."

The cascade of tears down Zara's cheeks has not slowed and Garrett pulls out a few more tissues to hand to her.

"Easy, Little One."

Taking the hair tie from her clenched grasp, he works to gather all of her loose tendrils in his hands and wrap the band around her hair.

Zara is frozen during the entire process. She knows that pulling away is not an option and maintains her position holding her breath.

"Breathe, Zara, breathe," he says, finishing his task. Garrett leans back against the couch to admire his job. "Not as good as you would do, but all the hair is up. I wish you had dried it. I don't want you to get sick."

Zara finds her voice again and manages a soft thank you. Wanting to look into Garrett's eyes again, Zara wipes the last of her tears and finds him looking at her. He begins to speak, only to be interrupted by the door opening at the opposite end of the plane sending Zara's eyes back to her lap.

Hearing the sound of someone coming, Zara braces for what will happen next; the unknown making every part of this journey scary. As the woman draws closer, Garrett leans into Zara to murmur, "Little One, please breathe for me."

Zara releases the breath she does not realize she is holding. The woman stops on the other side of the coffee table. She places two small napkins in front of each of them and places filled glasses on the napkins. She adds two plates and two sets of utensils wrapped in napkins.

"Mr. Dawson, will there be anything else for now?"

"No, Felicity, thank you."

Without another word, the woman pivots and walks back toward the door leaving Garrett and Zara to pick up where they left off.

Lifting the covers off the dishes, Garrett hands Zara a plate then picks up his and sits back against the couch.

"I chose sandwiches. I didn't know if you would decide to come with me or how each of us would feel. I hope that's alright with you."

Shocked, Zara whips her head to look at him and then down at her plate. She tries to process the words that have just been spoken. In her entire life, no one had ever hoped that something was 'alright with her' and she struggles to wrap her mind around it.

Almost done with half of his sandwich, Garrett places the sandwich on the plate and looks at Zara. Feeling his eyes on her, she carefully picks up half of her sandwich and begins to eat, only then realizing how hungry she is.

With her sandwich consumed, the exhaustion of the day falls upon Zara like a blanket. She can barely focus on Garrett's description of the college she will soon be attending. As hard as she tries to stay awake, Zara feels herself drift away from the last minutes of her eighteenth birthday.

CHAPTER 4

Zara blinks awake. She has no memory of disembarking the plane, driving to this house or getting into this bed, and a sense of panic begins to take hold. On the nightstand, a note sits with her name on the front. Tentatively, Zara brings the paper closer, nearly under the comforter, to read.

Your coffee is waiting for you in the kitchen. Garrett.

Zara eases out from under the covers finding comfort in Garrett's words. The sound of waves catches her attention. Rolling over, Zara's mouth drops open upon discovering a wall of glass revealing a brilliant blue sky. Zara gazes around the room realizing the room was designed to accentuate the view. The walls and furniture were done in soft white while the accents were the color of the sky. The art on the walls tied everything together with seascapes.

Zara heads to the balcony and pushes the glass wall open a smidgen. She steps out and finds the smell meets her head-on. Thoughts of the day's first cup of coffee are replaced by the glory of the view. With her hands on the rails, Zara leans into the smell and sounds radiating from the largest body of water she has ever seen. The sounds of waves washing over the sandy beach makes her smile stretch further across her face.

This is what he smells like. Lovely.

Even the noisy seagulls screeching on the beach add to the overwhelming beauty. Moments like these leave Zara wishing she could paint or draw to capture the view forever. Turning to abandon this prized spot, Zara squeezes back through the opening in the glass door.

Built-in shelves on either side of the big white bed hold knick-knacks with a beach theme. Zara walks to two doors standing closed side-by-side at the other end of the room. Opening the door on the right, she discovers the biggest bathroom she has ever seen.

At the end of the long narrow room sits an immense bathtub graced by a picture window providing another view of the beach. To the side is a shower encased in glass with built-in shelves stocked with a variety of products.

After several moments spent figuring out the shower, steam begins to fill the glass space. Zara begins to remove her clothes from the night before. Spinning around in her half-naked state, she opens the shower door to get a closer look at the products arranged in the shower. Once again her favorite body soap, peppermint Dr. Bronner's, has a place of pride. Zara looks closely and finds the men's razor that she has switched to recently after reading about it in a magazine.

"How?" slips out of Zara's mouth.

Pushing down the questions scurrying around in her mind, Zara steps into the shower under the rainwater spout. Head back and eyes closed, the water washes over her and clears away her thoughts. Breathing deeply for a few minutes, she feels her shoulders lower to a more relaxed position.

Reaching for her favorite shampoo, Zara opens the lid and takes a big sniff. Pouring more into her hand than she actually needs, she begins washing her hair.

The practice of clearing her mind is not working and thoughts of Garrett are front and center. His hair. His eyes.

Zara, this is the first step to you experiencing life on your own terms. Trust me.

Picking up a sponge and applying the peppermint soap, she suds it up to an aromatic lather. Zara drags the sponge up her arm and over her shoulder, leaving a trail of lather resembling the froth of the waves as they cascade onto the beach.

The contact of the sponge with her left breast sends a bolt of sensation through her entire body. Both nipples harden and immediately Garrett invades her thoughts. Covered with thick lather, Zara uses her free hand to caress the soap into small circles over her hard nipples.

A vision of Garrett running his tongue over his lips after taking a sip of a drink plays on repeat in her head. Zara's eyes close as her fingers go from a gentle caress to lightly tugging on a nipple. The sensation feels so good she drops the sponge back into the basket to free her other hand. Repeating the action of gently caressing her breasts, her eyes close and her head goes back rinsing away the conditioner in her hair and the thick coat of lather covering the top half of her body.

The image shifts to Garrett's hands kneading her breasts. The strong hands that helped her up and led her out of the Ceremonial Circle–

Zara's eyes fly open. The sexual thoughts are replaced with an overwhelming sense of guilt. She had one job to do in her family. One role to fulfill. She failed.

Zara steps directly under the stream of water to wash the tears away with the soap. Taking a deep breath, she attempts again to clear her thoughts.

Wrapped in a towel, Zara works through the rest of her morning routine without entertaining further thoughts of Garrett. Opening the drawer under the sink, she finds the 'wet hair' comb and leave-in conditioner and as she opens the door to the bedroom, the smell of coffee hurries her along.

On top of the dresser, Zara finds the three hair ties that she and Sloane made resting on three smooth stones. Wonderingly, she opens the top drawer of the dresser. Neatly folded in sets are several new bras and panties on the left and there are two rolls of Zara's old bra and panty sets on the right. Shifting through the items, it is apparent that only her favorites were brought. Grabbing the green and white set, Zara holds them to her chest.

No tears, Zar. None.

Pulling out each of the drawers, she finds the same arrangement continues. New shorts and tee shirts, sleep clothes, bathing suits and jeans on the left and one or two of Zara's favorite pieces on the right.

Putting the green and white panties set back where they were, Zara selects a new green and white polka dot bikini. In the bathroom she finds the suit fits a bit small in every way and a smile creeps over her face seeing herself in the sexy bathing suit from every angle.

After pulling on perfectly sized black yoga shorts and a pink tee from the left side of the drawer, Zara puts her hair up in the hair tie from last night.

Looking for shoes, she opens the door next to the bathroom and finds more clothes hanging up along with several pairs of shoes.

Pulling out a pair of black flip-flops, Zara stops to admire a pair of black pumps with red soles. They are one incredibly sexy pair of shoes. Setting them back on the shelf, she wonders briefly where she would ever wear such shoes.

After making the bed and hanging up the towel, Zara makes her way down a bright hallway in search of the coffee that seems to be mocking her. The sound of her flip-flops on the wood floor takes her back to her parents' house.

How many punishments had there been for running through the house in flip-flops? Way too many.

Father did not like noise in the house and over the years, the house got quieter and quieter. With her bedroom right next to her parents, there was no escaping the mandate of quietude. Sloane's father had the same aversion to noise. Since the two of them took turns staying at one another's home, near silence was the norm. Bending to remove her flip-flops, Zara stops at the entry to the main living quarters. This entire side of the house is made of glass with an unobstructed view of the beach and water.

One step down and Zara finds herself in an expansive room. A light grey sectional sofa big enough for two people to lay side-by-side graces the center. Two chairs sit near it, their backs to the water. Modern in design, the muted colors allow one's eyes to gravitate to the real feature of the room, the water outside.

"Good morning, Zara," a gravelly woman's voice startles Zara into dropping her flip-flops. "I'm sorry, child. I didn't mean to scare you."

"No. I am sorry."

Bending to pick up the shoes, Zara makes her way to the short round woman standing in the kitchen. Squaring the shoes up on the floor in the corner as far out of the way as possible, she moves quickly the rest of the way to properly introduce herself.

Extending her hand to the smiling older woman, she murmurs, "Good morning, I am Zara. Please forgive me for making so much noise."

The woman stares into Zara's eyes as if trying to read any secrets she is keeping.

"You're lovelier than your photographs. You look simply adorable in that tee shirt. I will have to tell Viv to get more in that style. And you certainly made no noise, girl. I know where Garrett and Warren are in the house at all times.

"I bet you're ready for some coffee. Sit… sit and I will bring you a cup. It's a fresh pot. I am glad you slept in. Yesterday must have taken everything out of you."

Zara's eyes must have gotten big before she could catch herself.

"Oh, yes, I know all about your decision to break the Circle. That was a very courageous decision you made. You are much stronger than you know. Hang on to that knowledge."

The woman sets a large coffee cup on the table in front of Zara. Before she can ask, a tiny plate with Splenda and a pitcher of 'Half & Half' is slipped beside it.

"Thank you. May I ask… how do you know how I take my coffee?" Zara asks in an almost whisper. Raised to never ask questions, she remembers herself and places her hands on her lap. Zara lowers her eyes and begins to blank her mind with a breathing technique bracing for whatever manner of punishment is to come as an official reminder.

"Relax, child. In any Dawson house, you are free to ask questions. Encouraged, actually. I have been with the family for over twenty years. The Dawson family has even been known to enjoy a heated debate from time to time."

"Been with–"

"Oh drat. Zara, I have been going off at the mouth. Forgive me, child." Sliding into the seat across from Zara, a standard coffee cup in hand, the woman takes a deep breath.

"I'm Trudy. I am the Dawson's family housekeeper. Well, I'm getting up there in my years so now I take care of running the houses and cooking mostly. Normally, I would be traveling with Warren and Charlotte but this was a big event for Garrett and I wanted to be here for him.

"We didn't know what you would decide to do so I decided to stay here and get everything situated for your arrival. Garrett told me how you like your coffee and that you are a bit of a coffee addict. I cannot have any coffee after noon or it keeps me up half the night."

"Garrett told you how I like my coffee? I don't understand. Why would he tell you that and how would he know?"

Trudy's smile lights her face as Zara finishes her questions.

"Child, Garrett has told me many things about you. All of your regular products and favorite foods. Anything that would help make your time with us more enjoyable. As for how he knows, well, that's a question for you to ask Garrett."

The look on Zara's face conveyed the question that she had been thinking non-stop since opening her eyes and Trudy rushed to answer. "He wanted you to be able to wake up and have a bit of time to yourself. We can't begin to imagine how exhausting yesterday was for you."

Getting up from her seat, Trudy moves at a slow but steady pace. Opening the refrigerator and pulling out a few items, she sets them out on the table. Zara stares at them without a word. In front of her sits her favorite recharge breakfast, each item neatly displayed on plates matching the one that was now holding two less Splenda packets.

Reaching for the utensils wrapped in a cloth napkin, Zara looks up to see Trudy staring back at her. A blush spreads over her face.

"Oh, now, enjoy your breakfast. Garrett went to run some errands." Looking at her watch, she continues, "He will be back in two hours. I am going to let you eat in peace. I have some calls to make. If you need anything, just pick up any phone and dial 11. That will ring me directly. To dial out, hit 7 and then the number.

"There is a Kindle connected to the Wi-Fi in the drawer of the nightstand in your room. The beach is always nice and it is private so you don't have to be concerned with anyone bothering you. The water is not really warm because we had a violently cold winter. Next to the door leading out to the beach, you will find a closet with beach towels, chairs, umbrellas, radio… basically anything you need for the beach.

"I would imagine you have a lot going on in your thoughts. Maybe even having trouble clearing your mind." The utter shock of her statement is obvious and Zara's reaction makes her chuckle. "Oh yes, Child. I was owned. My Master passed on twenty years ago. Warren Dawson was a student of my Master and took me in after. But that is a story for another day. My point, Zara, is that if you need to talk, I'm available. Your openness is safe with me."

With that, Trudy stands up again and places her cup on the counter next to the sink. "Leave your dishes by mine. That is an order, Child."

"Yes, Ma'am. Thank you."

"Zara, Garrett is a good man. He wants to ensure that you are comfortable and happy. He will never admit it, but he is as nervous as you are for what will happen next. Never doubt that, Child."

With a small nod, Trudy shuffles out. Halfway through the living room, she turns back. "One thing that I don't know about you is what type of music you enjoy. Would you like me to put on anything in particular?"

"I am... I am not familiar with much music. I would not want to disturb anyone."

"First of all, it's only you and I here at the moment and I will not be bothered by music playing. Garrett and his parents always have music blaring through the house. Any special requests? Rock? Country? Jazz? Classical?" She had returned to the opening of the kitchen and stood staring at Zara expectantly.

"I am sorry. I am truly not familiar with music. My parents did not like noise in the house so I never listened to it. But thank you." Zara stirred her oatmeal-on-the-go wondering why it tasted so much better than when she made it.

"Well, Child, it's time for you to get to know music. I will put on some classical and leave you to your breakfast. Remember, Zara, you can get me at 11. Any phone will connect us."

Without further ado, Trudy goes to a panel on the wall at the opening of the hallway, punches a few buttons and sounds of a piano concerto flood the kitchen. Suddenly caught up in the music, Zara fails to see Trudy leave.

Starting off softly, the concerto rises to a level that would send her father over the edge with anger. Without using any of the techniques from her training to clear her mind, all thoughts that are pushing for attention slip away as the music soars, each note so strong and confident in its placement with the others.

Zara sits staring out at the water, allowing the piano to transport her to another place. Before she knows it, tears are coursing down her cheeks, distorting the view of the moving water. The tears do not fall because of upsetting thoughts. As the song reaches its crescendo she realizes it is the music that brought them. Using the napkin to wipe them away, Zara finds her mind is clear.

As the piece ends and the next begins, Zara remains, still allowing the music to penetrate through her. Closing her eyes, she locks the moment into her memory knowing the peacefulness of this moment will be useful later as a technique to block out pain or discomfort.

As another piece ends, the task of searing the combination of the music and the movement of the water deep inside her draws her back to her surroundings. She realizes her coffee is cold and her breakfast barely touched.

She does not waste any more time. She finishes her breakfast and coffee and rinses the dishes, leaving them in the sink as ordered. On the counter, a travel mug sits under the open Keurig. Its blue light flashes to indicate the coffee is loaded and ready to be started.

Upon hitting the button to brew, the aroma of freshly brewed coffee puts a smile on Zara's face. She is ready to go explore the beach with a travel mug filled with doctored coffee in a matter of minutes.

Slipping into flip-flops and heading out the door, her only regret is leaving the piano music that has already found a place in her heart. Closing the door behind her, the sound of music is replaced by the sounds of the beach.

CHAPTER 5

Treading down a few stairs, Zara leaves the flip-flops on the bottom step and enjoys her first walk on warm sand. The sand slides underfoot with each step, but her single goal is to get to the water that spans as far as she can see.

The sand at the water's edge is packed tighter and takes less effort to move. The water glides over the packed sand and a white froth is left behind as the waves recede back into the lake. Zara walks into the surf but stops abruptly as cool water submerges her feet, dancing back out of the reach of the oncoming waves.

Zara stands still to take in the magnitude of the view. Seagulls fly overhead but do not stop to explore. With one deep breath, Zara walks into the water up to her calves. A sandy bottom is visible through the water and a small amount of seaweed floats in the water but not close to where Zara is standing. She feels the sand moving out from under her feet from the constant draw of the undertow. Two yards from the shore it takes effort to remain standing and Zara slowly makes her way back to the beach, each step a mini battle to beat the sand working against her.

Once she reaches the sand at the shoreline, Zara takes a deep breath releasing the tension in her shoulders, realizing she had more concern about making it back to the beach than even she was aware of.

Zara sits on the dry sand just past the shoreline traveled by each wave. Warm to the touch, the sand is soft and conforms to her body. Knees drawn up to her chest, Zara closes her eyes to enjoy the sound of the water crashing against anything in its way.

The rhythmic pattern of the water over the sand blends with the warmth of the sun and lures her into a deep sense of relaxation.

Looking over the water, Zara spots a boat coming from the right side of the horizon. She watches it move across the water. It is a large boat with sails and she can see several people onboard.

The muffled sounds of music dance over the water to where Zara sits.

With time and space to muse, questions return front and center in her mind.

Why did Garrett offer me this out? How did he get all of my belongings here? Why would he risk his position in the Community to do this? What is going to happen in the future?

Garrett had given her an out and as much as she appreciated the gift, self-doubt bubbled up from her choice. Her entire existence had revolved around being collared and making the best submissive wife to whichever Dom her father picked out. She could not help thinking, once again, how she had failed in epic proportions.

What is my father thinking of me?

Zara recalls that there had been something in her mother's eyes when Zara stood up holding Garrett's hand, but she had not been able to convey her thoughts before being ordered to assume the position. It had left Zara with a feeling of emptiness.

And what about Fredrik?

"Fredrik! Oh No!"

She gasps, sobbing and choking for air. For the first time since walking down the ceremonial path, Zara thinks of her younger brother. She had not even looked for him when she left with Garrett. The single most important person in her life and she did not say goodbye. Racking cries shake her body.

Oblivious in her grief, Zara does not hear Garrett approach. She only becomes aware of him when he gently lifts her into his arms and sits, holding her as she sobs. Zara presses into his body sobbing violently while Garrett rubs her back. Zara's tears stop falling as her breathing turns soft and steady and she feels exhaustion overtaking her.

Water.

The sound of waves crashing on the beach draws Zara from sleep. It is loud, almost as if she is lying on the beach right next to the waves. Opening her eyes, she finds she is in a darkened room. Running her fingers over the sheets and under the pillow it is clear this is not the bed she awoke in this morning. The feeling of missing her brother engulfs her again and the tears fall freely. Hearing the swish of footsteps approach the bed, Zara fights to stop the tears, only making the crying harder. Garrett stands at the side of the bed and gathers her into his arms.

"Come here, Little One."

Zara wraps her hands around his neck as he brings her to his body and walks toward the chorus of the beach sounds. Passing through a wide opening, he sits in a large chair, doing nothing more than holding her close as she cries.

Soothed by the harmony of the water meeting the beach and returning into itself, Zara nuzzles into Garrett's chest. The material of his shirt feels different than it did on the beach, softer and tighter to his body. Garrett shifts slightly and Zara pulls away to detach from him.

"Stay put, Zara." That is enough for her. She returns to resting her head on his chest and closes her eyes.

He shifts again, and lifts something up. She hears clinking in a glass and she senses him taking a large sip before returning the glass to its original resting place. Zara opens her eyes to find Garrett bringing a water bottle to her lips.

"Take a drink, Zara. You have been asleep for hours and need to hydrate." There is no question in Garrett's tone that it is time to take a drink. His voice is quiet and even, but his message is loud and clear.

"Thank you…" Zara takes the bottle and lifts away from his chest to drink. Garrett keeps his arms securely around her, suggesting he has no plans for Zara to sit anywhere else.

The water is cool and refreshing, and Zara quenches her thirst, drinking the full bottle. This morning's coffee is the last thing Zara drank. Garrett takes it from Zara's hands before she could stretch to place it on the small table next to his glass.

With his hands free, Garrett pulls Zara back to his chest. Without thought or hesitation, Zara returns to her place in his arms. His hand begins to slide up and down her back and Zara sighs, her body relaxing further into his.

"Zara, I would very much like to discuss what upset you this morning."

Zara tenses against Garrett's chest. "I am sorry."

"I don't want you to be sorry. I want you to feel every emotion that you have at the time each one occurs. It's my wish that you discuss them with me. Does that make sense?"

"Yes," she replies in a voice so soft it wouldn't have been heard by a person sitting in the next chair.

"May I sit in the other chair?" Zara asks without looking into Garrett's face.

His hand freezes in the middle of Zara's back then he releases his hold. She feels him looking at her as she places her bare feet on the floor, regretting the loss of the warmth of his body.

Zara tucks her feet underneath her as she sits in the chair next to Garrett. She looks out into the darkness toward the sound of the water and closing her eyes, hears Garrett pick up his glass.

Zara opens her eyes and looks at Garrett. Solemnly she begins, "I looked at my mother before I left the circle. We made eye contact and I saw something in her eyes before she presented herself. I don't know what she was trying to communicate."

Tears track down her cheeks as she continues, "I didn't look for Fredrik. I walked out of the circle without being collared and I have not thought of him. I did not say goodbye to my brother."

Zara stares out at the dark water, her tears continuing to fall.

"Why am I here?" She blurts. Zara tenses, moving to the edge of the chair and placing both of her feet on the floor, arms crossed behind her back. Her eyes focus down as she waits for the reprimand warranted for her slip.

"Zara Faith." Garrett sets the glass on the table and kneels in front of Zara without touching her. He begins to speak in a comforting, yet firm tone.

"While in my presence, you may ask any question freely without fear of reprimand. Am I clear?"

Zara gives the slightest nod.

Returning to his chair, Garrett picks up his drink and proceeds to answer Zara's question as if no interruption had taken place.

"Little One, you fell asleep before we could talk last night. You are here with me because your dorm room won't be ready for move-in until Thursday. Since I wasn't certain if you would choose to accept my offer or wish to continue with the collaring ceremony…"

Garrett pauses as Zara's right hand flies to her neck upon hearing the word collaring. Taking a moment, looking out into the darkness before he continues, "I didn't want to move ahead with the preparations until a decision was made."

"I will be living in a dorm? Do you live in the dorm as well?"

"No, Zara. You will live in the dorm room alone. The dorm is called Yakeley Hall and it's the oldest all-girl's dorm on campus."

Zara looks at Garrett. "All-girls dorm."

"Yes, Little One, an all-girls dorm. We may not be a collared couple but I don't wish for you to spend your evenings in a building filled with eager college guys. I was an eager college guy and that is not an option for you."

Garrett drinks the last of his beverage and stands extending his hand to Zara. "Shall we continue this in the kitchen and get some food?"

Zara takes his hand and stands.

He releases her hand when she gets to her feet and walks away two steps and turns on soft floor lights. He motions Zara to move past him into his bedroom.

Garrett waits patiently while Zara takes in her surroundings. She can feel him observing her and is careful to set her expression as she surveys his private space. Zara takes her time looking at his room, attempting to remember as many details as possible.

The space is double the size of the room she woke up in this morning, with a wall facing the water set in glass. Double doors lead to a balcony overlooking the beach.

The furniture in the room is modern, dwarfed by a platform bed facing the water. The bed is neatly made with the exception of the space Zara had slept in earlier.

On either side of the bed are platforms that have matching reading lamps. The side that is still tucked in with military precision has a couple of books stacked on the platform. Across from the foot of the bed and against the glass wall is a sitting bench. On the floor by the bench, sits a basket of wood and shells. The basket is all that could be considered clutter in the room. A closer look at the basket shows the items arranged in a particular order. There is zero clutter in Garrett's room.

Zara steps aside to let Garrett lead the way. The walls of the hallway are covered with frames in an organized manner, all matching and grouped in small clusters. It is not light enough to see the pictures, so Zara hurries ahead to catch up to Garrett who is already halfway down the first staircase.

"This is my parents' floor," he points down a hallway similar to the one above. There are more clusters of frames, this time in various shapes and sizes and a runner down the hallway accentuating its length.

Garrett continues to the ground floor and waits for Zara to join him. He waits in an identical hallway, but instead of one door, like the floors above, there are several. There are no frames on the wall in this hall.

Garrett opens the first door and Zara recognizes this is the doorway Trudy had slipped through after turning on the music. Reoriented, Zara knows the kitchen is all the way on the other end of the house and the room where Zara slept is down the hall on the other side of the sunken living room.

Walking toward the kitchen, Garrett pauses at the same control panel that Trudy had used to start the music. The entire floor glows as soft floor lighting fills the living room.

"Go change and I will get us something to eat." The schooled expression on Zara's face slips.

"Yes, Little One, I am going to prepare a meal. Go… I am hungry and I am guessing you are as well."

As Zara makes her way down the hall, another soft piano concerto fills the air. Pausing to enjoy it, a clank of pans from the kitchen sends her moving to do what Garrett instructed.

Opening the door to the room, Zara knew that someone had been in and straightened up the space. The bed that she had made before going to find the coffee now had the same military corners as Garrett's bed.

Taking off the hair tie as she walked into the bathroom, Zara noticed the towel she had used after her shower was no longer hanging on the towel bar. A replacement towel makes the stack exactly the same as this morning.

Turning on the shower, Zara quickly removes her clothes and steps under the warm spray, enjoying the water against her skin. There was something special about this rain stream spigot.

Washed, dried and in a tee shirt and yoga pants in record time, Zara makes her way back to the kitchen where three things catch her attention. First, Garrett has changed. He is now in a MSU tee shirt, sleep pants and is barefoot. Second, a wrapped present sits on the counter next to the coffee machine, and third, a black box in the center of the table. Of the three, Garrett in comfy clothes and bare feet top the list.

"May I help with the cooking?"

"No... no... no. Just talk to me and keep me company. It is almost ready." Garrett points to the table and returns to chopping vegetables.

"May I get a beverage?" Zara whispers.

Garrett pauses. Zara tenses and quickly sits in the chair closest to where she had been standing. Putting down the knife and cucumber, Garrett rinses his hands and picks up a towel.

Without a word, he dries his hands and tosses the towel on the counter next to the cutting board. He steps to the table to stand directly in front of Zara. Garrett looks deeply into her eyes, almost as if he is reading her thoughts. Without touching her, he kneels in front of her never taking his eyes from hers.

"Breathe, Zara." He waits for her to exhale and once satisfied begins to speak, never breaking eye contact.

"Zara, while you are in this house or any house that I sleep in, it is your home. Let me say that differently. You are free to do whatever you would do if you were in your own home.

"First, I am not your Dom. You are not required to ask me for permission to get a beverage or anything else. If you are hungry, eat. If you're tired, go to your room and rest. If you're bored with the conversation, change it.

"Second, if or when we do finish the Circle Ceremony, you will continue to have these same freedoms. I have never wanted a slave as a mate. I am a Dom and the Master/slave dynamic does not appeal to who I am."

Garrett continues to stare into Zara's eyes, as the tears begin to pool. She fights to keep them at bay but once the first tear escapes, several more follow. He reaches to wipe the tears off her cheeks but pauses just shy of making contact.

Standing, Garrett walks quickly to the pantry and pulls out a box of tissues. Returning to the table, he hands Zara the box and sits in the chair next to her. He waits. She rips open the cardboard and takes out a couple of tissues.

"Are you disappointed that I don't want a slave?"

"NO!" Zara answers firmly, but the lack of confidence in Garrett's voice when he asks the question throws Zara off balance. She hopes he didn't need her to give more of an answer.

Garrett reaches for the black box that had been sitting on the table. He doesn't say anything for a moment. Placing the box in front of Zara, he stands and returns to the knife and cutting board.

"It's important to me that you consider this your home and that you move around freely and without concern. I would like that very much." When he finishes speaking, he resumes his chopping.

Zara looks at the picture on the top of the box. It's an iPhone. She's never had one but smiles to herself. She picks up the box and opens it.

Zara looks up at Garrett and smiles when her eyes meet his staring back at her, "Thank you."

Placing the phone back into the box and setting it on the table, Zara rises from her seat and silently walks to the refrigerator. Opening one of the doors, she is happy to find several cans of her favorite Arnold Palmer with pink lemonade.

Looking around the refrigerator door, Zara finds Garrett pulling something out of the oven.

"Would you like something to drink?" she asks shyly.

"Yes, please. I'll try one of those Arnolds of yours." Pausing to look at her, Garrett smiles.

"Your house… Little One. And there are frosted mugs in the freezer," he states matter-of-factly, returning to his task at hand.

With a bit of hesitation, Zara gathers two cans and two mugs. Returning to her seat, she fills the mugs. Setting the cans aside, she takes a big drink of her favorite beverage.

"Mmmmmm," Zara enjoys the drink. When she looks up, Garrett is watching her again with the same look he had last night when she came out of the bathroom in her own clothes. A blush suffuses her face. There is no missing the soft chuckle from Garrett.

Zara unwraps the utensils in a cloth napkin and places the napkin in her lap waiting. Garrett has prepared homemade pizza that looks as good as it smells.

Garrett picks up the frosted mug and takes a small sip of the iced drink. Taking a longer drink, Zara watches him enjoy one of her favorite beverages.

"It is delicious. I wasn't impressed with the idea of mixing iced tea and pink lemonade, but it's good."

Smiling, Zara looks down at her plate. Her mouth waters in

anticipation of the first bite.

Garrett looks over at her, puzzled, "I thought you loved pizza."

"I do love pizza. I am waiting for you to start."

"Why?"

"It is what is right. That is how it is supposed to be."

"Zara, please take a bite of pizza."

Slowly, Zara reaches for her fork. Looking up at Garrett, she searches for confirmation of his intent. She had been trained to never eat her food first. Her entire life, her mother demanded that she wait for both her father and her brother to begin eating. It feels wrong to take a bite before the man at the table.

"Little One, we are not bound together. You aren't my sub. I want you to feel comfortable. Please try the pizza. Trudy worked really hard to make your favorite and I reheated it to perfection."

Zara cuts the pizza into small bites, her eyes filling with tears as she puts the pizza in her mouth. Setting the fork on her plate while she chews, the tears begin to run down her face.

"Zara, I am not sure how you were raised or what your expectations are as a sub, but we need to address this immediately. I do not want, nor have I ever wanted, a slave. Are you a slave in nature?"

Zara looks him in the eyes and begins to cry harder. "I don't know what I am. I don't know if I am a sub or a slave or even if I want to be in this type of relationship. I was born with my life predetermined. In one second, everything that I have known to be true changed.

"When I was little I wanted to go to college. Something I never in a million years thought I would have the opportunity to do. I don't know if I can do it. Everything that I was raised to be... I no longer am.

"I did not get collared as I was supposed to. Do you not see? I have failed at the one thing I was meant to achieve. I do not know how to behave in any situation because every situation was supposed to be different."

"Little One, you have been keeping this all inside. I didn't stop the Ceremony because I didn't want you. In fact, I want you so much that I am giving you the freedom to decide if you want *me*.

"I'm scared too. I'm worried that you are going to go on campus, have the time of your life and meet another man who suits you better. I'm afraid you will turn your back on the Community and on me, that I will lose you before I even had a chance to have you."

They sit together in silence thinking about what the other has said. Garrett speaks first. He stands up and grabs the present that caught Zara's attention when she came into the kitchen.

He holds it for a moment and returns to his seat. Silently, he sets it down in front of Zara.

"I bought this for you in the event that you decided to take this adventure and go to MSU. I attended Michigan State and had one of the best times in my life. I want that for you. If you meet someone or decide that the Community is not for you, I will respect that and I will help you in every way that I am able.

"Please open it. For me."

Her hand shakes as she picks up the perfectly wrapped present. Zara begins to unwrap the sides of the package, working slowly not to rip the paper. She uses the time to process what Garrett has just revealed.

He wants me.

That sends shivers all through her body.

Focusing on the job of opening her gift, Zara could feel Garrett's eyes on her as she works. She opens the box to find a silver necklace lying on a baby blue pillow of silk. Also in the box are two small pouches. Garrett takes the box out of Zara's hand and places it on the table next to the pizza.

Lifting the chain, he states, "This chain represents your journey of exploration. I ask that you wear it always. Please do not mistake it for my collar because that is not the intent."

Opening the blue pouch, a shiny pendant falls into his hand. Lifting Zara's right hand and turning it palm up, Garrett places a sparkly letter Z in the center. He opens the purple pouch and pours the contents into Zara's hand. A small silver circle shows a lower case 'g' engraved on its surface.

"The Z is for Zara. You are always to remember that this is your life to live and that you should make your own choices as you go. The G represents me. You can see the G is smaller, but still present. Little One, I will always be here for you. School may be overwhelming but I am going to be there every step of the way."

He takes the chain and threads the pendants. Garrett steps

behind Zara and lowers the chain in front of her, closing the clasp in the back. He carefully lifts her hair out from the chain.

Returning to his seat, he takes her hand in his. "I want you to find the answers to all the questions that roll around in your head when you get that far off look in your eyes. If and when you want to explore a relationship with me, we will do it privately and not before the entire Council.

"I swear to you that I will remain yours until you make the decision not to be mine. That does not mean that I expect you to live as a sub, but I would hope that if you meet someone that you wish to explore in an intimate way that you will talk to me."

Sitting back in his chair, Garrett stares at the Z that now hangs around Zara's throat. Her hand went to her neck like it had so many times during their brief stay together. This time her fingers found the necklace and wrapped around the charms.

"Thank you, Sir. Thank you for setting me free to seek who I am and what I want. Thank you for telling me why you ended the Ceremony."

"Zara, you should call me Garrett. When you call me Sir… I plan to be your Dom. Your one and only. Does that make sense?"

Zara nods silently to Garrett. Piano music fills the space between them, taking a hold of the moment.

Garret picks up both plates of cold pizza and places them on the counter. Opening the oven and sliding on oven mitts, he pulls out the other half of the pizza. A trivet from the drawer is placed on the table and the pizza pan placed between them.

"Let's eat. It's late and I'd like to take you to my favorite place tomorrow. If you are comfortable with that, Trudy won't be there. It will just be the two of us."

Zara is beginning to recognize the subtleties of expressions on Garrett's face. He is nervous about what her response will be. This smile is a mask for his uncertainty.

"I would very much like to see your favorite place. I feel perfectly safe with you. I thought we were alone here."

Garrett's full smile replaces the last before Zara finishes speaking. "Trudy has been here the entire time. She is available to you night and day if you would like to speak with her.

"Oh… your phone! That's your new phone." Garrett points to the black box with the picture on the cover. Zara picks up the box and hands it to him.

Garrett retrieves the iPhone out of the box and powers it up in seconds. Pointing to the warm pizza between them, he watches Zara take a new piece. Garrett picks up a piece and inhales a huge bite.

"HOT... HOT... so HOT!!!" He holds his mouth open to draw in cooler air.

Zara struggles to maintain her expression. Inside her thoughts are jumbled, one thought pushing its way to the forefront. She could not help thinking how adorable Garrett looks eating too-hot pizza in his lounge pants. And the bare feet...

Cutting each piece and blowing on it before putting it in her mouth, Zara feels her body begin to relax. It was so easy to be comfortable with him.

"Can we discuss why you were so upset on the beach today and again upstairs?"

She stops chewing the bit of pizza that is in her mouth and swallows hard. The relaxation that has settled in her shoulders evaporates with one question. Zara picks up her glass of Arnold Palmer and takes a long drink.

Zara nods.

"Hey... hey. Relax. We don't have to talk about anything that makes you uncomfortable. Allow me to say this one thing, your phone is charged. Sloane's mobile is already programmed."

Zara's head snaps up, the change in her facial expression unmasked this time. She is still going to be able to speak to her best friend.

Zara had not given much thought about whether communicating with her best friend from her old life would be permitted. In the last twenty-four hours, there had been very little time to process any of the monumental changes.

Garrett didn't mention her family's numbers being programmed into the phone. Zara schooled her expression and shifted her focus onto the phone. Looking at Garrett, she knows he perceived where her thoughts had drifted.

"I haven't loaded any music yet because I don't know what your favorite bands are. I have a lot of music on my computer and I'm almost positive I'll have something to get you started. You can load it up when you have some free time at school."

Zara's blank stare gets a confused stare in return.

"I do not have a favorite band. I do not know much about music. We did not grow up with music in our house." With a wave of her hand towards the speaker she continues, "This is nice. I like this a lot."

Garrett finishes his piece of pizza and drinks more of the Arnold Palmer. Zara feels like she has said something wrong and suddenly has no more appetite.

"Aren't you going to eat anymore?"

"I am finished. Thank you."

Popping the last bites into his mouth, Garrett stands and picks up the pizza pan. Zara jumps up and carries the mugs to the sink. While Garrett puts the cans into the pantry, Zara clears the remaining dishes off the table.

Leaning against the counter, Garrett listens to the music. "As an only child, life can get lonely. My parents gave music to me early. There is always music playing in the house, car, office... everywhere. I love music. I wanted to be a pianist for a while as a kid.

"I probably liked saying pianist more than anything," he chuckled to himself. "My piano teacher sat my parents down and explained as gently as possible that I was not talented enough to play the piano professionally. They never knew I was listening in the hallway.

"They never told me what he said and there was a new piano teacher when it was time for my next lesson." His words trail off and it seems Garrett is reliving the experience in his head.

"It's late. You look like you are going to tip over. Come on, off to bed with you." He says changing the subject.

"I will just wash these few dishes first."

"You will do no such thing." Zara jumps at the voice behind her. She hadn't heard Trudy's entrance. Putting the phone back into its box, Trudy hands the box to Garrett. "JG, take Zara to bed immediately."

"Gram has spoken. Goodnight and thank you," he whispers the last part as he bends down to kiss the older woman on the cheek.

Gesturing for Zara to lead the way out of the kitchen, Garrett follows a step behind. This is completely new for Zara and she pauses to move out of the way twice in the distance between the kitchen and her bedroom door.

"Here, let me show you how to make a call before you go to bed." Garrett stands at the doorway of Zara's room but does not step inside. It only takes a quick lesson for Zara to call his phone using the preprogrammed number.

"Goodnight, Zara. I'll see you in the morning." With that, Garrett turns around and walks back down the hallway. Zara stands in the threshold of her bedroom, holding her new phone and its box.

Despite a long day filled with new information and gifts, one thought lingers in Zara's mind.

Why is he not touching me anymore?

She steps further into her bedroom and closes the door, then walks to the militarily-made bed and sits down.

Pulling the phone out of its box, she texts Sloane.

> Hello. I wanted to let you know I am okay. I have a lot to talk to you about. Please do not worry. I will call you on Thursday. PS My hair ties are here. Oh, this is Zara.

The ding and then vibrate alert to an incoming text, makes Zara smile.

> I'm really glad you're here. Sweet dreams.

A second ding and vibration announces a second text.

> I have been worried. You better call me. PS HOW?

Zara puts the phone on the nightstand next to its box. So much has happened since leaving the Circle. The presence of her hair ties and all of her favorite stuff has not been explored. And they aren't the last thoughts on Zara's mind as she slips into sleep.

He is glad I am here.

CHAPTER 6

Upon waking, Zara makes her way to the kitchen to the aroma of freshly brewed coffee and the sound of music playing. It is not the soft piano of yesterday, but something light and airy with a woman soulfully singing.

Zara pauses hearing Garrett's voice mingled with another voice, foreign to her. Uncertain, she waits to enter the kitchen. Garrett catches a glimpse of her and makes his way to her side. He has an unfamiliar smile as he stands in front of her. With a start, Zara realizes she is disappointed she is not alone with Garrett this morning. His not touching her comes as a surprise so she schools her features the way she has been taught. Zara smiles up at Garrett.

"Good morning. You look amazing." Feeling uncertain about responding her hand goes to her neck, her fingers sliding down to the end of the chain to grasp the pendants.

"Good morning and thank you. I can come back later if I am interrupting."

"What? Never. You could never interrupt. You remember my mother. My parents arrived very early this morning. Come. I want you to meet her."

Garrett reaches for her hand then withdraws abruptly. Zara's heart sinks.

Why? Why does he stop?

She searches his eyes for answers, but finds only a practiced smile and an empty stare.

"Lead the way."

Garrett steps aside and follows close behind as Zara makes her way into the kitchen. At the table sits a woman with manicured blonde shoulder length hair flashing the same brilliant smile as Garrett's. She stands and meets Zara with a bear hug.

"I am so glad that you are here with us, Zara," she says with quiet sincerity. "As is my son, who has been looking forward to meeting you for a while."

"Mother!"

Zara laughs in delight at Garrett's childish tantrum. She begins to take a chair between them, and then remains standing as an afterthought.

"I'll get the coffee," Garrett says motioning for her to take a seat.

Zara's attention returns to Garrett's mother when she asks, "How do you like Michigan so far?"

"I like it very much, thank you. Your home is lovely. Thank you for allowing me to stay."

"Nonsense. This is your home now. The Ceremony may not have been completed, but you decided to come here with Garrett. That makes you family."

As Garrett places large cups of creamy coffee before her and his mother, tears once more pool in her eyes at the disappointment. She has let them down by not going through with the Ceremony. Eyes down, Zara concentrates on the music playing.

"Zara, would you be interested in going for a drive?" Garrett asks.

She nods slightly.

"I'll be right back."

Zara drinks a little more of her coffee listening to him retreat behind her. Alone with Garrett's mother, she has no idea what to say or what protocol to follow.

Breathe. There is nothing that can be done. Eyes down. Breathe, Zar.

"Zara Faith, please don't feel embarrassed for one second. You did a very brave thing choosing the path you know nothing about."

Zara looks into her eyes shocked to discover a hint of tears that mirror her own. Garrett's mother reaches out and warmly takes her hand. The contact is more than she had received from her own mother in many years, adding to the inundation of feelings Zara is experiencing.

"Sweets, you are not the first one to decide not to complete their Circle Ceremony. In fact you now know three women that have done it and all have survived. Although one has not survived as well as the other two."

Zara is unable to suppress her look of surprise.

"That's right. I refused to go through with the Ceremony until I met my Sir. Trudy stopped the planning of her Ceremony." She held up her fingers as she went through the list. "And your mother is the third."

The silence is deafening. Both women stare at one another for several minutes. Zara searches for more answers in the eyes staring back at hers.

"Zara, breathe dear. You are going to pass out."

"I don't understand. My mother?"

"Zara Faith, that's not my story to tell and I'm sorry that your mother hasn't shared her story with you yet. I will, however, share mine with you though I don't think now is a good time. Just know everyone here has a great deal of respect for the courage it took to walk out of the Circle without a collar."

Zara's fingers fly up to her neck as if to verify a collar had not been placed there without her knowledge.

Reaching for Zara's hand, Garrett's mother cradles it in both of hers, "It will be alright, Zara Faith. The unknown doesn't mean it's wrong or forever."

"Thank you." The concern gives Zara a sense of closeness she had not felt with her own mother in years. Before Zara can ask Garrett's mother more, a frown passes over her face.

"Sweets. I can hear you thinking all the way over here. Please let go of the information I have shared with you about your mother. In time she will open up and tell you her story. That is my hope, anyway. There is no point in allowing it to run rampant through your thoughts."

Blushing, Zara looks down at the coffee remaining in the cup. She slowly brings the cup to her lips and takes a long sip. Even at a lukewarm temperature, Garrett's coffee is the best Zara has ever tasted, including her many trips to Starbucks with Sloane.

Knowing her thoughts of Garrett have betrayed her, Zara's blush deepens.

"Well, Zara Faith, it is not your mother turning your cheeks pink. It must be my very handsome son. Isn't this an interesting turn of events," she declares. "What is your most pressing question? I know you are bouncing several around and are not sure if you should ask. Here in this house, you should always ask."

"He stopped touching me," Zara coughs in surprise at the

bluntness of her question, rushes on to explain but falters in the end. "From the moment we were in the Circle until last night, he touched me. He would hold my hand or lay his hand on my back. Now he has stopped– not even brushing up against me. I don't understand. Forgive me, please. This is not a subject I should be having with his mother."

"Let's start with you calling me Charlotte. I'm actually the perfect person for you to talk to about this since I, too, am a submissive. Trudy is also a resource for you. Anytime. Let me ask you a question. At any point between the time you were in the Circle and now, did you pull away from Garrett or ask not to be touched?"

"Last night I requested to get off his lap. I was upset and he wanted to talk about it but I needed space to discuss what was wrong. I only needed it for that conversation." In a voice barely above a whisper, Zara realizes she has discovered the reason for his retreat. "I did not know it would stop all the closeness."

"Ahhh..." Charlotte nods. "When a Dom is not in a collared relationship with a submissive, there are certain protocols that must be adhered to at all times. Garrett is very attracted to you and has been for quite some time. I see you're surprised to hear this. He knows you much better than you are aware.

"When you asked Garrett to release you from his hold, you set a boundary that he will not cross. You may have intended it for just that conversation, but to him, you requested space between the two of you. Until you remove that boundary, Garrett will fight with every fiber in his body to respect that. Never mistake his respect as disinterest."

Male voices can be heard coming closer and Charlotte, reading the concern on Zara's face, rushes to say, "Zara Faith, the only way to change the boundary that he perceives that you want is to talk to him about it."

Charlotte's last sentence dances around in Zara's mind as Garrett and an older version of him walk into the room. They are smiling and it is obvious they have just finished a conversation meant only for them.

"Dad, this is Zara. Zara, this is my dad, John Warren." It is impossible to miss the joy Garrett feels making the introduction. Charlotte and Zara stand as he approaches them, his face lit with a huge smile. He stops briefly behind Charlotte to caress her shoulders, then moves toward Zara.

"Zara Faith, it is a pleasure to meet you. Please call me Warren. Before we go any further, I would like to let you know that in this house I have only one sub and that is Charlotte. Since you are collared by no one, you are here as part of our family. I would ask that you conduct yourself as freely as you possibly can. Now give me a hug."

Unsure she has just heard everything correctly, Zara slowly takes a step forward, then suddenly finds herself engulfed with her first hug by a man other than her little brother in as long as she can remember.

"Okay... okay... okay. Dad, let Zara go." Warren releases her and walks over to Garrett and enfolds him with the same embrace.

So... this is the difference between a dad and a father. A dad would have been nice.

"I have to run. I love you, son. Be careful to remember that while Zara is with you, she is your complete responsibility in every way. Have fun today."

"Will you still be here when we get back?" Garrett asks his dad after extracting himself.

"I don't think so, but Trudy will remain here until you head back to the city. Call if you need anything. Zara, it has been a pleasure to meet you. We will make more time to talk next time. Charlotte, I will be in my office."

With that, Warren turns and walks out, returning the same way he came. Charlotte stands and gives Zara a quick hug, then embraces Garrett for a few beats longer.

"I love you, Son. Please take care of our Zara Faith." Grabbing her cup of coffee off the table, Charlotte gives a last wink and follows after her Dom.

Mulling over how the interaction in this family is nothing like her own, Zara startles at Garrett's voice just behind her. "Do you have your phone?"

Zara nods and then follows Garrett out into the sunshine. Zara closes her eyes and turns her face up to the sun, reveling in the warmth of the morning. She is spending some time alone with Garrett.

They walk to the open top Jeep. Garrett mistakes the source of her smile and chuckles, "So you like Jeeps then."

Closing the door behind her, he reaches in to hand her a hair tie from his pocket. She pulls her hair into a messy bun. Uncertain about so many things in her life, Zara is certain the distance between she and Garrett will be gone by the end of the day.

Garrett climbs in, turns the ignition and cranks the stereo so loud Zara cannot hear herself think.

Perfect.

Zara finds a peaceful confidence in the rhythmic pulse and the woman's conviction, appreciating the power in her voice as she takes hold of the song. The song ends way too soon and Zara considers begging Garrett to replay it.

Sitting side by side, the loud music becomes the conversation between them. A couple times, Garrett turns the music all the way down to ask if the song that is playing is okay. Responding with an enthusiastic head nod, he sends the volume soaring back up.

Enjoying a puffy white cloud scurrying across the deep blue sky, Zara leans her head back against the head rest to soak in the woman singing *Here's to Us*. Enjoying the scenery whipping by, a feeling of disappointment replaces Zara's relaxation as the Jeep pulls back into the driveway.

CHAPTER 7

Trudy suggested that I begin writing some of my thoughts in this journal. She said that after so many years of being taught to not express how we feel it will be a safe place for me to explore how I feel. She also said my situation is radically different from anyone else's because they all stayed within the safety of the Community. Feels strange to write my thoughts and feelings.

The look on Mother's face when I turned to walk out of the Circle will not go away. Although her body was in absolutely perfect presentation position for my father, her expression was completely mine. In the instant we had, I saw no anger or sadness for the loss of a daughter. I saw disappointment in her eyes. There was a great disappointment in a daughter who had failed her so publicly in front of the Community but, more importantly, her Master. All those years of trying to make her proud of me have been erased.

My Fredrik. How I miss you, brother. This beautiful place has been a paradigm shift. I have spent the last four days virtually alone with my thoughts on the beach. The family has been very welcoming and you would like them very much. I miss you so much. When I lay in bed at night, I wish for those three knocks of yours before you open the door and come in to talk. Tomorrow, I leave here to go to college. I am so nervous. Scared even. I hope you know that you are in my thoughts.

Clipping the pen to the cover of the journal, Zara lays back on the blanket listening to the sounds of the water lapping over the shore and retreating. The screeching of birds as they search for food and the occasional boat horn from across the lake. After hours on the beach, it all resonates into an evenly balanced chorus that allows Zara to relax her wandering thoughts.

A shadow appears over Zara, it is Trudy standing in a big floppy hat and large glasses. "Mind if I sit with you?" Trudy asks.

Sitting up quickly, Zara replies, "I would like that." She moves over to give Trudy room on the blanket.

"Hold this, would you please?" Trudy hands Zara a straw bag before slowly easing herself down onto the blanket. "It has been a month of Sunday's since I've been out here."

Once she is settled, Zara hands her back her bag. Trudy takes out two travel mugs and gives on to Zara. "Iced tea."

"Thank you."

"Seems this is it." Trudy takes a long drink of her tea.

"I have never spent so much time alone."

"Well, Child. Garrett felt that after everything that you needed time between leaving your family and the Circle and starting at State to just take a breath. We all wanted you to have your space."

Zara looks at Trudy.

"Well, now."

Zara stiffens.

"Child, he will be back this evening for dinner. He just went to his cabin for the day."

"Cabin?" Zara's asks with definite interest.

Trudy nods and continues, "Garrett has a cabin left to him by his grandparent. It is his retreat. He often goes when he wants to get away and think. Much like you seem to be drawn to the water, he is drawn to the woods of his cabin."

Why did he not take me to the cabin with him?

"It's been nice having you around the house these last few days." Trudy interrupts Zara's thoughts.

"Trudy, I am nervous about going to State."

Reaching around Zara, Trudy draws her into a half hug. "Child, you are supposed to be scared. This next chapter is unknown to you. But, you do have one thing going for you…Garrett."

Zara looks back out over the water. Trudy places her hand on Zara's shoulder and leans on her to stand up. "It's hot out here. I don't know how you kids do it."

"Child, tomorrow morning you are going to wake up and Garrett is going to drive you to State. You will join a lot of other kids who are feeling the same way you are. Remember that my number is programmed in your phone and you can call me day or night, even just to say you are scared."

With that Trudy, started her slow ascend back to the house.

From several yards away, she turns back to Zara. "You will be ok. Child, you will be far better than ok."

Zara draws her knees up to her chest and wraps her arms around them tightly. Resting her cheek on her knee she closes her eyes.

Funny how someone I just met can try to comfort me but my own mother never could.

CHAPTER 8

Everything about this moment is exactly as Garrett said it would be. Zara takes a deep breath and squares her shoulders, looking down at the white access card in her sweaty hand. Feeling her car door open, Zara exhales one last time before stepping from the Jeep.

"This is it. Yakeley Hall."

Zara slowly takes the first steps toward her new home. Glancing back, she finds Garrett is leaning against his Jeep. Making no move to accompany her, she replays the detailed instructions he gave her while at the beach house and, again, on the drive over. His waiting at the Jeep until she was inside was not mentioned, yet she finds it is a welcome addition.

I wish we were still at the beach house.

Squaring her shoulders more confidently, Zara takes in her new home. Yakeley Hall is a lovely old red brick building with a plethora of windows, the lush greenery different than what she is used to in Chattanooga. Marbled steps lead to a set of wooden double doors with iron handles and stained glass mosaics in place of windows.

Zara waves the access card over a black electronic box above the iron handle and a tiny red light turns green. Quickly pulling the handle, Zara opens the door to her new life, barely believing how much has changed since waking up on her eighteenth birthday four days earlier.

Pausing long enough for one more deep breath, Zara walks through the entryway, resisting the urge to see if Garrett is still leaning against his Jeep. Inside the door, Zara looks up at the ceiling and closes her eyes.

Come on, Zar. You are not allowed to already miss him. You should have had the conversation with him. Now, when will you see him again? FOCUS! THIS IS YOUR LIFE!

This moment marks the beginning of a dream she had never dared dream. Zara reaches for the pendant Garrett had given her only a few days prior and finds some comfort in squeezing it in her hand. Needing to feel more control, she empties her mind and pictures a grain of sand.

Feeling calmer, Zara opens the inner door to the smell of an old building and books, bringing to mind the small public library she visits near her parents' home. Many hours were spent in that library reading to Fredrik when he was smaller.

Smiling at the memory, Zara hardly notices a bank of metal mailboxes in the wall across from the "front desk" area Garrett described. The 'Welcome to Yakeley' banner would probably have led her to the correct location without his thorough instructions.

Growing up, Zara had imagined students milling about the halls discussing science and philosophy. Much to her surprise and disappointment, she is the only person in the lobby, making her feel smaller than normal.

A student dressed in a pink MSU tee shirt and cut off shorts sits staring at a computer screen as Zara approaches the desk. Not wanting to interrupt, she stands silently in front of the counter and patiently waits to be noticed. Observing a room off the lobby with several couches and comfy chairs, she is startled when a door in the lobby opens and an older woman walks up to her with a welcoming smile.

"Hello, have you been waiting long?"

"No, Ma'am. I just arrived a moment ago. I am here to check in. My name is…"

"Zara. My name is Kaye. I am here to help get you to your room. Beth, this is Zara. Zara, this is Beth."

Kaye gives the girl at the counter a stern look. Beth gets to her feet, her annoyed expression replaced with a smile that doesn't quite reach her eyes.

"Very nice to meet you, Zara. Welcome to Yakeley. Thanks for choosing our dorm this year."

Sliding a green laminated folder in Zara's direction, Beth continues with her exaggerated niceties.

"Here's a copy of the dorm's rules and regs as well as the university's, and a schedule of dorm meetings and events. The temporary entry key you somehow already got your hands on must be returned once you get your student ID. Your ID will be your access key. If you have any questions, I will be waiting at this desk until you are as comfortable as ALL your money can make you."

"Beth!" Kaye touches Zara's arm to motion her to follow her. "Come this way, Zara."

Walking away from the desk, she continues, "I understand you're from down south. I'm not hearing an accent. Were you raised elsewhere?"

"No, Ma'am. My parents felt an accent was not appropriate for their children so we worked to minimize our accent. Linguistics lessons at a young age helped and we were required to speak without the use of slang." Zara's voice dwindles off at the end as a look of consternation crosses Kaye's face. Conversations with her mother about 'outsiders' come rushing back.

Using a technique her mother had taught her, she changes the subject, "Is there anything you might tell me about Yakeley Hall?"

Kaye smiles broadly, "Yakeley Hall is the only all-female dorm remaining on campus here at Michigan State. Built in 1948, there is no elevator or air conditioning. Of course, you will not have to worry about that."

"Here we are. This is your room. I am going to let you get settled. If you need anything, Beth will be at the front desk."

As Kaye walks away, Zara worries her social skills pale in comparison with the other students at Yakeley. Home-schooling and limited friendships to fellow community children had insulated her life.

The first thing Zara sees as she walks into her room is a vase overflowing with daisies. Just inside the door to her left, strings of beads form a white curtain. Tentatively, Zara runs her hand through them enjoying their tinkling tune and remembering her recent introduction to Chopin's *Spring Waltz*, a piece Trudy and Charlotte loved.

Zara moves silently to the center of the room, spinning once in a tight circle. For a brief moment, she contemplates lying on the floor with her arms and legs stretched out to see if she is able to touch both sides of the room.

Zara is transported back to the beach house by the freshly painted walls done in light blue complimented by a twin bed resembling a big fluffy cloud with its oversized comforter and two puffy pillows. Along with the white dresser at the end of the desk, the room feels light and airy.

Zara moves closer to the desk noticing two matching black frames sitting on the corner of the desk to either side of the vase of daises. Zara picks up a frame holding a picture of her family.

Her mother had insisted on having a family picture taken at the beginning of the summer. All the other photos in their house are candid. Her father didn't like the fuss of organized photo shoots. Actually, he often made it clear he didn't see the point of pictures.

Never had Zara witnessed her mother so adamant about anything like she was when begging to take these family photos. She had been willing to endure a serious punishment for pushing Zara's father to the point beyond what he would tolerate. In the end, there was both a punishment and a photograph.

Zara was touched to find it since she would be leaving behind everything as she began her new life with her Dom. Zara's job would be to do what she was told when she was told to do it. Her mother had prepared her well for her new life.

The second picture is one from her nightstand of her and Sloane astride horses taken the first day of lessons.

Zara gently stroked the image of Sloane's face, suddenly missing her friend and her family. Well, her brother. She missed Fredrik. Her parents... well... they are her parents and she loves them, but there was always a distance between her and her parents. She could not recall the last time either her mother or father had given her a hug, a stark contrast to Garrett's parents who freely demonstrated their affection with bone crushing embraces.

Feeling her phone vibrating in her back pocket stops the futile attempt at recalling a memory of her parents that just doesn't exist. Garrett smiles at her from the phone's display.

"Hello."

"How's it going?" he inquires, uncertainty in his voice. A long silence follows as Zara nods but is unable to answer. "Zara, are you alright?"

"I think so," she pushes out. Garrett sighs and she rushes on, "I am trying to be."

"Zara, listen to me. If at any point you don't want to be there, you call me and I'll come and pick you up. Do you understand?"

"Yes. Thank you."

"You belong in that dorm and at this school, Zara. Don't be afraid."

"Thank you. I… I will be okay."

"Zara. Repeat what I said."

"Don't be afraid."

"What else?"

"If I do not want to be here and want to leave… you will come and get me."

"Right. I'll check on you later," Garrett says firmly.

Zara nods and in the space of dead air, Garrett lightly chastises, "I can't hear you when you nod, Little One."

Garrett hangs up and an alarming thought enters Zara's mind. Where would she go if this doesn't work? Would her family allow her to return after failing to complete the Circle Ceremony? Her father is on the King Council. Would returning home be an option without being the sub that she was raised to become?

An envelope sticking halfway out from under one of the pillows catches Zara's eye. Picking it up, she stares at the handwriting, appreciating the casual flourish of the 'Z' in her name. Before she has a chance to open the letter, Zara's notification goes off.

Recognizing Sloane's number, Zara sets the letter down and reads the message.

    Is this a safe time?

Zara replies smiling and nodding.

    Yes. I miss you.

A moment later another text shows up.

    Miss you too. What the hell is going on? I
    am worried sick about you.

While waiting for a response, Zara had looked out the window seeing a street lined with ancient maple trees. In a parking spot under one of those trees, a Jeep was sitting with the top down.

Is that Garrett? Is he still here?

Zara's heart jumps into her throat. The alert vibrates again.

    So what is going on? Details!

Zara quickly texts back saying she will call her in a couple of hours.

Grabbing her key from the desk, Zara heads for the door. She rushes out of the building, and then pauses. The trees she had seen from her room are not in front of her. Rushing around the corner, she repeats to herself, "Please still be there. Please still be there."

When he recognizes her running toward him from around the corner of the building, he jumps out of the Jeep to meet her halfway. Zara leaps into his arms. Held in his tight embrace, she whispers into his neck. "Thank you for still being here."

"Zara, I'll always be here. I'll never leave. I wanted to be close while you explored your room."

"I am nervous," she confirms.

"Let's walk around campus and talk for a bit?"

Zara nods.

Taking her hand, Garrett leads her down the tree-lined street. He begins to speak in a low tone that requires Zara to block out all the other sounds to concentrate on his words.

"Everyone is scared when they come to school for the first time. I was terrified the day my parents dropped me off. But... I was also excited. My hope is that you have that same combination."

Crossing the street, Garrett guides Zara down the sidewalk toward a tall tower. A heavy aroma of flowers fills the air.

"This is Beaumont Tower. It's a working bell tower."

Zara stares up at the tower.

"It is beautiful. There is so much greenery, but I smell flowers."

Garrett squeezes Zara's hand, smiling, "It's a plant lab."

Throughout their walk, Garrett continues to enthusiastically point out the highlights of campus, the museum, library and Stadium.

Campus is definitely his favorite place.

Zara feels her hand slip free from Garrett's moments before he steers her by the upper arm into a small opening in the thick vegetation.

"Zara... watch your step."

Nodding, Zara marvels that she is standing at the top of three wide marble steps looking out over a spectacular garden. Lush flowers adorn a small pond with a quaint walking bridge over it. A chorus of birds brings the hidden garden to life.

Overwhelmed by the beauty, Zara turns to look at Garrett standing just behind her. "Sir, may I ask why this is referred to as the 'plant lab'?"

"Garrett," he chuckles and continues, "Beal Botanical Gardens. It's the oldest working plant lab in the country. You seem enthralled. Shall we walk around the garden?"

"Si… That is not necessary. I appreciate you showing me this. I would rather continue your tour."

"Okay. Another time."

Leading her back out of the garden, Garrett points out locations recalled from his campus days, sharing short accounts of his experiences. Zara silently hopes she will find friends and make memories of her own.

"May I ask, where are all the students?" Having only seen a handful of people around campus, Zara wonders if she is missing something.

"Main student check in is on Saturday. Upperclassmen check in tomorrow afternoon."

"But how did I get to check in? Will I be alone in the building until Saturday?"

With a shrug Garrett responds, "I made arrangements for a student worker to be available for you to move in early. I wanted you to have time to get settled before the other students overwhelmed you."

Zara cannot disguise from Garrett the horror recalling Beth's comments earlier suggesting she was entitled by wealth for early access. Raised to never question or react, Zara suddenly finds herself completely off balance. Needing to be away from him to find her center and yet drawn to be near him, Zara feels she is losing her ability to mask her emotions.

The rest of their walk is done in relative silence. Garrett points out landmarks while Zara listens, but cannot stop thinking about the special arrangements Garrett has made for her comfort. Her years of training are no match for the break in the mental wall that is occurring.

Arriving back at the Jeep, Zara looks up toward her room to see if it is as visible to Garrett as he was to her. She finds it is and that pushes her further off kilter. For the first time since leaving the

Circle, Zara feels a desperate need to be alone with her thoughts.

"Little One, your face is giving you away. Would you like to go to dinner and talk?"

"Thank you for walking with me. I need to get settled in as you mentioned the arrival of all the other students will be overwhelming. It would be better for me to return to my room." Zara plasters a smile on her face that she hopes radiates happiness and contentment.

"Very well. A student employee will be staying in the building tonight so you'll have someone available if you need anything. Dinner has been arranged. I will take you to breakfast in the morning. Please be in front of the dorm at 9:30.

"Now, get going. I will wait here until I see your light in the window." The lightness in Garrett's voice was unmistakable.

"Thank you." Zara says. Garrett tilts his head and stares into her eyes with concern as she continues. "Thank you for giving me this opportunity. I do not know how to express how thankful I really am."

Emotions held too long at bay are beginning to take over. Turning, Zara walks quickly toward the entrance of her new home. Just before turning the corner, she hears Garrett say, "Goodnight, Zara. You're welcome."

CHAPTER 9

Safely inside, and knowing Garrett is outside, Zara moves the curtains to the side allowing him a glimpse of her arrival. Quickly closing the curtains, Zara collapses on her bed, everything about the last several days overwhelming. A lifetime of training for the Circle Ceremony had not prepared her for this loneliness. In the past, Fredrik would have bound into her room to push her worry away. Zara pictured how he looked at her before she got out of the car the morning of the Ceremony.

He was smiling. Exuberantly, happy she was exiting his life to embark on a new journey and start a different life, a life away from a dominating father. Zara had felt so angry seeing his joy and knowing the opportunities as a new submissive to visit your family for the first few years was nonexistent. Traditions within the Community were hard to change and Zara knew that she did not have what it took to change them. Ironically, she grew up not knowing if she had what it took to live a life as was dictated by the King Council.

Zara had spent hours questioning Sloane why she thought things were the way they were. The history of the Council was not normally exposed to younger members. Sloane never questioned the traditions. She just expressed relief that her future had already been charted out. Romantic to her core, Sloane was confident whomever her father and the Council chose for her would be her soul mate.

Suddenly remembering her promise to call, Zara reaches for her phone. Sloane picks up on the second ring and Zara hears the happiness in her best friend's standard perky greeting.

"Hello... Hello... Hello."

"Hello."

"And whom do I have the pleasure of speaking with this evening?"

Smiling at the warm familiarity, Zara removes her shoes and crawls under the soft white covers of her bed. Closing her eyes, she transports herself to Sloane's comfortable bed.

"Still just Zara."

"Are you alright? Seriously, are you okay?"

"Yes. I am alright." Swallowing hard, Zara does her best to keep her voice even. The last thing she wants is to make her best friend worry. With so much distance between them, as well as the distance Zara imagines being placed between them by the Council, there is nothing Sloane would be able to do to help.

"You are trying too hard. I already know that you are not doing okay. Please do not underestimate how well I know you Ms. Zara Faith Evans. Talk to me. Tell me everything and the nothings, too."

Over the next several hours, Zara takes Sloane through the entire story of how she came to be lying in a dorm room alone. Listening closely, Sloane would chime in with a well-placed question, typically, for clarification on a point. Her questions all revolved around Garrett and if Zara had been paying attention, she would have realized that Sloane was leading her to a particular point with the line of questions.

Exhausted with telling her story, Zara needs answers to her questions. Carefully thinking of what is truly important and what she is willing to do without knowing, Zara dives in headfirst.

"Sloane, how is Fredrik? I never got to say goodbye."

Sighing, Sloane is quiet for a moment. Knowing Sloane like a sister, Zara waits for her to determine how to best respond in a way that will make it seem like everything is going to be okay.

"Zara, your father was embarrassed. Your mother's expression never changed. The Kings left first and were all muttering to themselves. Your father led your mother out. When I was walking out of the hall, I saw your father arguing with your Dom's family.

"Wait. Not your Dom. I'm so sorry. I don't know what to call him. We left immediately after that and I could not get anyone to tell me what had happened. Zar, I was so scared."

"I know. I am so sorry. I contacted you the moment I was able. What about Fredrik? Have you spoken to him? Is he alright? Did you tell him I was alright?"

"Zar, I have not been able to get in contact with him. I started texting him and calling the minute I left the ceremony to see if he knew what was going on and where you were. I went over to your house, Zara. They are gone."

"Gone? What does that mean? Gone? Did you ask my mother? What is gone?"

"Zara, I have been over there every day. I have called Fredrik's number and the house phone. I have tried different times of day. I even went to your father's place of work."

Zara gasps, alarmed that Sloane would go to see her father at work. He is very private and from the earliest time she could remember, she was told that when father is at work, he was unreachable.

Her father was good provider for the family. They lived in a beautiful home and both of her parents drove top of the line cars. Zara and her brother were home-schooled and she didn't know other kids to draw comparisons of their home life, but she always felt like she had what was needed.

As a member of the King Council, her father was proper in every aspect of his life. Often, he would comment that it was up to him and the family to be examples for the Community. All rules set by the King Council were to be followed. This meant complete obedience for Zara and her mother.

Fredrik was the bright light in Zara's home life. Being only 18 months apart, they were friends as well as siblings. Zara would ask Fredrik to sneak into her room when she was on punishment. Or "in training", as her mother referred to it.

Zara would light up when Fredrik was around. King Council by-laws were law in their house and he was the only one she could confide in about her real dreams and fears. Fredrik had a few years yet but eventually he would be heading toward the ceremonial circle to collar a submissive of his own and join his father on the King Council. As the Dom, he would be privy to the selection process and be able to contribute feedback on the pool of applicants. Like Zara, the potential submissive would have no knowledge of who their future Dom would be. This was always bothersome for Zara, as the Council and her father expected this to be a legal marriage to the outside world.

The night her mother came to her room to inform her that she had been paired, Zara rebelled. She screamed at her mother that she was being sold to the highest bidder and that there was no way her mother could love her if she would allow this to happen.

Sitting, rock still, her mother waited for her to finish and then calmly continued going over the details; the date and events of the ceremony were already known by all. Tradition dictated it was to be her eighteenth birthday. The first night of being an adult she would be given to a stranger to begin her new life.

With tears rolling down her cheeks, Zara fell to the feet of her mother and asked her why. For one moment, the schooled expression slipped and Zara was granted the opportunity to see the immense hurt in her mother's eyes.

In a blink of an eye, the well-trained sub slipped the mask of control back into place and stared at her hands resting gently in her lap. That had been the last time Zara ever questioned her mother on the traditions of their Community.

That was five months before her eighteenth birthday and what little relationship Zara had with her mother grew more distant after that night. By the day of the Ceremony, the two of them only spoke about traditions and exceptions.

Silent tears fall onto the pillow as she remembers that night. Zara had never shared that conversation with Sloane. When she had told Fredrik, they had both cried. It was one of only two times she had seen him get emotional. To be honest, Zara did not know if he was crying for her or his mother's pain.

"Zara, are you still there?"

"Mmhm," she snapped back to the conversation with Sloane. "I am here."

"Sweet girl, I know your family is fine. I am sure they went on vacation that night. You know it is common for the Dom's family to send the family away to give everyone time to adjust to the transfer."

"Sloane! Transfer?! We are not property. How is this still happening? How can you be alright with this entire process?"

"It sounds to me like you already have feelings for your would-be Dom. You talked about him for three hours. His hair, the way he smells, even the fact that you miss his touch when he removes his hand from yours. Yet, you ask me how I can believe in the process that paired the two of you together?

Her tone switched to admonishment, "Seriously, Zara. It was a really selfish decision not to go through with the ceremony. Everyone is talking about you. It is our role to carry on the traditions and ensure that the Community grows and stays secure. How could you not want to do your part?"

There is no mistaking the anger elevating Sloane's voice. Zara blinks away the tears falling from her eyes. Silence overcomes them and they sit listening to the other breathe. Sloane finally breaks the silence.

"Listen, I am glad you are safe. I am also glad that you are getting to follow your dreams and go to school. Your family is fine. Mother told me tonight I have been paired and will have a lot to do in preparation for my Ceremony.

"I think it would be better if we did not talk for a while. My parents are not going to allow you to attend my Circle Ceremony because you have fallen out of the good graces of the Council. I was not going to tell you tonight but we may as well get it all out now.

"I love you. I always will, but I believe in our traditions and I am looking forward to having my collar placed around my neck. I am sorry you do not feel the same way. I have to go. Enjoy college, Zara."

The phone clicks in Zara's ear. She slowly brings the phone to her lap. Sloane is gone. Pressing a fist against her lips, heavy sobs escape as Zara's anguish at losing her best friend a second time in so few days, as a result of following her own dreams.

Her best friend. Her family. Her Community. Zara closes her eyes and works to still her mind. She focuses on the sounds of the waves rolling over the shore at the beach house, the smell of wet sand under her bare feet and the warmth of the sun on her shoulders. Taking deep breaths, Zara replaces the thoughts causing her such pain with a moment in time that is hers and hers alone.

The rhythmic sounds in her mind send Zara into a fitful sleep, the last thought of Garrett, and the wonder at how a short amount of time together was all she needed to feel a sense of belonging that she had not expected.

Zara wakes a few hours later, confused by her surroundings. Gathering her thoughts, she rises and opens the door to her bathroom. No longer surprised to find her favorite color or supplies, she steps onto a plush pink floor mat and opened the new toothbrush. Grabbing toothpaste and dental floss from under the sink, Zara brushes her teeth.

Exploring her dorm room, she pushes the bead curtain strands aside to see what is hiding inside. Discovering a silver half-circle loop on the side of the closet, she tucks the beads in the loop.

Zar. Look at all of that. Everything is so perfectly perfect.

Zara steps back, struck by the organization. Shoes, boots, blouses, sweaters, sweatshirts, sweatpants, shirts, and dresses fill the space. Overwhelmed, Zara goes to the dresser and opens a drawer at the bottom. Sleep clothes... just like at the beach house. Pulling out her all-time favorite pink tee, matching sleep pants and a pair of fuzzy pink socks, she begins to change.

Lifting her shirt over her head, she is astonished by a knock at her door. A muffled voice announces, "Hey. I have your dinner. Your Highness."

Surprised into stillness, it takes the person pounding on her door to pull Zara from her trance. She opens the door. In the hall stands Beth, from the front desk. She looks even more annoyed than she had earlier.

"Apparently, I am your personal delivery person now." Handing Zara two large handle bags, Beth turns and walks back down the hall. Not given a chance to respond, Zara says thank you in a voice that would not have been heard if Beth had been standing beside her.

"Whatever," Beth snapped back with a wave over her head.

Zara peers into the two bags and retreats back into her room, closing the door and placing the bags next to the flowers on the desk. Not wanting to eat but knowing there is a good chance Garrett will inquire about her dinner, she opens a bag. Inside are salad, bread, and dessert in Styrofoam packages. The second bag has two heavier containers of chicken parmesan and lasagna. Zara loves Italian but even on a good day, she would not be able to finish the food and this had not been a good day.

Zara takes out the chicken parmesan, adds bread to it and puts a bit of salad on the lid of the container. Re-bagging the rest, she grabs her key and takes the excess food with her. Thinking that her mother would be appalled that she was leaving her room looking this unkempt, she forces the thought away and heads to the lobby.

Sitting behind the desk reading a book, Beth doesn't look up when Zara approaches. Setting the bags down on the counter, Zara turns and walks away, tossing over her shoulder. "I cannot finish all the food so you can have it if you would like."

Already to the opening of her hallway before Beth responds, she hears a quick thank you. Waving her hand above her head, a smile on her face, Zara mimics Beth. "Whatever."

HA! You were not expecting a bit of kindness were you, Miss. Beth.

Unlocking the door to her room, the scent of warm Italian makes her stomach growl. Zara is ready to eat her first meal as a college student. Zara opens the mini fridge for the first time, knowing what she will find before the door is open. She pulls out a can of Arnold Palmer, and then sits at her desk, silently eating the best Italian she had ever had.

Picking up her phone, Zara locates Garrett's name and sends him a text.

> Thank you for dinner. It was too much but delicious.

A moment later she receives a reply.

> Glad you liked it. Everything okay?

She quickly taps back.

> Yes, thank you.

Another immediate reply.

> Little One, what is going on in that head of yours?

Ruefully, Zara sends another message. She did not mean to make him worry.

> Everything is good. I am sorry to have bothered you. Good night.

The phone rings. Knowing it has to be Garrett, Zara smiles and answers it, but before she says hello, he says, "Zara Faith. You can't be a bother. I am at dinner at the moment but I can be at the dorm in about 30 minutes."

In the background, Zara hears the clink of silver and a woman's voice, "Garrett, I need to make a call. I will be right back."

The smile slides off Zara's face.

Ummmm... who is that?

"Okay. Sorry, Zara. As I was saying, I am just finishing up dinner and I can be at the dorm in 30 minutes."

Wondering what she interrupted, Zara shakes her head. "Little One, I cannot hear you when you nod. Talk to me, please."

"Everything is fine. I am fine. The room is perfect. I will talk to you later." The volume of her responses decreases with each sentence, the last is barely audible.

"I will be out front at 9:30 for breakfast. Get some sleep."

"Ok." She whispers.

The phone disconnects. Holding it in her hand for a while, Zara wills Garrett to call her back. When the phone doesn't ring, she places it on the desk with her daisies.

What have I done?

Crawling under the covers of her new comfortable bed, Zara finds her pendant and encases it in her hand, closes her eyes and searches for something to focus on, but the sound of the woman saying Garrett's name keeps playing in her mind.

Feeling alone in every way she considers the choice that brought her to this point. Her reality would be dramatically different had she declined Garrett's offer and he placed the collar around her neck. He wanted her to choose this. And if he wanted this, then the only conclusion Zara could ascertain was that Garrett did not want her as his submissive. Garrett did not want to marry her.

CHAPTER 10

Waking to a pounding at the door, Zara jumps out of bed and flies across the room to open the door. Wondering if she is late for breakfast with Garrett, she is surprised to find Beth standing in front of her. The smell of coffee trumps asking what Beth is doing at her door.

"I don't know how you take your coffee or if you even drink it, but I got you a latte. You can dump it if you don't want it." Thrusting the coffee into Zara's hand, Beth finishes her statement with a shoulder shrug.

"Thank you. My addiction is full blown."

"Whatever."

Beth turns and walks down the hall back toward the front desk, leaving Zara standing in the doorway and holding a steaming hot latte.

Zara giggles as she makes her way back to bed with the hot cup of coffee, knowing today is going to be a much better day. Pushing the curtain back, Zara checks the parking spot for Garrett's Jeep. No Jeep, but the forgotten letter sits waiting to be opened. Climbing back into bed, Zara sips the latte and opens the letter.

> *Dear Zara Faith,*
>
> *I have arranged your class schedule this semester, as there was not time for you to select your own classes. I will leave that to you in the future. All relevant information is located in the backpack.*
>
> *Also in a wallet in your backpack is a bankcard. I have arranged an account for your use at the Michigan State University Federal Credit Union. Please feel free to make a withdrawal whenever you wish. Currently, there is a balance of $1000.*
>
> *A credit card has been ordered and should arrive within the next week. This will be for any larger purchases you wish to make. I committed to taking care of your needs*

while you are at school and I intend to live up to my word.

You will find other campus related items in the backpack, including season tickets for football and basketball. Even if you are not a fan of sports I encourage you to attend, as they are a part of the college experience and that was your dream.

My intent is to give you the time and space you need to explore yourself and enjoy school. Enjoy your new space and if there is anything you find you need, please do not hesitate to contact me. As you know, my number is programmed into your phone.

Regards,

John Garrett Dawson

Zara rereads the letter. It is informative but the tone distant, a man fulfilling a duty. This is not the Garrett she had just spent time with at the beach. Where was the warmth she had felt when she ran into his arms yesterday?

As she slips it back into the drawer, Zara wonders if she is misinterpreting the closeness between them. There is so much Zara does not understand about Garrett. With a jolt, the sound of the woman saying she would be right back echoes in her mind and the self-doubt from last night comes crashing back with a vengeance.

Forcing the unwelcome thoughts away, Zara picks up her backpack. She begins to remove the items finding a laptop and a wristlet with a bankcard in it. The bankcard has a picture of Beaumont Tower on it reminding her of the tour Garrett took her on the day before.

Suddenly, remembering he was due to pick her up at 9:30am, Zara looks at the Breakfast at Tiffany's clock on the wall, shocked that it is already 8:30am. Zara quickly combs through the rest of the items laid out on her bed. The wristlet has a key ring with several keys, a paper copy of an MSU student ID and a pack of sweet mint gum. Flipping through the official MSU student planner, she finds a typed class list with times and locations attached to the inside cover.

Going to today's date, Zara sees there is an appointment at 10:00am in the Hannah building. She also discovers her first college class is Biology and it begins on Monday at 10am in Wells

Hall. Closing the planner, Zara attempts to remember where Wells Hall was located. Garrett had mentioned the building, but there were so many buildings and landmarks she could not recall its exact location.

Zara picks up her new laptop, carefully opens the top and hits the power button. Rather than get too comfortable, Zara sets the computer on the bed and walks to the bathroom. Meeting Garrett with furry teeth is not an option.

Turning on the shower and undressing, she takes a moment to confront herself in the mirror. This is her bathroom. This is her dorm room. Satisfied she is in control, Zara steps into the shower.

Standing under the stream of hot water, Zara's thoughts turn to the relaxing piano music that had been played at the beach house. Wondering if there was a way to get that on her phone and listen to it while showering, it didn't take long for all of her thoughts to be of Garrett.

She thought of how he stood at the stove in lounge pants and bare feet, a Michigan State University tee-shirt accentuating the muscles in his upper body, and how strong his arms were when he picked her up and held her.

Zara works the shampoo through her hair, rinses and reaches for conditioner, as she recalls his lips on her forehead and her hand held warmly in his. She picks up the natural sponge and pours some Dr. Bronner's on it. Starting with her neck, Zara lifts her necklace out of the way and soaps her body with the sponge, enjoying the strong scent of peppermint as she covers her body in a thick lather.

Unconsciously, Zara returns the sponge to the basket and runs both of her hands over her breasts. Her nipples harden as she caresses the under sides while picturing Garrett taking his tee shirt off and standing in front of her at the kitchen table.

Zara imagines running her hand over the muscles in his chest, brushing his nipples with her thumbs. Closing her eyes, and letting her head fall back, her hand slides down her stomach to the smooth area between her legs. She remembers Garrett leaning close to her asking her to leave with him.

Lightly spreading the bare lips, Zara's fingers brush the nub between them, a small moan escaping her lips. Holding her lips apart, Zara enjoys the cascade of water over her most sensitive parts. Having only touched herself a couple of times in the past, she explores with trepidation, the memory of Garrett kneeling before her spurning her on.

Zara uses one hand to brace herself against the shower wall. Her other hand continues, wet fingers spreading herself wide while lightly running her middle finger up the center of her clit.

Feeling a pressure begin to build, Zara allows it to happen. Until the thought of her mother's disapproval invades her thoughts. Even in the privacy of her new bathroom, miles from her home, she knows going any further is out of the question.

Washing herself thoroughly one more time, Zara rinses the conditioner from her hair and steps from of the shower. Standing in front of the mirror, Zara takes a longer look at her entire body. She is considered tall at 5'7" but only because both her mother and Sloane are much shorter. Beside Garrett, Zara feels like the perfect height. Releasing the pendant she had not realized she was holding, Zara considers what Garrett has chosen. He had picked out a 'Z' that is so much bigger than the g. For a Dom, it is an unusual thing to do, but then Garrett is not the 'usual' Dom Zara had been raised around.

In exasperation, Zara wonders if Garrett is the only thought she is capable of having in her head.

Where did he go last night? How far is his house from here? Why is the letter written in such a cold manner? How would he feel touching her nipples in the shower?

The last thought makes Zara's eyes pop open. She goes to the window to grab her coffee, wondering if she will find Garrett's Jeep outside waiting for her. She is disappointed when she peeks between the curtains and it isn't.

Sighing, she turns to get dressed. It hits her that what she is feeling is how it feels to miss someone you want to be spending time with. Talking aloud to herself, she reasons, "Ok. I like him. I want to spend time with him. I want him to be here... outside looking up at my window."

Finishing hair and make-up, and wanting to look extra special for their breakfast, Zara tries on one of three floral maxi dresses hanging in the closet. The fit is perfect. She picks out an adorable pair of strappy sandals that buckle halfway up her calf.

Ready and waiting, Zara picks up the laptop and sits down on her bed, pushing herself back to the headboard. Moving her finger over the pad, the computer comes to life, the image bringing a wide smile to Zara's face.

It is a picture of her standing at the edge of the water looking down the beach. Whoever took the picture had perfect timing since Zara didn't recall looking down the beach. The blues in the picture are a perfect match to her wall color. Taking a closer look, Zara sees for the first time that the rug under bed is the color of the sand on the beach, the white of the foam the color of her pillow. Garrett has replicated the beach for her. Zara closes the laptop and takes in the room with an entirely new appreciation.

Realizing the time, Zara places everything back in the backpack and makes her bed, ensuring the room looks as it did when she entered yesterday. Outside the building, Zara finds Garrett standing against the stair rail looking down at his phone. Hearing the door snap shut, he looks up from his phone. As he looks her up and down, Zara is happy she had taken the extra time to look a bit nicer.

"You look amazing. I love this dress."

"Good morning." Zara responds softly.

"Really. I really love this dress. You should get a couple more of these." Zara smiles and nods.

Garrett gestures for Zara to walk on ahead of him. She smiles as she feels his eyes skim her backside as thoroughly as he had her front. Not seeing the Jeep, Zara pauses and looks back at Garrett.

"We are over here", he points out as they make their way to a large white sedan. Zara looks around and notes an increase in people in the area. Students are walking on the sidewalks and standing in small clusters.

Garrett opens the passenger door and Zara slides onto the soft leather seat. The driver's side has so many controls and buttons that it seems like a spaceship. Garrett opens his door and gracefully slides in. The steering wheel lowers into position.

"We are going to get you checked in and get your student ID and then head to breakfast."

There is never a question with Garrett. Zara trusts that Garrett knows the best thing to do and when. It is not that she has to ponder the idea, it is what she is raised to believe. It would never sit well with her parents if she were to tell him that was a stupid plan.

Pulling up to the Hannah Building, Garrett jumps out of the car and feeds the meter. Walking to Zara's side, he opens the door and offers her his hand. Accepting the assistance, Zara climbs out of the car.

In silence, the two of them walk to the building's entrance. Inside, Garrett leads the way to the student services office. Zara is asked for her license. She looks up at Garrett with a look of panic.

Garrett touches her arm to ease her fear. "Ma'am, this is Zara Faith Evans. She does not have a driver's license yet."

Pulling out his wallet, Garrett pulls out a piece of paper and hands it to the woman behind the counter. Reading it over, the woman shakes her head and tells Zara to step on the 'X' on the floor and look above the camera. Without any warning, Zara's picture is taken.

Garrett waits at the counter then pulls her close as she returns. Welcoming his warmth, she allows her body to fall into his, feeling safer and more secure. The woman walks over and places Zara's new student ID on the counter. Garrett nods for her to pick it up. Smiling, Zara looks more relaxed than she felt and the colors in the dress accentuate her sun-kissed skin.

Holding the small laminated card, Zara feels as if she is her own person for the very first time in her life. She never had a license. Her father felt it was a decision for her Dom whether Zara should be able to drive or not. Her whole identity as a child was wrapped up in her parents. After them, her entire identity was to revolve around her Dom.

Zara is amazed that this little card has the power to make her feel like a whole new person. Standing in the Administration Building on the campus of Michigan State University, Zara belongs to no one. She has to obey no one. For the first time in her life, she is going to call the shots for herself and the man standing next to her made this possible. Garrett is as important in this moment as the card Zara holds in her hand.

"What would the newest Michigan State SPARTAN like for breakfast?"

He asks such an easy question, a question anyone would be able to answer. Yet, as Zara stands next to the counter holding a card that makes her feel like her own person, she is unable to answer. Garrett touches her elbow to guide her from the counter.

"I don't know if I can do this." Zara blurts the words out then slaps a hand over her mouth.

Pulling her hand from her mouth, Garrett leads her outside to the car without acknowledging Zara's confession. Secure in the passenger seat, Zara sits in the seat with her hand resting in her lap. The card sits in her lap under both of her hands.

Garrett turns to face Zara at the first red light; his serious expression is unreadable. Zara glances at him then draws her eyes back down to her lap. Garrett says nothing and Garrett resumes driving when the light changes. Garrett sighs. Zara's body tenses in fear of Garrett being unhappy with her.

Garrett unclips his seatbelt but remains in his seat after pulling into a parking spot.

Finally opening his door and stepping out, Garrett takes his suit coat off and lays it across the backseat. Strolling around to Zara's side, he opens the door for her to climb out. Taking her ID and room key from her, he places them in the center console.

"Where's your phone?"

"I forgot it in my room."

"Zara Faith, it is critical you carry your phone. At all times… for safety reasons. Is that clear?"

"Yes. I am sorry." Zara says in a whisper standing next to the car unable to make eye contact.

Gently touching Zara's elbow, Garrett guides her to the patio of a green building. 'Golden Harvest' is painted on a sign. The smells swirling around are heavenly but all Zara can concentrate on is the fact that she has displeased Garrett. He gestures her to sit in one of the patio chairs and moves another one next to her but the opposite in the direction she is sitting. Zara can see a line of people at the front door of the building but Garrett is facing an abandoned building across the street.

When he sits, she realizes the positioning allows them to look at one another and speak without needing to raise their voices. Sitting in front of the restaurant with a line of customers waiting to go in, Garrett and Zara are able to have an intimate conversation without worrying about being overheard.

"Zara Faith. Do you know why I gave you the option of not completing the Circle Ceremony with me?" Her eyes grew to the size of saucers at his blunt question. Shaking her head only slightly, she is surprised they are having this important conversation sitting outside with people around.

"Little One. I've known about you since I was around ten years old." Zara eyes jump to meet Garrett's.

With an audible gasp, Garrett nods and continues. "Your mother and my mother are friends. As you know, the Community doesn't allow a submissive to maintain her relationships with her past lives without her Dom's permission. Your father refused, so their friendship was terminated.

"When you were born, my mother was the only person your mother asked to be notified. The information given was limited to your date of birth and the fact that you were a healthy beautiful baby girl named Zara Faith. My mother would always talk about you like you were an angel in a faraway land that I would someday meet.

"When the time came for me to go through the selection processes, you, Zara, were the only candidate I was interested in researching. Traditions within our Community are very shortsighted for future submissives. As you know you receive no information about the man that you are paired with. But for the Doms, it is a different story. Information is shared freely about the pool of submissives. When I began to research the adult you, there were indications you were not sold on the idea of being collared."

For the first time since Garrett began speaking, Zara looks away, embarrassed he knew of her lack of commitment to the Community and the traditions she had been raised in and humiliated that her feelings about the collaring ceremony have not been kept private.

"Little One, it's okay. I don't blame you for not wanting to be given to a man you've never met and know nothing about. Not knowing what kind of Dom I would be, what type of relationship I want, it's almost a relief that you questioned our ways."

"NEXT!" shouts a tall, lean man standing in shorts and a tee shirt. With the door held open, loud thumping music spills out. Garrett stands and quickly moves his chair back to its original location, gesturing for a stunned Zara to follow him inside the door.

"John, good to see you. Who have you brought with you

today?"

Garrett shakes the guy's hand. He then steps to the side and allows Zara to enter. "Zara, this is Timmy. Timmy serves the best coffee in the city and never allows your cup to get past half empty. Timmy, this is Zara. Zara is a lover of coffee like I have never. Seen. Before."

"Well, sit sit sit. You're in the right spot." Timmy is already filling the mug that is sitting on the table in front of the seat that Zara sits in. "Ms. Zara, take a second and look over the menu, Vanesa will be right over to take your order. Oh and check out the specials on the board. Zane is creating masterpieces this morning," he says with a wink. Then Timmy buzzes off to pump coffee and take time to speak with all the customers.

Looking at the board of specials, Zara is determined to choose her own breakfast and not disappoint Garrett a second time. She reads through the first three items and as she gets to the fifth, her confidence lessened. By the end of reading all twelve specials, she is overwhelmed.

"The waffles and pancakes are awesome. Would you be interested in splitting a waffle and ordering your own breakfast?"

A lovely woman wearing combat boots walks up to the table, "Hey John, welcome back. Hi. I'm Vanesa."

"Hello. Zara. It is very nice to meet you."

"You guys know what you're having?"

Turning to John with a look of desperation, Zara's eyes beg for Garrett to save her. He orders her a breakfast burrito with hash browns and a Polish omelet for himself.

As Vanesa was preparing to rip the check off the pad, Zara whispers. "And a waffle to share please."

"I'm sorry, Darling. You are going to have to speak up in here."

"A waffle. We would like to split a waffle, please."

"Sounds good. Now where are you from Zara? I thought I heard a bit of Southern sweet in you."

"Tennessee. Chattanooga." Zara said lightly with a bit more authority and no hint of a southern accent that time.

"Beautiful city." Vanesa says, walking towards the grill behind the bar.

"This place is unique," Zara remarks, looking around.

"Ahhhh. The Golden Harvest is one of Lansing's pride and joys. It's the only place locals are willing to wait in line in all types of Michigan weather. We do that because once inside, we know that we'll be treated to a wonderful eating experience.

"Vanesa and Zane own the place. It's a neighborhood staple. Years ago, it caught fire and the customers came out day after day to help put it back together. We missed the food, atmosphere and company so much that a lot of us would come here after working all day and pick up paint brushes.

"Several of their long-time customers took vacation days and were here every day to help wherever they could. Some have a neighborhood bar where everyone knows their name, here we have a neighborhood diner that serves the best food in the entire city and everyone is a friend.

"This is my favorite place to eat. You'll see. My favorite is a painting that hangs between the bathrooms. It reminds me of the old television show, *The X-Files*. I used to watch it all the time online. Have you seen it before?"

Giggling, Zara shakes her head no. Listening to Garrett sing the praises of the establishment, Zara is able to clear her mind of the conversation they had outside and enjoy being in his company.

Vanesa sets a waffle between them and gives Zara a huge smile, "Enjoy!"

"No, I have not heard of the files," Zara tells Garrett after Vanessa backs away.

Garrett freezes. "You have not heard of *The X-Files*? Oh, we are definitely going to have to introduce you to Mulder and Scully."

Shaking his head, Garrett picks up syrup. Lifting his eyebrow, he seeks Zara's permission before smothering the waffle and hands her a fork from a mason jar in the center of the table.

Garrett and Timmy chat about old movies, neither of which Zara is familiar with. Laughing as they make their way out, Garrett assures Timmy he will see to it personally that Zara gets an immediate introduction to *Dancing with the Stars*.

I want to come back. I have a new favorite restaurant in Michigan.

Back in the car, Garrett's tone becomes serious. "You will be able to do this college thing. Only someone raised to be put into a specific box, and who wants to break out of that box, would have made the choice you made not to finish the Ceremony. Zara… you are much stronger than you think you are. I see it every day that we spend time together. I know you will make friends and do well in your classes. What I am less sure of is whether you will choose me at the end."

Zara keeps her eyes in her lap as she processes all of Garrett's words. He believes in her. He believes she can handle all the new challenges that school will present. His only is concern is that she will discover there was something or someone else out there for her. The rest of the drive to campus is silent, both replaying the declaration Garrett had made.

Recognizing they are pulling up to Yakeley, Zara turns a bit in her seat. "I am so very thankful for this opportunity. I am nervous but I am excited. I will be living as my own person for the first time."

Zara watches Garrett put the car in park and turn to look at her. "Thank you for coming to breakfast with me. I am going to let you jump out without walking you to the door since it's move-in day and I shouldn't take up the space. As I said at the beach, I am going to allow you to determine when and how often we talk. You don't have a purse. Why don't you have a purse?"

Reaching into the center console and pulling out her room key and student ID, Garrett looks at her picture and smiles before handing them both to her. Blushing, Zara does not answer his question.

"Okay. Take the credit card and go shopping this weekend. There are several good stores across from campus where you can pick up some items for yourself, including a purse. Am I clear?"

Zara nods. The nervousness that was gone the whole time she was with Garrett, bubbles to the surface. People are everywhere.

"Thank you for taking me to Golden Harvest. I liked the people and the food was amazing. I hope that we can go back." Zara uses the moment to take a deep breath and square her shoulders.

"You've got this, Little One."

CHAPTER 11

SUVs, U-hauls and cars jammed with students and their belongings wedged onto campus for the massive drop-off. Doors that had been closed before now stand open, ready to be filled. Zara politely excuses herself over and over as she makes her way through the crowd to the safety of her room.

Catching glances, Zara is conscious not to stare at the small groups of girls excitedly laughing and hugging after a long summer apart. A wave of loneliness catches Zara off guard.

Gone is the quiet emptiness and peace of the dorm. Concentrating on every step, the hallway seems much longer than when she left before breakfast. Grasping the pendant around her neck, Zara focuses on the hypnotic sound of loud music playing from the room nearby. After a few seconds, she realizes someone is singing every word over the artist

Errbody wanna be a dope boy

Errbody wanna be a coke boy, errbody gotta choppa

Errbody get money, errbody say they from the hood

Errbody real but they not boy

Err'bitch say that she a bad bitch

Zara continues down the hallway toward the music. She looks in open doorways until she is directly across from her room watching a short curvy woman in the middle of the room singing and dancing with her back to the door.

Zara unlocks her own door and slips in, shutting out the sounds behind her. Making her way across the room, Zara sits on the bed and clutches the pillow to her stomach, not sure she is ready to experience the journey she has started on.

Zara is startled by a loud knock at the door. She smiles to herself at the thought of Beth popping by to see her again.

"HI! I'm Ella and this is Liliana. We're your hall mates. We share the room across the hall. We wanted to come over and introduce ourselves to you and your roommate. You're stunning! Love that dress. Wait… are you alright? Hey… how are you all unpacked already?"

Zara stands wide-eyed, confronted by two strangers blasting her with information and questions. "Zara…"

"Your room is blue. I didn't know we could paint. Lil, did you know we could paint? Hey, where are you from? I'm a junior in 'I'm not quite sure' and Lil is majoring in engineering. What's you major? What year are you?"

"Fuck, El! Let her absorb all the questions you're throwin' at her. Shit. Sorry, this is Ella. Ella has only two gears, fast and faster. Welcome to Ella's world." Liliana speaks at a pace easier for Zara to follow as Ella works to look around Zara into her room.

Fearing she's about to push past her way past, Zara relents, "Would you like to come in for a moment?"

Ella passes before the words are out of Zara's mouth. Standing in the middle of the space, Ella slowly spins in circles.

Liliana causally follows her in and peers into the bathroom. Liliana shakes her head, "I would have never thought of a bead door for the closet. It gives more space but still provides a visual barrier. Nice. Excellent thinking."

While Liliana wanders around commenting on the various space saving units in the room, Ella hops on the end of the bed and makes herself at home. Zara turns to close the door realizing her guests have no plan to leave any time soon.

"Oh, just leave it open. Then we can see if anyone stops by." Zara is puzzled by the comment but yields to Ella's request.

Removing her sandals, Zara climbs onto her bed and leans against the headboard.

"What year are you again?" Ella repeats pausing for Zara to reply.

"This is my first year. I am a freshman."

Ella and Liliana glance at each other and look back at Zara. Liliana walks over and sits in the desk chair.

Liliana approaches the subject again, "So, you're a first year, but it looks as if you have a single. And you scored a room in the upperclassmen wing. Who are you really?"

"Yeah. Tell us. We will keep it just between us. You know…

hall mates," Ella chimes in leaning toward Zara to hear her response.

Zara's body tenses and her eyes find her hands that are resting in her lap.

"My name is Zara. I am from Chattanooga, Tennessee," She responds in almost a whisper. "I am not sure why I was given this room. Garrett just said that I was..."

"Who is Garrett? Father? Boyfriend? Pastor?"

"Ella. Stop. We just met her. Would you give it a rest?!" Liliana scolds.

"Shit... music stopped." Ella bounces off the bed and heads over to their room. With the music started, Ella races back in and leap onto the bed.

Ella is speaking, but Zara's attention is captured by the hymnal quality of the music.

"Excuse me. What is this song?"

Zara watches Ella and Liliana glance at each other as if mentally discussing what she just asked.

"This is *Take Me to Church...* by Hozier," Ella says with a dramatic drawing out of the names.

"Hozier is just the 'IT GUY' at the moment. Forgive, El. She grows on you. Give her time," Liliana smiles at Ella and Ella sticks out her tongue in reply.

"Don't they play Hozier in Chattahoochie? What are you into?"

"I was not raised with music. My parents did not like music in the house."

"What about at school? Your friends?" Ella questions with hopefulness.

"My brother and I were home-schooled. I did hear some wonderful music when I arrived in Michigan. I do enjoy it," Zara says.

Clapping and bouncing up and down, Ella plasters a big smile on her face, "Hooray, you will be our blank canvas."

Again, Liliana comes to the rescue. "Zara, if our music is too loud, just let us know. We'll turn it down. Ella tends to play it on full blast. There will be no hard feelings."

"It is not a problem at all. I don't hear anything once my door closes and..."

"What?!" Ella leaps off the bed again and shuts the door. As the latch clicks, all sound from the hallway is muted. Ella looks at Liliana and raises an eyebrow in the silence.

"NO FUCKING WAY!"

Liliana meets her at the door and begins opening and closing it over and over again. Zara sits staring in confusion at the strangeness of their behavior.

Liliana turns and gestures toward the door with her hands. "Your room is soundproof! How in the hell did you get a soundproof room? Why do you need a soundproof room? Ok... what the hell is going on?"

"I do not know. I thought all the rooms were similar. Are you positive your room is not soundproof?" Zara asks in a shaking whisper.

The question brings laughter that Zara is not accustomed to and she wonders if they are laughing at her. "Our room is definitely NOT soundproof. The walls are paper thin in this old building. Where's your stereo? I'll show you."

Ella looks around. "Wait... you don't have a television or a stereo in here. What are you going to do for entertainment?"

Shrugging her shoulders, Zara is beginning to feel self-conscious. "I was not raised with a television either. I read a lot. I will study, I guess..."

"Well, thank Christ that you found us!" Ella states matter-of-factly. "We have TV, music and video games. The door is always open if we're home. It's kind of a dorm thing... you'll get used to it. You'll come over and chill with us all the time."

"Trust me, Zara, it's so much easier to just say yes. She is short but mighty," Liliana proclaims with a giggle. "And she's correct. You're welcome anytime."

"Thank you. I would like that." Zara forces out a small smile on her face.

"Oh, hey, Sara! We're in here!" Ella yells at two blonds dressed in MSU tee shirts at the door of their room.

"Cool as FUCK room... score!" says Sara. Zara admires her waist length hair and blue eyes.

Walking in behind her is one of the most breathtaking women Zara had ever seen. With hair a darker blond than the first girl, her magnetic eyes and seductive smile make Zara forget where she is for just a moment. When the girl winks at her, Zara has to give Ella her undivided attention to regain her composure.

"Zara… these are more of your hall mates. Zara? Hell–O?"

"Yes…" Zara drags her eyes back to Ella.

"Sara… this is Zara and Zara's room. She is a freshman from Tennessee. She has no music baggage and no bad TV show habits that we need to break. She is a perfect addition to the hall."

"It's very nice to meet you Zara. I am lovin' your room. How did you get on an upperclassmen floor?" Sara asks walking further into the room with a wave and sits on the floor next to the bed.

"No point in asking… she is not giving up any info. Zara… this is Christine," she finishes and moves on to a new conversation with Sara and Liliana.

Christine joins Zara at the side of her bed where Zara locks eyes with her. With a slight shift, unobserved by the rest of the room, Christine's posture changes. Immediately, Zara casts her eyes down and modifies her sitting position to that of a submissive. In this moment, she realizes all her secrets have been told, for she knows she is in the presence of a Domme.

"Zara… it is a pleasure to meet you. Please let me know if there is anything I can assist you with."

Zara nods, unable to reply. Without another word, Christine turns and walks from the room.

"I guess we aren't staying to chat. See ya." Sara stands and follows Christine out.

"We need to get to unpacking too… Ella. That was the deal."

"It was very nice to meet you both. Thank you for coming over and introducing yourselves everyone." Zara stands, grateful for the alone time to process what had just occurred.

"You can still keep your door open and listen to the music. Or come over and hang out in our room while we unpack," Ella states with a lift in her voice.

Zara smiles back at her. "Actually, I am going to go shopping for a…"

"SHOPPING! We love shopping. Lil, let's go shopping and put the room together later. We cannot let our new friend go shopping alone. Please… please… please," Ella hops up and down in front of her roommate.

"Let's shop!" Liliana concurs, giving Zara two new shopping

companions and zero alone time.

In a matter of moments, they gather what they need and lock up their rooms.

From the hallway, Zara can hear the music from her hall mates' room clearly. "Told you, not soundproof."

At each open door they pass, Ella introduces Zara as her new friend that they have to get to know and by the time the three make it out the door, Zara has been introduced to over twenty-five new people.

"Don't worry. I don't remember any of their names. That's Ella's specialty. She knows everyone and remembers everyone she meets," Liliana whispers in her ear.

Smiling as they make their way out, Zara cannot wait to tell Garrett that she has made new friends. For the first time since coming to college, excitement is outweighing the fear of being at Michigan State on her own.

CHAPTER 12

"Fuck! Look at the lovely 9 Series. I have not seen one of those around these parts." Liliana exclaims, pointing to the white sedan parked at the curb as they make their way closer to the front of the dorm. Shifting the bags from their recent shopping expedition from one hand to another, Zara recognizes Garrett's car.

As they get closer, the door opens and Garrett steps out angrily walking up to Zara. Both Ella and Liliana stop dead in their tracks, mouths open and unable to speak. For the first time since Zara has met her, Ella is not talking a mile a minute.

"Zara Faith, where have you been?"

"I went…"

"Where is your phone?" Zara set the bags on the ground in front of her.

Her body tenses. "I forgot it in…"

"You forgot the phone again. The phone that I have asked you to keep on you at all times. Is that what I am to understand?"

Zara's eyes drop to the ground and her shoulders hunch over in shame because she has upset Garrett for a second time in one day. Awaiting the pending punishment, she realizes Garrett has picked up the bags she set down.

"Take these to your room. Call me when you get inside."

Zara takes the bags and stands shaking before him. Having never seen Garrett so angry, she is unsure what is coming.

"NOW, Zara Faith!"

Without a word or backward glance, Zara heads to her room, her key out of the wristlet before she reaches the hallway. Inside her room, she immediately picks up the phone with her free hand.

Looking at the screen, Zara sees there are ten missed calls and just as many texts. Before she can dial, the phone rang. Knowing it is Garrett but afraid to speak, Zara swipes to answer the incoming call. While the packages crinkle in time with her quaking.

A deep breath precedes a calmer voice. "Little One, please go to the window and look out."

With her packages in one hand and the phone in the other, she goes to the window and pulls aside the curtain.

"Put the bags down, Little One. Go on, I'll wait."

Another deep breath whispers in her ear as she sets the bags down. "Little One, I am sorry I raised my voice at you. I am sorry that I spoke like that in front of your friends. That will never happen again. Please forgive me.

"Listen, you are in a new city, a new state and I am the only person that you know. If you were to get lost and scared, that phone is your connection to me. But, Zara, it's also my connection to you. I brought you here. I put you into a situation that you never expected to be in. I need to know that you are safe and handling the situation.

I worried when I couldn't get a hold of you. When you walked up smiling and laughing, my worry came out as anger. I behaved badly. Can you please forgive me?"

Zara nodded. Not sure yet if she going to be punished, she remains silent as Garrett continues.

"Little One, if anything happens to you, I would never forgive myself. Does that make sense? When you have your phone you're two buttons from all the help that you could possibly need. Without your phone, you're helpless if something happens to you."

"I am very sorry. I will never go anywhere without my phone again. I promise. I have learned my lesson," she whispers.

"Zara." The exasperation in Garrett's voice unsettles Zara leaving her feeling as if she steps from one landmine to another.

"Just be more careful to keeping the phone with you. Please." He hangs up.

Zara watches Garrett pull out of the parking spot and drive away, panicking at the thought that the only person who knows her has left in anger.

Zara remains in the window for a long time, watching for Garrett to return and make her feel safe. Waiting at the window, Zara is reminded of how alone she is in her new home. Garrett has brought her here, but he has also left her here.

The light of the day fades away as Zara stands waiting in the darkening dorm room. Hearing a soft knock at the door, she knows it is not Garrett and does not move to answer it. After a minute, the knocking stops.

An hour later, still standing in the window, Zara has replayed every word that she and Garrett had exchanged that day. She had disobeyed his one request. He had given her so much, asking for only one thing in return and Zara had failed him.

Zara collapses onto her bed crushing her phone in her hand. Fully dressed, no desire to eat or drink, tears accompany her exhaustion into sleep.

Jolted awake at the sound of an incoming text, Zara releases the grip on the phone and reads the message.

"I hope you're okay. I'm not angry with you. I was very worried."

Zara sits straight up and turns on the reading lamp beside her bed. Her fingers fly over the keyboard to pull up his number and hit the call button.

Hearing Garrett answer, Zara begins, "I am so sorry. I was forgetful and made you worry. It will never happen again. I promise."

"You had bags. You shopped." Zara nodded. "Little One, you understand that I can't hear you when you nod over the phone. Can I see what you purchased or are you too tired?"

"Outside? Are you here?" She turns off the lamp and jumps out of bed to open the curtain. The streetlight illuminates the empty parking spot.

"No, Little One, I'm in bed at my house."

"Alone?" Zara slaps a hand over her mouth the second the word slips out. Closing her eyes and holding breath, Zara waits for Garrett's response to her inappropriate question.

After a moment, she realizes he is laughing. "Yes, Zara, I'm alone in my bed at home. I'm not in the habit of having women in my bed. I definitely wouldn't have someone in my bed while I was speaking to you."

Smiling, Zara walks to the other side of the room and flips on the light switch next to the door. The sudden brightness of the room makes her squint and shield her eyes.

"I thought we could Skype." Zara nods as she takes her laptop off her desk and climbs onto her bed.

"I would like that very much," Zara responds realizing the

silence is from her lack of response.

Booting her computer and opening Skype, Zara's computer rings immediately with an incoming video chat.

"Hanging up now." The phone clicks and Zara lays it on the bed next to her.

The video window reveals reclining in bed with his arm behind his head. Seconds pass in silence, both looking at one another thinking their own thoughts. Seeing him without a shirt, Zara blushes at the intimacy.

"Little One, did you get dressed again to Skype me?" Zara shakes her head. "Please take a few minutes and change into your comfy clothes. Turn the laptop toward the wall."

Hopping off the bed, Zara pulled the dress over her head that she had worn out shopping earlier. Running to the bathroom, she grabs the sleep clothes from last night and throws them on.

Zara rushes back to the bed to get comfortable against the headboard. Placing a pillow on her lap and the computer on top, she is ready to talk.

"Okay. What did you buy?"

Holding her finger up and smiling, she puts the laptop back on the bed and grabs the bags from where she had dropped them.

Over the next thirty minutes, Zara shares the exciting details of her day and displays two purses, a pink Michigan State sweatshirt, and a pair of yoga pants. The pants have Spartans across the butt and Garrett requested Zara wear them the next time they hang out. She rushes on telling him about the music she heard in the dorm.

"I saw something while I was shopping and I will understand if you would prefer that I return it."

"Zara, I told you that you could purchase whatever you wanted. If you wanted to buy a car, I would hope that you would allow me to go with you and assist you in getting the best deal, but that is your choice."

Zara just stares at Garrett in the video. She would never spend that kind of money. There was a part of her that hesitated to spend the money that she had today. Seeing Garrett's excitement about each item helped to relieve her nervousness.

"No. It is not a major purchase. I purchased this for you." Zara lifts the Hozier CD up to show him. There was a silence. Zara looks from the CD back to Garrett and back to the CD.

Disappointed, she tells him that she will take it back in the morning.

"Hell no, you will not return my present. I love it. The computer froze. Hold it up again. Please."

Happy that he is pleased with all of her purchases and seems to like his surprise, Zara sinks into the bed a bit further. "Little One, move your purchases off your bed. I will wait. I want to be able to tuck you in. Smiling back at him, Zara nods and does as she is told.

Turning off the overhead light and turning the reading light on, she crawls under the covers this time. Taking the laptop off the pillow and placing it next to her, Zara gets cozy in her bed.

"Thank you." In a moment of panic, Zara runs her hands over the covers until she finds the phone. Holding it up, she finds Garrett chuckling at her. She does not say anything for a moment. It feels nice to just be with him even if it is through a computer.

"I met two friends today. The two you saw me with earlier. Liliana is a junior majoring in engineering. Ella is a junior but is still deciding what she is going to focus on. They are in the room across the hall. When I came back from breakfast, they came over and introduced themselves to me.

"That is how I learned of Hozier. Ella says that he is the hottest guy these days. I like that song, *Take Me to Church*." Garrett laughs and Zara pauses in uncertainty.

"Little One, you've talked more in the thirty minutes on Skype than in the four days we spent together before I dropped you off at MSU. I think I am going to have to make a point of Skyping you. It sounds like you had a great day. Until you saw me, that is. Again, I am sorry for that."

Looking down at the keys on the laptop, Zara searches for something to say when Garrett continues.

"You know I met my best friend, Branden, the day I started at MSU. He was my roommate. We went in blind and ended up being the best of friends. He is family to me. His sister, Vivian is also family. They are both looking forward to meeting you. My point is that I hope that you meet life-long friends while you are at State. It sounds like you have a good start with your hall mates."

Zara yawns as she nods. "Okay, Little One, time to say good night. Sleep well. Call me when you want to talk again. Thank you for my CD. I love it. Night."

"Good night."

CHAPTER 13

Zara wakes up to a sunny room and a smile on her face. After showering and slipping into a pair of jean cut-offs and a tee shirt, she feels ready to go in search of coffee, knowing the purchase of a coffee maker was in the near future.

A wall of loud music meets Zara at the door, accompanied by her hall mates wearing expressions of concern.

"Good morning. I am…"

The opening is all Ella needs to begin firing questions. "Are you okay? Who was that? What did you do? Can I get your number?"

"Yes. Of course you may have my number." Zara reaches into the side pocket of her pants and withdraws her phone. Not knowing her new number, it takes her a few button pushes to locate the number.

"Here let me call your phone. Then you'll have mine. Who was that? Why was he yelling at you? Is that your BF?" Dialing didn't prevent Ella from drilling Zara for answers. "I hit Lil's too. Cute shorts. Where are ya' going? So, why all the secrets about the guy?"

Zara looks from Ella to Liliana and back again during the barrage of questions. As if on cue, the quieter hall mate comes to her rescue. "Fuck, El. How is she going to answer you without you shutting up?

Pushing Ella aside, she continues, "Zara, good morning. Ella is a bit worked up this morning. We waited to hear from you all night and she was a little worried."

"Whatever, Liliana. You were worried too. Nice try." Crossing her arms, Ella leans against the doorway to their room. Zara senses she is waiting to have all of her questions answered and preparing to go another round if the answers are not up to her standard of curiosity.

Confident that neither of the two girls looking back at her had been raised in a Master/slave household, she pauses, uncertain how to respond.

Taking a deep breath and squaring her shoulders, Zara looks into the two sets of eyes before her and smiles, "That was Garrett. We are friends. He was upset with me for not having my phone with me for safety. He and I talked last night and things are good. I am in desperate need of caffeine. If you want to go with me, I am buying."

Liliana nods and retreats into their room but Ella takes a step closer to Zara. Hands on her hips and looking her directly in the eye, she speaks softly and slowly, "Never allow a man to speak to you that way again. Women are to be cherished and respected. There are ways of showing concern without being a dickhead. If he can't find those ways, walk away."

Zara watches as Ella spins around and disappears into her room. Standing alone in the hall, Zara considers Ella's words. A moment later, Liliana walks back through the door and joins Zara. She softly shuts the door behind her, leaving Ella alone inside.

"Ready?"

Pulling her own door closed, Zara nods and follows Liliana down the hallway wondering why Ella has not joined them. They walk in silence for several minutes then Liliana begins to shed some light on the situation.

"Ella was in an abusive relationship her first year here. It began with him yelling at her for not calling or picking up when he called. The last time she forgot her phone in the dorm, he beat her up... bad. She would stay at his apartment off and on so I didn't think much of it when she didn't come home.

"I knew her phone was in our room with me so I called his phone to check on her. He told me she fell asleep and that she was staying the night. I never gave it a second thought."

Opening the door of the coffee shop, Zara was too preoccupied to soak in the aroma of coffee. She was horrified at the thought of someone hitting Ella. Obviously, it is bothering Liliana to talk about it. She patiently waits to see if Liliana will continue.

Coffee ordered and seated in the back corner of the shop, Liliana gazes into her coffee cup as she continues.

"She was gone for a total of three days and two nights. When she walked into our room, she burst into tears at the look on my face. I should have controlled my expression but I would never have thought it possible. I mean, I knew he was on her ass but I just thought it was how their relationship worked. I took her to the clinic and called the police.

"It's been two years and she is mostly back to her old self now, but it took a while. I don't know what happened to her while she was in his apartment. She has never wanted to talk about it and I've never pressed. She has been going to a shrink for a while." Taking a sip of coffee, Liliana turns her attention to Zara.

"She watched that guy step out of the car and saw the change in your body language and relived what she went through with her ex. She waited up all night to see if you would come out of your room. She fell asleep sitting on the floor just inside the door." Tears filled Zara's eyes as she stares down at her coffee listening.

"She wanted to stay back at the room to get some rest, now that she knows you are okay. I'm sorry she was all over you like that. You don't have to tell us anything about him."

"I am so sorry she worried. You too. Garrett is very good to me. He was concerned that I could get into a situation and be unable to call for help without my phone. He works in security and worries. Please forgive me for leaving you both to worry last night."

Shaking her head, Liliana put her coffee on the small table next to her, "There's no need to apologize. I only told you about Ella because of the similarity of the situation with the phone and so you understand why she gets overprotective.

"She knows I am telling you about this. It is hard for her to relive it and discuss it, but wanted you to know. The guy was arrested and charged with assault. He was expelled from State and sentenced. He didn't serve enough time."

Silently, Liliana and Zara sit sipping their coffee. Zara knows her childhood involvement in the Community is not a topic she should discuss with either of her hall mates any time soon.

Finishing her coffee, Zara stands and asks Liliana if she wants a refill. Together they head to the counter so Liliana can get a coffee to take back to Ella.

CHAPTER 14

Goodnight, Little One. Sorry it's late. I
hope you have a great first day of
classes.

Zara tosses her phone on the bed after re-reading Garrett's text
for the fifth time since waking up. Checking the mirror after
changing outfits for the twelfth time, she sees fear and doubt
reflecting back at her.

Pacing, she searches her closet for a different outfit. Careful to
put everything back exactly as she finds it, no one would know she
had tried on eleven outfits before the current one. A soft knock
stops Zara's search for the perfect first day of school outfit.

Opening the door, Liliana stands dressed once more in yoga
pants and a tee beside Beth who is holding a bouquet of daisies, a
cup holder with four coffees, a small bag and a box.

"Looks like someone is trying to start your day off with a
bang," Liliana says as she walks into Zara's room.

"Seriously, I'm your personal delivery bitch now. The
instructions state I am to bring them inside the dorm room.
Apparently, handing it to you in the hall is not quite good enough,"
rolling her eyes, Beth makes a grand gesture requesting to enter.
"Thanks."

Beth hands Zara the coffee carrier to better balance the rest of
her load. Liliana voluntarily removes the burden of the donuts
from Beth, leaving her with only the flowers to place on the desk.

"Will there be anything else Your Royal Highness?"

"Umm Beth, this bag has your name on it." Liliana says
laughing.

"WHAT?"

"Oops… this coffee appears to have your name on it as well,"
Zara holds up one of the large cups from the carrier.

"Hey Beth, looks like there's a little bit of princess in all of us today… thanks to Zara," Liliana takes the cup of coffee from Zara and hands both the coffee and bag to Beth.

Beth walks to the door and pauses, "Thank you very much, Zara." With that, Beth disappeared down the hall back to the front desk.

"He thinks of everything," Zara shrugs in a hushed voice.

"I take it the daisies are for you. And by the shit eating grin on your face, I think you and this guy are more than 'I don't know what we are exactly.' I am not even going to ask because when El gets out of the shower, you are going to get interrogated."

As if Liliana's words magically summon her, Ella walks through the door singing. She stops in her tracks, mouth hanging open at the sight of a new bunch of daisies and Liliana eating donuts. Walking to Zara, Ella gently lifts the pendants on the necklace hanging around Zara's neck. Zara freezes as Ella examines each letter. Placing them back against Zara's chest with a light pat, Ella walks over to Liliana and takes a coffee. She picks out a donut and gets comfortable on the bed.

Zara watches her every move and braces herself for a list of questions, but Ella happily eats her donut, humming softly to herself.

It is near silence while all three enjoy the breakfast of coffee and donuts. Zara and Liliana keep looking at Ella expecting an outburst of questions, but the questions never come.

Finally, Ella stands up and walks to the door. "Be ready in five minutes. Lil and I are walking you to your first class."

"Ella. You do not need to worry. I found all my class locations already."

"Z. Five minutes. It's your first day. You're nervous. We've been there. We're taking you. Now… change into some comfy clothes and let's do this. Wait… I have something for you."

Ella darts out of the room.

"She's right. Everyone is nervous on the first day," Liliana smiles and heads over to her room to get ready to go.

Ella comes bouncing back in. "Here. It's for your wall. You have to put it somewhere you will see it all the time. It'll help."

Handing Zara a brightly colored piece of paper, Zara reads, "EVERYTHING YOU WANT IS ON THE OTHER SIDE OF YOUR FEARS."

Zara reads the quote several times, the words getting harder to see as the tears in her eyes well. When the first droplet hits the paper, Zara tries to hide the fact that she is not only touched by the quote, but also by the fact that Ella wants her to have it. Without warning, Ella grabs Zara and gives her a hug. Zara hugs her back, squeezing her as hard as she can. Ella returns to her room.

Zara wipes away the other tears making their escape. For the first eighteen years of her life, she could not remember ever being hugged, yet since making the decision to accept the opportunity Garrett presented, she had three in just over a week.

Quickly washing her face and changing into a pair of white shorts and a peach drape front tank, Zara takes a final look in the mirror. The sound of her mother's disapproving voice rings loudly in her head, "Zara Faith, you must always be mindful that your body belongs to your Sir. It is not appropriate to flaunt it. Until you are presented to your Sir, ask yourself if your father would approve."

NO! Today, I am dressing for me.

"HOLY SHIT!" Ella exclaims returning to the hallway. "You do comfy well. Okay... sexy, hot freshman, let's get you to your first class."

"Too much?" Zara rushes to her closet.

"Wipe that horrified look off your face. You look amazing. We look like straight bums walking next to you, but you look fantastic. Perfect, in fact," Liliana explains.

"Grab your stuff and let's goooo," Ella insists.

Zara pauses at the door of her first class to take a deep breath and square her shoulders. She recognizes nothing in her life had prepared her for this moment. Her stomach flip-flops with concern that the education her mother gave her at home will not be enough to keep up with college classes.

Zara slowly pushes the door open and makes her way to an empty seat as more students begin to trickle in the door. Zara takes out the journal Trudy gave her and flips past several entries to the first clean page.

I am sitting here waiting for my very first class to begin and I wanted to thank you for giving me this opportunity. This is a completely foreign life that you have provided for me, one I have neither training nor preparation to navigate. I worry I will not be able to keep up with the studies. I do not want to disappoint you.

Please know that I will do my best at this every day. I will not waste the opportunity that you have handed me. Thank you.

"Hey. Are you saving this seat?" Zara looks up and shakes her head no.

"Super. I'm Nina." Slipping past Zara to the seat on the other side of her, Nina opens her bag and pulls out a thick notebook and a purple pen. "I'm freaking out. I couldn't find the class. I suck at science and what is my very first college class? Biology. What's your name?"

"Zara," she responds, closing her journal and sliding it back into her backpack.

"Zara. Ooh... I like that. Well, Zara, how are you at science?"

"I like science."

"Score. You are my new science friend. I may need some help. Don't worry... I'm totally not a slacker. Science just freaks me out completely."

The professor walks to the front of the lecture hall and begins class. Turning to a fresh page of paper, Zara begins taking notes as the lecture gets under way. In what seems like no time, Zara's first class at Michigan State is behind her.

Sitting back in her chair, Zara reviews her notes.

"WOW. Are you a professional note taker?" a guy asks as he leans forward from the seat directly behind. "He wasn't even supposed to lecture today."

Zara replies at a whisper, "No."

"Seriously, Zara, you and I are totally setting up study sessions together," Nina states, packing her stuff into her bag. "Finding you was a gift from the college gods."

Placing her notebook back in her backpack, Zara feels a blush begin to cover her face. Keeping her eyes cast down, Zara stands to leave.

"Wait for me," Nina rings out.

"Oh… okay," Nina gathers her bag and follows Zara toward the door.

"Ladies, wait for me," the guy behind them calls out stepping over a couple of girls still in their seats chatting. Both Nina and Zara turn to wait for him to jog down the steps toward them. "I'm Ollie. Did I hear mention of a biology study group being formed? I'm in."

"I'm Nina… this is Zara."

Zara stands looking back at them looking at her expectantly.

Without waiting any longer for a reply, Ollie says, "Super. We can work out details on Wednesday. I have no idea how many chapters he covered today, but I already feel behind."

"He covered chapters one and two," Zara volunteers quietly.

"Fuck… I'm already way behind," Ollie exclaims.

"It was very nice to meet you both but I have another class. I must get going. Thank you," Zara says quietly.

"See ya, Zara. I'm glad I sat next to you today," Nina tells her with smile.

"Me too," Zara replies softly.

On her walk to her next class, Zara smiles at how well her first class had gone. Growing up down the street from the University of Tennessee at Chattanooga, Zara had often watched girls walk around the campus in small groups. She had grown up dreaming of attending college, even if for many years, she was not sure what that really meant.

Making her way back to the dorm following classes, Zara finds herself by the hidden garden. Walking in, she once again is overwhelmed by its beauty. The sounds of campus become muffled until birds and bubbling water are the only sounds Zara hears.

Zara heads down the steps to explore the garden. The lush green grass creates a thick carpet for each step. The flower beds look meticulously groomed and are clearly labeled with the name of each plant. Deeper in the garden, Zara discovers an open area where a couple of people are sitting on the grass reading quietly. Finding a spot far enough away from everyone else, Zara sits in the grass.

Placing the backpack beside her, Zara removes the phone from her pocket and lays it on top of the backpack. Drawing her legs to her chest, Zara rests her cheek on her knees and wraps arms around her legs. The nerves of the first day are over, leaving her with a longing to speak with Garrett and tell him about her classes.

"Stop it, Zara. This is an incredible opportunity. You are where you always wanted to be... COLLEGE!! Stop with the 'I need a connection' with someone. First day of class, and already you have been asked to form a study group. Liliana and Ella wanted to walk you to your first class. You are in college. This is your life now. All you have now is you," she mutters to herself under her breath.

Zara runs her fingers though the grass. Memories of her waking up the morning after the Ceremony in Michigan begin to flood her thoughts and, for the first time since arriving on campus, Zara allows herself the freedom to think about them.

The vibration of an incoming calls jolts Zara from the beach house back to the hidden garden. As Zara sits daydreaming, her phone rings.

Releasing her grasp on the pendant, Zara picks up her phone and answers quietly, "Hello."

"Little One, is everything okay? Are you back at your room?"

"I am on my way back there now." Zara explains standing to quickly make her way to the garden entrance. "Everything is fine. Thank you."

"How'd classes go?"

"Very well. Liliana and Ella walked me to my first class. I met some fellow students to study with in biology. Thank you for breakfast. We all enjoyed it."

Garrett chuckled, "You're welcome. Sounds like you had a good first day. Why did you sound so sad when you first answered the phone?"

"I was just deep in thought. The phone call startled me," Zara says in a hushed voice.

"Mhmm... Do you wish to share what you were thinking about so deeply?"

"I was thinking about my first day at your beach house. It is hard to believe it has only been one week since..."

"Since your life went in a completely unexpected direction," Zara nods as Garrett finishes her thought. "Zara, do you remember what I told you when I gave you the pendants that night?" Zara's thoughts traveled back to her first night at the beach house when

Garrett gave her the pendant.

"Zara! Zara! Are you alright?" Garrett booms in her ear.

Startled, Zara is suddenly alarmed by car horns and people shouting.

"Zara!" Liliana yells running full speed toward her. Still holding the phone to her ear to hear Garrett firing questions about what is happening and who is there while Liliana wraps her arm around her and walks her across the street and up to the dorm.

"Zara, come on. Let's get you out of here. What's going on? You look lost. Who is on the phone?"

"Garrett," Zara whispers.

"Great. Can I say hi and thank him for the coffee this morning?" Liliana asks gently reaching for the phone.

"Little One, go inside and let me talk to your friend for a minute."

Zara nods and hands Liliana the phone and continues into her room.

Closing the door, Zara sets her backpack on her desk and goes to the window. Hoping to find Garett parked beneath one of the big trees and on his phone talking to Liliana, a flood of disappointment fills Zara at not seeing him.

A knock at the door rouses her from the window. Zara plasters a smile on her face before opening it.

"Hey, Z. Here is your phone back. Garrett has a meeting but said he will call you later. What the fuck happened today? Why were you in the middle of the street?"

Taking the phone, Zara steps aside and Liliana comes into her room making herself at home. "Better me than El, you know that, right?"

Zara closes the door and takes a seat on the bed. "I was deep in thought and lost track of where I was. All of a sudden the horns and yelling started and I froze." Exhaling, Zara looks off into the space of the room.

"Are you okay?"

"Yes. It was a stressful day," Zara responds in a soft, clear voice.

"Alright. I am here if you need me," Liliana stands up and makes her ways toward the door. "How were your classes?"

"Good. I have a lot of reading to do."

"Welcome to college. Yeah, there are parties and fun but it's mostly studying." Opening the door, Liliana greets a couple of the girls from down the hall as they returned to their room. "Take a shower. El will be back any minute. We can all get food and study. The fun begins today!"

Later that night, when Zara is sitting with Liliana, Ella and several other girls from the dorm in the large study room reading, her text notification makes everyone look up. Blushing, Zara reaches for her phone.

Please check your email when you have time.

Puzzled, Zara reads the text again. Gathering her books, Zara heads back to her room to read the email alone.

Zara Faith,

Congratulations on completing your first day of college. With the exception of a minor traffic incident, it seems you had a very successful day. I had no doubt that you would make it through today with ease. Hearing that you have already established friends reassures me that you are going to do very well at MSU.

You mentioned thinking about your time at the beach house earlier and, I must admit, I have been thinking about our time together as well. I am glad that we had that short amount of time to get to know each other before you started school.

Now it's time to discover who you are and what you want. It's time for me to give you the space to explore your time as a college student.

Little One, I will always be here for you. If you need anything, you just need to contact me. But no more staring out the window, I will not be out there. Everything that you need is inside the room and inside you.

Garrett

Zara numbly closes her laptop. Grabbing her backpack and phone, she returns to the great room to continue her reading with the other girls. Opening her textbook on her lap, Zara finds herself staring out the window into the darkness of night.

"Z, you alright?" Ella asks in a hushed voice.

"Yes. Thank you for asking," Zara says more forcefully than intended, and then adds a smile to attempt to soften her response. Ella looks from Zara to Liliana and back. Nodding, everyone returns to reading and a peaceful silence falls over the great room.

Later, as Zara climbs into bed, she tries to summarize the material that she read for biology, but the science materials are replaced by images of her father correcting her mother's misbehavior, her mother disappearing before her eyes and leaving Zara to care for her newborn brother so her father could have his slave.

Sitting up, Zara takes deep breaths and brings a relaxing image of the beach to mind until she can hear the sound of the waves crashing against the shore, and the smell the wet sand being baked by the sun. Slowly, the images of her father ordering her mother to sit on the floor while everyone else sits at the table to eat dinner fade away.

CHAPTER 15

Zara finds a sense of relief by the end of her first week of classes. The amount of homework is far less than what her mother had demanded of her and her brother. Her current knowledge on her subjects surprises her, by far exceeding the requirements of her courses.

Having so many new people around has transitioned from overwhelming to welcoming. Zara works hard to get to know all the girls in the dorm by name. Some of them are warmer than others, but all maintain a level of social politeness that Zara appreciates.

As each day starts and ends, only one thought refuses to be suppressed. From an early age, Zara had been taught to place her emotions into a box and place the box in the deepest part of her inner self. Garrett could not be wrestled into a nice neat box.

Zara's daily thoughts of Garrett begin when she wakes up in the morning, checking her phone in hopes of receiving a 'good morning' text or any type of communication from the man she had spent so little time with, but who had left such a lasting impression.

Meeting Ella and Liliana had been a wonderful surprise and an enormous help. Today, when Zara opened the door to say good morning to her best friends, Ella rolls her eyes at Zara's maxi-dress and scandals. She looks down at herself, to see what is wrong with her outfit.

Liliana giggles. "It's Friday, Freshman. No classes." Zara shrugs her shoulders in confusion.

"You don't dress up to bum around!" Ella admonished with exasperation. Zara looks at both of them and notes that they are in yoga pants and MSU tee shirts. No makeup.

"I thought we were going off campus for breakfast this morning. Ella mentioned shopping," Zara says puzzled.

Pushing Zara back through her door, Ella holds both of her

hands and looks into Zara's eyes. "Breakfast and the mall. We're gonna wait while you change out of this stunning outfit and put on a pair of those yoga pants. Put your hair in a pony, too. Trust me... you need this!"

Ella pulls the door closed behind her, leaving Zara wide-eyed and mouth open. Zara stands in that spot for a long moment before pulling out a new pair of yoga pants and a "Spartan 4 Life" tee shirt. Slipping on her flip-flops, she pulls her hair into a neat sleek bun. Applying a couple of spritzes of hairspray, she picks up her purse and pulls her phone out with a hopeful glance at the screen; she sees there are no messages from Garrett, drops it back inside and opens the door.

Ella snaps a picture of her, "I am going to print this out and post it on your mirror as a reminder that comfy is good!"

Moments later, the three friends walk out the front door and head for the diner for much needed coffee and breakfast. Zara smiles to herself as she walks a step behind them.

"What are you so smiley about this morning, Freshman?" Ella quips, glancing back at her.

"Just thinking how lucky I am to have been assigned a room across the hall from the two of you." Zara feels the heat of a blush creep over her face.

"DAMN right... you're lucky!" Ella laughs. She wraps her arm around Zara's waist and pulls her forward.

The aromas of greasy food and freshly brewed coffee hits Zara as she steps in the door of the diner. Packed with students nursing their first "Friday morning away from home" hangovers, the girls join a table with Ella's classmates. Ella introduces Zara as their resident freshman and everyone at the table laughs and says hello. Once coffee is poured and orders placed, the conversation turns to the upcoming football game.

Quietly sipping her coffee, Zara sits listening to the friends chat and laugh. Ella jumps up when the food is delivered and begins taking pictures of the table. Laughter breaks out when one of the girls points her fork, loaded with pancakes, at Ella and threatens her, "If any of these pictures see the light of day on social media, you are a dead woman."

After breakfast, Ella declares they are doing a photo shoot. Neither Zara nor Liliana feel like having their pictures taken, but

Ella insists. Not even the promises of a trip to the mall sway her, but they agree to go to the hidden garden. Zara holds her pendant while Liliana further tries to talk Ella out of taking pictures. Ella glances at Zara and declares they are going to the hidden garden.

Zara and Liliana explore the garden, while Ella roams around snapping pictures of whatever moves her. Eventually, Zara finds a spot to sit in the grass near the walking bridge and Liliana joins her.

"This is my favorite place on campus so far," Zara says softly. She runs her fingers through the freshly cut grass. Staring off into space, thinking of her special place in Tennessee and how happy she is that she has found a place that brings her a sense of peace. A soft breeze brushes her face bringing with it many different scents of the surrounding flowers.

"A penny for your thoughts," Liliana says. Zara looks at her without saying anything. "Z, this is where you start to tell me where you went just then. You disappeared in your thoughts. You do that a lot."

Zara draws her legs to her chest and wraps her arms around them. Resting her cheek on her knee, she is careful to keep her eyes diverted from Liliana's penetrating stare. "I was thinking what an amazing opportunity this is for me."

It comes out sounding sadder than Zara intended, but before she has a chance to continue, Ella begins to snap pictures at them mimicking a professional photographer giving direction.

"Z, lay back on the grass for me and look straight up. Wait… Lil, lay down with the top of your head touching the top of Z's."

When she notices that Liliana has not made any movement in the direction requested, she sighs and says, "Seriously, Lil the faster you give in, the faster we can wrap this up and move on to the next adventure of the day."

Crawling on hands and knees into position, Liliana lays down with the top of her head resting against the top of Zara's head. "Our freshman is ready to experience all that MSU has to offer."

Ella stands directly over the top of them and begins snapping away. "Okay, I think I got what I need there. You both can sit up now. What's this about Z experiencing college life to its fullest?"

Zara sits up and takes a deep breath, "Coming to college is a big opportunity for me and I need to take advantage of everything it has to offer."

"You are clutching that pendant awfully hard, Freshman. Ready to tell us about that yet?" Ella queries in a soft voice.

Zara shakes her head no, feeling tears begin to collect in her eyes while she stares down at the grass. What could she tell them? Missing Garrett was confusing and scary. The idea of explaining all the facets of the relationship is overwhelming.

Standing up and brushing herself off, Liliana pats Zara on the shoulder. "Hey, when you are ready, we are both here to listen. Until then, we'll help you experience State. That journey begins tonight... FOOTBALL! We should go get you a ticket for the game tonight."

"I have season tickets," Zara quietly replies, then brightens at the possibility of seeing Garrett in a few hours.

CHAPTER 16

Ensconced back in the student section and dressed in another new football tee shirt, Zara pays little attention to the game. For the fourth game in a row, Zara finds herself scanning the faces around her for a glimpse of the man who has captured her thoughts. Her eyes stop their progress when they fall upon Christine staring back at her. Blushing, she slowly draws her eyes away and continues her wayward search. When the scoreboards flash 70,401 in attendance, Zara knows spotting him in this week's crowd is again impossible.

"GO GREEN! GO WHITE!" Zara chants along with the crowd.

"Freshman, we are 'GO GREEN!' this time," Ella reminds over the continuing back and forth cheer.

A timeout is called and the crowd settles back into their seats. Zara pulls out her phone to text Garrett but when Ella notices the phone in her hand, she offers to take her picture. Holding her phone out to Ella, she spins Liliana for a cheek-to-cheek shot. Ella hands the phone back and returns to cheering with the crowd as the quarterback makes a successful pass for thirty yards.

Zara looks at the screen, admiring the picture Ella has taken.

"You should send it to him. You aren't going to find him in the stands. Too many people. Text him." Zara stares at Ella frozen. "Come on, Freshman. You know you want to."

Zara pulls up the text and attaches the picture, then adds a message.

> Because we have not seen each other in a
> few weeks.

Feeling the vibration of an alert, Zara sees the message is from Garrett and does a little happy dance.

> Bring your friends over to The Club
> entrance.

Puzzled, Zara asks, "What is The Club?

Liliana squeals and shrieks reading the text pushing Zara and Ella back down the aisle before she has an opportunity to explain their hasty departure.

Liliana leans in and says, "The Club is an exclusive viewing area where people who have way too much money watch the game."

Passing a guy from her Art History class, Zara says, "Hello, Dan."

"Hi! Likin' the game?" he asks as she pushes past.

"Absolutely! I am still confused about what is going on, but it is fun," Zara replies. Liliana clears her throat.

"Hey, my frat is having a party tonight. You and your girls should come. It will be fun. Very casual. It's the Theta House. Any time after 9pm."

"Thanks. We will try to make it. We gotta run," Ella says, chuckling. She pulls Zara in the direction away from the moment of awkwardness.

"I just… I…"

"It's fine, Zara. Some guys have that effect on us girls. It was just super fun seeing it happen. Come on. The Club awaits us." Liliana is still giggling as she rushes them around the stadium to the exit closest to The Club.

"Text him! Tell him we are here. Tell him." Liliana hops up and down in place. Having never seen her so animated about anything, Zara laughs, and quickly texts Garrett that they are outside the door of The Club.

The security guard opens the door and asks for 'Zara Faith.' Liliana pushes her forward into the man's arms. "Hi, I am Zara. These are friends of mine, Liliana and Ella."

Gesturing them inside, the guard guides them to the elevator. The door opens immediately when the button is pushed. Liliana steps inside and happy dances again pointing at the button with a Spartan helmet and the words THE CLUB next to it.

"El… if you don't get your camera out and take pictures of the first picture-worthy event that we have had this year, I am going to kick your ass."

Without further encouragement, Ella begins snapping picture after picture. The twenty second trip in the elevator yields at least thirty pictures.

When the doors open, Zara finds Garrett is standing across from the opening leaning against the wall. She steps out of the elevator as Garrett steps to her. She wraps her arms around his neck and feels his arms find their way around her waist. She leans in, whispering in his ear, "I have missed you."

Hearing the clearing of a throat, Zara releases Garrett and steps back. Blushing, she looks down to gather herself. Garrett takes her hand and introduces himself to Liliana and Ella then leads them away from the elevator as he continues.

"I'm very happy to meet you both. Zara speaks about you every time we talk. I owe you an apology for the last time we interacted. I was upset with Zara for not having her phone and I allowed my concern for her safety to overrule my manners. Please accept my apology, but know that Zara's safety will always be my first concern."

Liliana smiles broadly at Garrett and Ella steps closer to extend her hand to him. He shakes it and smiles back. "So, shall we head inside?"

"Hell yeah!" Liliana squeals.

Garrett places his hand in the small of Zara's back and guides her inside, led by Liliana's and Ella's oo and ah at the surroundings.

The Club is very different than the student section where they had watched all the previous games. The carpet is so plush it feels like Zara is wearing sneakers rather than her flat-soled sandals. Sliding glass doors face the football field and open out to a sitting area with comfortable seats, affording its patrons the option of watching the game from the comfort of inside or enjoying it in the elements with all the other fans.

Opposite the wall of glass are tables upon tables of food, with waiters hovering by in tuxedo shirts and black pants. Two bars ensure fans will not have to travel far for a refill on their cocktail of choice.

Garrett works Zara and her friends through the crowd to a round table occupied by several people. Two guys stand up as they reach the table, while a woman between them remains seated.

"Zara, this is Branden Jacobs, Kegan, and Branden's sister, Vivian. Everyone… this is my Zara Faith." As Garrett introduces

Zara, she feels his hand sliding up and down her back and she leans into him letting him also introduce her friends.

"Forgive me, ladies. This is Ella and Liliana. They are Zara's hall mates. They have been kind enough to show Zara the ropes on campus. Kegan, Liliana is an engineering major in her third year. And, if am not mistaken, Ella, you are in your third year and still deciding your major. These are two of my college friends, Branden and Kegan, as well as Vivian, who also graduated from State."

Turning to the girls directly, he asks, "Have you eaten? There is plenty of food. The second half is just starting so we can take your plates outside if you wish."

Zara gazes up from her spot in his arms with her back against his chest. Hearing the familiar sound of Ella's camera clicking, Zara knows she is the object of the picture and smiles into the camera. Oblivious, Garrett leans down to whisper in her ear.

"I'm glad you texted me. It hasn't been easy knowing you're so close sitting in the student section. Plus, I would have missed seeing you in your very cute football shirt and very short shorts."

Giggling, Zara tilts her head further to the side to give Garrett access to her neck. To her delight, he plants a lingering kiss just below her ear.

Please do not stop ever.

Branden walks around the table and speaks to Zara's friends loud enough so Garrett and Zara cannot miss a word. "Since Garrett is completely wrapped up with the dear Zara, would you mind if I escort you to the buffet?"

When Zara pulls away in deep embarrassment, Garrett thanks Branden and slaps him on the back. All five of them head to the buffet, Zara and Garrett following the rest. His hand finds her favorite spot for it at the small of her back.

The buffet has a lot of choices. Liliana is in seventh heaven. Ella wanders to take pictures.

"Zara, get a plate. You've hardly eaten anything today," Liliana states as she fixes her plate. Hearing this, Garrett turns Zara around and lifts her chin. Eyes locked on each other, she feels as if he is trying to measure what she has ingested through her eyes.

"Zara Faith. Are you not eating enough? Don't like the food at the dorms?"

Unable to drop her eyes with his hand on her chin, she slowly lifts her eyes from his lips back up to his eyes where she is met with an 'I know what you are thinking' smirk.

All of her attempts to stop from blushing fail. "I eat. I eat a lot."

Liliana gives a '*humph*' from the end of the table. Drawing his eyebrow up, Garrett waits for Zara to finish. "I'll get a plate."

"Perfect." He reaches for two plates and hands one to Zara. "What do you think the budding photographer would like?"

As Zara puts a little bit of this and a little bit of that on her plate, Garrett fills a plate for Ella. Back at the table, Zara sits quietly and listens as Garrett and his friends talk about the game and other teams' successes and failures.

"So Zara, it's great to finally meet you. How do you like MSU? How's your dorm?" Vivian asks across from Zara with a warm smile on her face.

She is absolutely lovely.

Smiling, Zara nods. "I love my room. It is so warm and cozy. I have been to a few other rooms and they have an institutional feeling. The best part about my room is the space saving techniques. I cannot begin to explain them but it's as if someone made a list of everything that I would ever need and created a space for each item.

"There is this tall corner cabinet that is amazing. It has different sized shelves and they adjust. It is the coolest thing ever. Oh… wait. I have a picture of it on my phone. I was trying to explain it to someone in class and ended up just taking a picture. They have been trying to locate it online…"

Zara opens the picture section on her phone and starts to flip back past the ones Ella had taken in the stands.

"May I see your phone please?" Garrett asks. Looking up, Zara sees his hand extended and waiting. She slowly hands it to him.

"Viv knows what the cabinet looks like. She picked out everything for the room. I thought I told you that already. She also picked out the clothes at all the houses," he says as if it is common knowledge that she has clothes in other locations.

"I… I didn't realize. I am sorry. I should not have gone on so." Abashed, she looks down at her plate feeling scolded by Garrett.

Laughing in a way that draws attention from the people around them, Vivian stands up from her chair and walks around the table to Zara. She gives her a big hug from behind. "Never apologize for going on about my work. These two don't value my efforts very much so it is great to hear some positive feedback. Are those shorts a pair I purchased?"

Walking up behind them, Ella answers for Zara. "Nope, I made Zara get those when I dragged her out shopping with me a couple days ago. It was my way of not feeling guilty for purchasing the amount that I did. God bless student credit cards."

Picking up a fork and taking a melon off Zara's plate, Ella has not noticed that she has the attention of everyone at the table except Garrett who is looking through Zara's phone. "These are really good pictures of you. Ella… did you take all these pictures? You have an amazing smile when you don't think anyone is looking."

Shaking her head in response and continuing to pick off Zara's plate, she gives a happy squeal when Zara slides a full plate in front of her. "Those aren't even the good ones," she explains. "Zara is a great subject. She has great bone structure and is a natural. She just allows me to do what I am going to do without becoming rigid in front of the camera like… where is Lil?"

"She took her plate out to watch the game with Kegan," Zara replies accepting her phone back from Garrett. Turning to Vivian, she asks, "Where is the restroom located?"

Vivian gestures for Zara to follow her and as they leave the hearing range of the others, leans in to say, "So, you and Garrett. I'm glad you didn't go through with the whole collaring thing. That says a lot about you."

Zara loses a step hearing a reference to her ties to the Community and rushes into a stall, her heart racing, and her palms sweaty. Shaken anyone here knows about their life within the Community, Zara has no idea how to respond.

Finishing up, Zara takes a deep breath and squares her shoulders then opens the door to the stall where she is met with Vivian standing at the sinks.

Careful to avoid eye contact, Zara washes her hands and dries them. She asks Vivian a question about the color on the walls of her dorm room and Vivian gracefully acknowledges the redirection and allows the subject change.

Rejoining Garrett, he asks if Zara and her friends want to go out after the game. Branden has invited them over to his place.

Before Zara can think of how to answer the request, Ella drops a bomb she had forgotten existed. "Zara, remember Dan invited you to his frat party tonight? The Theta House... wasn't it?"

"Of course. Well, I hope you have fun at the party. Perhaps another time," Garrett's voice remains as even as if he is ordering off a menu. There is no indication that he has any opinion of Zara going to a party to meet another man.

Zara's shoulders slip a bit. The recording that Zara had packed away comes to the surface on maximum volume.

Garrett, I need to make a call. I will be right back. Would she be there tonight?

"Z... Zara! Say goodbye. We need GO!" Ella insists.

Zara draws her eyes up from her lap to find Ella's warm protective smile. Before she can say a word, Ella takes her hand and squeezes it. Zara returns the squeezes. Liliana smiles warmly and gives Zara's shoulder a quick pat.

"Garrett, it was a pleasure to meet you. Thank you for having us up here. It is amazing." Liliana continues, "Ella is not feeling well so we are going to head back to the dorm."

"Ella, can we get you anything here? Club soda? Vernors?" Garrett inquires.

"Thanks but I just need to lay down for a bit. This was fun." Ella stands and gathers her camera. "Z, we'll be downstairs."

Zara nods.

Garrett stands and waits for Zara to stand. Before getting up to leave, Zara looks around the table and says, "It was very nice to meet all of you. Thank you for allowing us to join you today. And, Vivian, I really do love my room. Thank you."

The elevator ride was silent. It was not the comfortable silence they had shared at the beach house. For Zara, it was strained.

I do not want to say goodbye again. Please, do not say goodbye.

"Little One, it was good to see you. You look beautiful. College is definitely agreeing with you. Take care of your friend." Garrett steps back toward the elevator. "Zara, please eat."

Zara stands there as he steps back into the elevator and the doors close.

He left.

CHAPTER 17

Liliana stops in her tracks seven feet from the exit. "Someone is going to tell me why I just left The Club and Kegan before the end of the game. Seriously, what the fuck just happened? PS, Zara, your boyfriend better get us back in there for another game this season."

With head lowered and eyes on the ground in front of her, Zara whispers, "Garrett is not my boyfriend."

"Oh, Honey. That man wants you badly. He may not be your boyfriend yet but that is clearly on you." Ella walks into Zara due to her stopping so abruptly. "Zara… please tell me that you realize that he's completely hung up on you."

Zara stands staring at her with her mouth open.

"He had no reaction when you told him about Dan's party tonight. If Garrett is interested, why was he not upset? Why would he allow me to go to the party?" Zara asks as she kicks a pebble off the sidewalk.

"Oh, yes, Garrett would throw a temper tantrum and stomp his feet. Maybe even tie you up and tell you that the party is off limits… if he was fifteen years old. Zara, he obviously respects you. It seems he is patiently waiting for you to pick him. I gave you an opportunity to do that but you…"

"When?" Zara asks angrily placing her hands on her hips. There was never a chance to pick Garrett. Ella had even told him about a party another guy had invited her to.

"The party. I only brought it up so he would know he isn't the only guy interested in you. I figured you would choose to skip the party and go with them. I thought you wanted to be with him by the way you two were looking at each other. Plus, Lil here was all flirty with Kegan, so I was prepared to take one for the team tonight."

At the stunned look on her face, her hall mates start laughing.

"You didn't know I was lobbing the ball to you, did you? Well, my bad, Zara. I did try. I got some great photos. Did you get the digits?" Ella asks Liliana. "Number, Zara. Phone number!"

Liliana shakes her head, "Nah, no worries. I took one look at Zara and I knew we needed to jump. What upset you?"

Knowing there was no stepping around this one, Zara mournfully replies. "He just sat there and told me to have fun at a party with a different guy. I thought it meant that he had no feelings for me. I just..."

"How many boyfriends have you had, Zara?" Zara rolled her eyes miserably and Ella persisted, "Okay, how much do you like Garrett? Scale of one to ten?"

"Twenty-six," Zara whispers keeping her eyes lowered. Her friends wrapped their arms around her from each side as they walk back to the dorm.

"Only one thing to do," Ella smiles. "We are going to a party."

Ella and Liliana wait behind Zara for her to unlock the door. Ella pushes by and marches to the bathroom. Liliana moves the bead curtain to the side and starts searching through the clothes. Once Ella finishes, she joins Liliana to discuss the options for tonight.

They pull out and hold up one item after another. Once they get to the shoes, the tone suddenly changes. Ella pulls out a pair of six-inch black pumps with red soles. "DO YOU KNOW WHAT THESE ARE??"

Relaxing on her bed while the pair ransacks her closet, Zara nods. "Zara Faith, what are these then? And can you walk in them?"

"Heels? Yes, I am able to walk in heels," she responds feeling less confident than before, less certain that she has the correct answer.

"These are NOT heels, as you so casually called them. These lovely never-worn-before pieces of art are Christian Louboutin, specifically Louboutin So Kate. They're the most delicate of the pumps and guaranteed to make any legs irresistible. These? These are your secret weapon. We are going to take one more look at the lovelies and then put them back in their home."

"Should I wear them tonight?"

"NO!" Ella and Liliana exclaim in unison.

"Those are the weapon you use when you go in for the kill. Tonight is just the beginning of the hunt. Tonight you go with an 'I didn't put in much effort but I look incredible' outfit. These do NOT come out of the box until you are ready to hear the words. Are we clear?" Ella looks as if she is teaching a class and Zara is her prized student.

With a heavy sigh, Ella glides her hand gently over the two pieces of art, closes the box and slides it back into its designated spot in the closet.

"Here we go!" Liliana states in a resigned manner. She carries two hangers with clothes on them over to the other end of the bed and sits down expectantly as if there is going to be a show.

"El?" Liliana holds up a bright multi colored skirt and a white off the shoulder top.

"Perfect!" Ella does her happy dance. Zara giggles at the two of them. Watching them, Zara has an overwhelming feeling of being blessed.

"Thank you. You know, for everything," Zara's voice quivers as she speaks but Ella cuts her off immediately.

"Stop right there. Don't thank us yet. You have just enrolled into the Lil-El boy boot camp. You better wait to thank us because there may be some aspects that you regret. Now, we have a party to get to."

The choice of flats is a good one. The six-inch pieces of art would have been lovely, but the walk to the Theta House in them would have been difficult. Reaching the frat house, Zara pauses to let Ella and Liliana walk in before her. She is surprised to see they just walk in without knocking or ringing the doorbell.

Once inside, the reason is clear. There are people everywhere. Hard thumping music accompanies three guys who walk up to Ella. One picks her up to swing her around. Another guy says hello to Liliana who tilts her head in return.

"What are you guys doing here? I didn't know you were coming tonight," the guy who said hello to Liliana asks Ella.

Ella points at Zara and waves her to come closer. "Our freshman was invited by Dan and there was zero chance we were going to let her come to this house alone."

Wrapping her arm around Zara and giving her a half hug, Ella looks around the house. "Not much changes around here, huh."

"El, a lot has changed, and that happened in his apartment not in this house. We DO focus education and we hold mandatory classes to talk about it. We are all sorry. It is so good to see you back here. I think Dan is in the meeting room. Make yourself at home. Your freshman is safe here, El. You have our word."

He is looking at Zara when he speaks but is talking to Ella. She just stands there holding onto Zara. Liliana walks in between Ella and Zara and the guys. "If you are too uncomfortable, we are out. No pressure. We will leave when you're ready."

Ella nods, a smile plastered on her face. "Zara, I would like you to meet AJ, Marcus and Russ. They are the head guys at Theta House. Two rules when you are in this house. You do not ever go upstairs during one of their parties. I mean it... ever."

She waits for Zara to nod her assent. "Second, get your own drink. Do not accept one from anyone. If you have to put your drink down, then consider it done. Never pick it up and drink it again. If anyone makes you feel uncomfortable, look for Lil or me. If you can't see us, then find one of these three guys. They will get you back to me unharmed. Do you understand?"

Ella turns to the men with a serious expression, "If anything happens to my freshman in this house, all three of you will pay dearly. Am I understood?"

"This is a party. Now that we have been served our orders, can we get to the partying part? Let's go get cocktails," Marcus says as he lifts Ella off her feet and carries her deeper into the house. Liliana and Zara follow while the other two guys bring up the back.

Zara feels completely out of place. The only parties she had ever attended had been collaring ceremonies. The Community had other parties but her parents felt that her position as the daughter of a King Council member negated attendance.

She and Sloane would organize their own private parties, gathering food and making non-alcoholic drinks for themselves. A few times they dressed up with makeup and up-dos, and even wore heels, even though they were just chilling out together. Recalling their fun, Zara wonders if Sloane would enjoy this party, but before her thoughts travel too far down that path, she forces them away. There is no time for that tonight.

Squaring her shoulders, Zara readies herself for her first

college party. Walking past the stairwell that she had been forbidden to use and down a hall, the hall opens to a huge room full of more people. The music is different. It is harder.

Ella and Liliana are mobbed as soon as the one of the guys announces "LOOK WHO'S IN THE HOUSE!"

Zara take a step back with each person that comes to greet her protectors. Before long, she is several feet away from the only two people that she knows and her level of comfort begins to decrease.

The heavy beat shakes the walls and a small circle of people shout along with the words while jumping up and down. Turning to walk back, Zara feels fingers wrap around her upper arm. She pulls away while turning to see who is touching her. Dan is smiling down at her.

"Come on," he says, drawing her deeper into the crowd of moving bodies.

Dan has blocked her view, leaving her unable to look around for Ella and Liliana. Zara looks at his hand grasping her arm.

Uneasy with being touched this way, Zara looks up into his eyes trying to judge his intent. Dan takes a long drink out of a red Solo cup. When he is done, he lowers the cup to Zara and offers her a sip. Shaking her head, she tries to say she would like her own cup but the loud music muffles her voice.

Zara resists the motion of Dan moving in closer to her and pressing against her body. He lowers his mouth to her ear in an attempt to kiss her. Zara backs away from him, but the crush of bodies and his arm around her stop her from breaking free. Laughing at her discomfort, Dan puts the cup to Zara's mouth again.

Zara freezes when the lights go off and the crowd in the room begins to cheer. Glow rings are lofted above the crowd, but for the most part, it is pitch black in the room filled with undulating bodies.

Tossing his cup into the crowd, Dan pulls Zara to him, tightly encircling her in his arms and pressing his hips into hers. She puts her hands on his chest and begins to push away, her heart pounding so hard she thought she could feel it through to her fingertips. His hands slide down her back to her ass and he squeezes her hard.

Unsure what else to do, Zara cries out for help, but her voice is lost to the roar of dancing bodies and loud music. Zara continues to struggle as Dan leans into her ear and shouts he is glad she came because he really likes her.

He runs his tongue down her neck and up to her ear where he gives it a tug. In sheer panic, Zara slaps him crossed the face, and then suddenly feels herself being ripped away from him. She is pulled from the mass of moving bodies into the dimly lit hallway.

Moving blindly, tears streaming down her cheeks, Zara realizes she has someone on either side of her. At the door, Zara begins to register Ella's screaming and Liliana pushing one of the guys that led her out.

"He's been drinking. He was excited that she came. He really likes her. He didn't mean to scare her," AJ says in a calming voice. "El, it is not the same situation as what happened to you. Come on. She is fine."

Liliana wraps Zara into her arms.

Ella continues to scream at the top of her lungs, "Nothing's changed in this place! Are you fucking kidding me… we were here for less than 15 minutes! I'm calling the cops!"

Liliana grabs Zara's face in both of her hands. Blocking out every other noise, smell and light, Zara focuses on her eyes and her words, "Did he hurt you?"

Zara shakes her head violently, but knows the tears escaping down her cheek are suggesting a different story.

"Zara, give me your phone."

Reaching inside her handbag with a shaking hand Zara pulls out her phone and hands it over to Liliana.

Watching her tap away on it, Zara shutters, "He wanted me to drink out of his cup. Ella said no drinking. I tried to tell him I wanted my own cup."

Liliana slips the phone back into Zara's bag and grabs her into a tight hug and is surprised by the voice so close behind her. "Zara, you are always going to be safe with Ella and me. We will never allow anything bad to happen."

"Lil… get her out of here."

Several people were standing around them now curious what was going on and asking if everything was okay when Zara hears Dan call her name. Her eyes grow to the size of saucers and her shaking becomes visibly noticeable. Before she can reply, Ella whips around on her heels and starts yelling.

"Say one more motherfucking word to my girl EVER and I will bring your entire world to an end... are you understanding me? You little piece of shit. ONE SINGLE MOTHERFUCKING WORD! AJ... Marcus, one word and this house is GONE."

Zara is lead out of the house by Liliana and Ella as they walk back to Yakeley, but she does not say a word. As they approach the spot that Garrett had parked in a week ago, Zara breaks down crying and the girls silently embrace her in a hug allowing her tears to fly.

CHAPTER 18

"Zara Faith."

The sound of his voice makes every fiber in Zara's body come alive. Pushing past Liliana and Ella, Zara is met by Garrett running up the sidewalk toward her. Zara takes off running toward Garrett, stopping as she draws near and resuming her natural position of looking down.

"Little One, tell me you are okay. I need to hear you say it."

Without words, Zara slowly lifts her eyes to look deep into Garrett's. She raises her arms and he pulls her into his chest. Her arms wrap tightly around his neck and she whispers hoarsely into his ear, "I was just scared. He didn't hurt me. I promise. Ella and Liliana were there and they brought me home."

Garrett squeezes her tighter before letting go. Zara tries to step back but he pulls her under his arm. "No, Little One you stay close to me tonight. Please."

Zara wraps her arm around him removing any space between them. Zara finds Branden standing off to the side talking quietly to Ella and Liliana. Garrett guides Zara to where they are gathered and catches Branden mouthing something to Garrett.

Garrett turns them around and walks toward his car. Opening the passenger door, Garrett puts Zara into the car and shuts the door. He jogs around the car and slides into the seat next to her while she leans back into the supple leather. As Garrett drives Zara away from campus, she takes a deep cleansing breath and feels the unpleasantness of the last hour roll off her as she exhales. Closing her eyes, she finds herself sinking into the music on the stereo and the warmth of being close to Garrett.

Music begins to play and she allows it to fill her mind with both its melody and captivating lyrics.

You've felt this way for far too long
Waiting for a change to come

You know you're not the only one

"I like this song. I can feel it deep inside." Zara opens her eyes wide and lifts her head, astonished at her sudden openness.

"This is Kodaline. I love this song. Wait… listen to this one."

The new song has a haunting undertone but an uplifting beat on the top. Zara allows the music to fill all the spaces of her mind. No talking, only the sounds of Kodaline singing 'The One' can be heard in the car.

Zara looks out the window watching the city pass by without any narrative from Garrett. When the song comes to an end, he asks if she would like to listen to it again.

"Please."

The car glides down the street as the song repeats. Turning down a heavily wooded street, Garrett turns into a hidden driveway and comes to a stop in front of a glass building that is all but lost in the darkness. It would be overlooked by anyone who did not know it was here.

Opening her door, Zara takes Garrett's extended hand and steps from the car and walks to the house. The skin on skin contact causes the surroundings to blur and fade away. The disappointment that hits when Garrett releases her hand causes a shock to her system.

Eyes cast down, Zara is lost in the brief moment of contact she was awarded only moments ago. Garrett turns to her at the door of the house and asks if she heard him. Confused, Zara looks up into his waiting eyes. Illuminated by the porch light, she is mesmerized by their slate hue.

They stand staring at each other until Garrett breaks eye contact, looks at the door before them and reaches for the handle. Opening the door, Garrett moves aside to allow Zara to enter.

Zara stands in the doorway of a modern, elegant showplace. Free of any clutter, the living space resembles an art gallery with soft lighting placed strategically to accentuate the artwork. Windows on either side of the long room would brighten the dark wood during the day but, tonight, it gave the space a warm feeling.

Zara welcomes the feeling of Garrett's arm slipping around her waist. "Welcome to my home. I have been wanting to show you the house since we arrived in Michigan. Are you up for a tour or would you prefer to put it off until tomorrow?"

Zara's stomach flips at the implication of what Garrett has just asked. "Tomorrow, please."

Zara feels him squeeze her hand. They pass through the living room and down a hall, past rooms with closed doors to a den lit with soft lighting near the top of the walls. A leather sectional compliments a large television on the wall while a comfortable desk sits next to a window.

Garrett releases Zara's hand as she moves to take a closer look at the items in the room. She walks over to examine a sideboard on the opposite side of the room and gently runs her hand along the grain. She bends to take a closer look at the clean lines then stands up and takes a step back to admire the entire table. She senses Garrett as he walks up behind her and taps the surface.

"This is the first piece of furniture that my parents purchased as a married couple."

Zara turns to look at him, a question formed on her lips, but suppressed. Garrett quirks an eyebrow at her as he pulls his phone from his pocket and hits a button. A gentle piano refrain floats softly though the room.

"You have a question. Please ask."

Confused, she reverts to her training and casts her eyes dart downward. She is in the home of a Dom – the Dom chosen to collar her. With sudden dawning, Zara realizes she had been seeing his space not as his submissive or his wife, but as her true self and the lack of clarity of their relationship rushes up to her.

"Little One, where did you go in those thoughts of yours?"

Zara's eyes falter and return to his. "I thought that when a submissive joins her Dom, he is already established. It is my understanding that she is coming into his life. Therefore, it would be his furniture. You said it was the first piece your parents purchased as a couple."

From a very young age, Zara was taught that as a submissive you could not have anything of your own. Zara hears the confusion in her own voice. Garrett grabs two water bottles out of a hidden mini fridge, and gestures for Zara to follow him to the sectional.

From the moment Garrett has been thrust into Zara's life, she had felt a surprising level of comfort. Growing up, she would lie in bed at night and wonder how her chosen Dom would treat her. Sloane believed whichever Dom was selected for her would be her prince charming, that they would have immediate affection for one another.

Zara had expressed that her only hope, was that the Dom she would be paired with would be kind to her. The tradition of pairing the daughters of King Council members had been in place for several generations and the reports of mistreatment by a Dom were few and far between.

On the rare occasion abuse did occur, the matter was dealt with swiftly and by the Community. Incidents were not kept from the members of the Community in the region where they occurred. Once a year at the Regional King Council conferences, a record was distributed to each member attendee.

Corrective measures were never reported, as that was a matter between the Dom and the Council in their region. Zara understood the purpose of the report was to demonstrate to the members that reporting was encouraged and that any type of abuse had no place within the walls of the Community.

For Zara, the traditions and history of the King Council and the Community were unimportant. She knew from an early age that her life had already been predetermined. Asking questions and paying attention to the inner workings did nothing to abate her importance and in response, she quit prying. Sloane was the exact opposite.

She was able to recite the history of the Community as well as the lineage of the regional community that both of them were from. It was not uncommon for Sloane to beg Zara to practice the Circle Ceremony when they were younger. For every, 'I do not care about that' that Zara would tell Sloane, she was bombarded with ten more facts.

Zara often wondered why they had such a different outlook on their future and the role they each played. Both of their families were conservative and required precise adherence to all protocol, but whereas Sloane's parents doted on her as an only child, Zara's mother grew more distant the closer Zara's Circle Ceremony came.

Sloane and her mother were so close her mother had shared with her the details about life, as her father's submissive. Zara's mother, on the other hand, had given no details of life with her Master and Zara never sought that information from her. Watching her mother be ordered onto her knees was hard enough, witnessing her transition into her father's slave leaving her and her brother to fend for themselves, was painful and confusing. She could not understand why her mother would choose to remain in that relationship.

Never had there been a time when either of the siblings was in danger, but emotional abandonment during a moment of need was bewildering. Zara's worst fear was that her father would pair her with a Master like himself and her life would play out like her mother's. Every night, as Zara drifted off to sleep, she fervently wished for a freedom from her eventual commitment.

The waving of Garrett's hand catches Zara's attention.

"Hey, Little One. Tell me what you are thinking about."

Her hands tense in her lap and she scans the carpet in front of her. Zara begins to share the thoughts that had taken her away from the here and now, "I was thinking about my parent's relationship."

Feeling him staring at her, she knows he is waiting for her to continue. "I was raised by Master/slave parents and thinking I do not know much about them. In my parent's house, everything belonged to my father, including my mother. There would have been no chance that she could have assisted in picking out furniture."

Zara looks at the table that brought about these thoughts of her parents.

Garrett stands and walks to the table, resting his palm on it, "Is that the type of relationship you are hoping for?"

"No," she answers tersely.

"It occurs to me that you and I have never discussed what it is we would like in a marriage. You are clearly not interested in a Master/slave relationship." He pauses and leans closer to her. "The million dollar question is, are you a submissive?"

"I was raised to be a submissive."

"That wasn't the question." Garrett leans in until he is only an inch from Zara's ear and breaths. "Are you a submissive?"

Zara takes a deep breath to calm her rattled nerves intensified by his scent of cool mint, summer breeze, citrus and crashing waves all dancing around her senses.

"Being a submissive is all I know about myself," she begins slowly. "That is what my place in my family has always been."

"I disagree, Zara." Swallowing hard, Zara looks at Garrett as he continues, "I know that you enjoy learning, your friends, the color pink, music and experiencing new things. You have not been submissive since we met."

Zara works hard not to smile, but she cannot halt the blush flushing her cheeks. Feeling Garrett take her chin in his hand, she lifts her eyes to his.

"Little One, this is your time to explore. Find yourself. Discover what it is that excites you. But do not discount all the parts of you that worked in harmony before you entered that Circle. I certainly never will."

His hand leaves her chin and Zara holds his gaze for a moment longer before searching for something else to occupy her line of vision. "I like the water. Being at the beach was magical. The sound of the waves crashing on the beach. The smell. I loved it."

"Excellent. The beach it is then."

Sitting together in a comfortable silence, Zara replays what Garrett said; how his touch made her feel. Soft sweet piano suffuses the room. He turns to look at her as he takes a drink. A smile lights up his face.

"You asked me a question and I have not answered it," Zara confesses.

"It doesn't seem you are ready to answer it yet."

"I… I…"

"How about we put that question on hold for now?"

"Thank you," she whispers, swallowing.

"Little One, I'm not pleased by the circumstances but I have enjoyed spending this time with you. I was planning on emailing you to invite you to spend Thanksgiving break here if you hadn't already made plans. The dorms get rather empty during the break."

Zara nods, taking a long drink from the water bottle.

Thanksgiving. So… this is it. We are not going to see each other until Thanksgiving. I am sitting in the house that I would have lived in as your submissive and I am going back to school to be a regular student. Am I submissive? Zar… are you? I am going to miss everything about him.

CHAPTER 19

"Well... look who is doing her very first walk of shame. I am not even going to ask how you have fresh clothes. BHAHAHAHA... I am totally going to ask but let's wait for Lil to get out of the shower so you don't have to tell the story twice. She is going to want the deets too. Coffee shop outing or dorm room? Your choice."

"Coffee shop," Zara states, entering her own room, and shutting the door. She flops on the bed and buries her face in her pillows, not ready for the questions the girls are going to fire at her. How do you tell your friends that the man you are in love with wants you to take time to explore and figure out what you really want?

Sitting up, Zara begins to pull herself together for the pending knock on the door. She ponders how she is getting everything she ever wished for but now is not sure she is ready to live the dream. Perhaps, if she had known there was a possibility of her wishes coming true, she would have been more careful about what she wished. Falling for Garrett had not been part of the plan.

Zara closes her eyes and tilts her head back. She sifts through her thoughts for 'her plan'. A long-suppressed memory of becoming a doctor rears its ugly head but Zara shakes her head to send that fantasy back to its rightful place in her childhood stories. The uncomfortable truth is, there is no plan. Her only wish had been to be free of the Circle Ceremony. College had been too far out of the realm of reality to hope for.

All this opportunity and all I really want is Garrett.

Zara hesitantly opens the door after continuous knocks from Ella.

"One minute, please."

She walks over to her desk and picks up the frame with the picture of her and Sloane. She was no longer her confidant.

Removing the picture, Zara put the frame in the drawer and slipped the picture into one of the colorful boxes at the bottom of her closet. Picking up her key, phone and backpack, Zara joins the girl in the hallway and shuts the door behind her.

"Wait... Z. Are you sure the coffee shop is the right place? Are you okay? You seem sad as fuck? Swear to GOD, did he hurt you?"

"El, please let Zara take a moment and talk to us. She looks tired but fine. Would you chill for a moment? I have spoken to Garrett and so have you. You know he is not going to hurt her. FUCK... CHILL!" Liliana scolds as she continues to walk down the hallway. Zara follows behind not ready to be in the middle yet.

The walk to the coffee shop is silent. Zara knows they are waiting for her to relax and just start talking. Liliana gets in line to order the coffees while Ella tells Zara to follow her to the back of the shop to save the comfy sitting area. Zara does as she is told and takes a seat on the big purple sofa. Looking around, she decides this will be her study hall for the day.

"Here we go, Freshman. Veranda with half and Splenda." Liliana hands her a cup.

Looking down at her coffee, Zara takes a deep breath and squares her shoulders, knowing they are waiting out of concern. "He wants me to take the time I need to explore who I am and what it is that I want before I make the choice to settle down with him."

Silence.

More silence.

"Wait... so let me get this straight..."

"El!" Liliana interrupts in a warning tone.

"I know, Lil! I know. He came and picked you up last night. I presume he took you to his house... yes?!?"

Zara nods.

"You spent the night together," she continues, stressing the word, "and today he tells you that he wants you to take the time to 'find yourself' and decide what you want?"

Zara squirms in her seat. "We did talk last night and this morning but I slept in a room he set up for me."

She takes a sip of coffee to hide the embarrassment of having to talk about such things openly.

"OH! Well, that's different. A room set up for you? You have a room in his house? I assume there are clothes for you in the room–"

Liliana interrupts her. "Z, how do you feel about the whole 'time to explore and find yourself'? I know for a fact that you have feelings for him. It seems like he is intending for you to date. Is he seeing other people while you are exploring?"

"I don't know. He says that he is stepping back for a while to give me space to enjoy college life. Garrett has provided everything I will need but says right now I should focus on discovering who I am."

"He is older. Maybe he is looking for a wife and wants to make sure you are ready for that kind of commitment. Zara, he is definitely into you." Ella reaches over and places a hand on Zara's knee.

"It says a lot that he has a room in his home for you. I've never heard of that before. That has to make you feel special. And let's not forget the necklace that you hold every time you think about him."

Zara nods as she glances down to find she is grasping the pendants.

"Well, maybe Garrett is right and it is time for you to experience college life. Now… Lil and I have a head start on most of this and can help. I say you jump in with both feet and see where you land. What do you say?"

Eyes wide and taking a big swallow, Zara forces a smile, "Thank you, Ella. I think I am ready to do this."

Both Liliana and Ella start laughing. "Freshman, there's no way you're ready to do this but I like your optimism. First up, striptease class. It is great exercise, but more importantly, it's fun as hell. Someday, whether with Garrett or some other guy, you will WOW them with the moves you've learned while staying in shape. What do you say?"

Liliana puts her hands up in response to Zara's dubious expression. "Z, if you hate the first class you never have to go back. It was not for me so do not feel like you have to do it."

"Lil… you didn't even give it a chance," Ella whined.

"I would like to try it," Zara states as the two hall mates begin bickering back and forth. That stopped them in their tracks.

"Ready to go back?" Liliana asks.

"I think I am going to stay and do some reading here," Zara replies, setting her coffee on the table in front of her and picking up her backpack.

"Freshman, are you sure? You know there is a massive study session planned in the dorm later in the great room. You don't want to go explore for a while with us?" Ella says lightly in a concerned voice.

"Ella, I will be alright. I am going to read a couple of chapters and then head back over. I like it back here. The couch is comfortable and they offer refills," Zara says with a big smile attempting to convince them she will be fine.

"Do you have your phone?" Liliana questions firmly.

Zara lifts her phone out of the outside pocket of her backpack and lays it on the arm of the sofa.

"If you get hassled by anyone or if you need anything, call us. I know you are going to call Garrett and you should but we are closer and can get here in minutes."

"Fucking A... Lil! It's Starbucks. What the fuck is going to happen to her at a Starbucks? You're going to creep her out. What is wrong with you? This is usually my area of expertise. We totally need to pick contact pictures to save in your phone for each of us. OMG... the pictures from the game turned out so cute. The ones of you and Garrett are adorable." Ella stops talking and Zara can tell by the look on her face that she feels badly for bringing him up again.

"I would very much like to see them. If there is one that is really cute of the two of us, I have a frame ready to go."

Ella is all smiles. "We can go through them tonight. Your walls are in need of pictures and the first football game is the perfect place to start. Okay, Freshman, we are going to leave you to your reading. Check in with Mother Lil every so often so she doesn't fret."

"Yes, Ma'am."

"You are so obedient. I like that about you," Ella says as she and Liliana walk toward the front of the coffee shop.

Sighing, Zara leans her head back against the sofa and closes her eyes.

If you only knew.

Sitting alone, Zara pulls out her Biology textbook and stares into space. After only a moment, she reaches for her journal. Knowing that the only way to purge her thoughts of Garrett and concentrate on her studies is to express them, Zara finds the next blank sheet and begins to freely write.

> *Garrett,*
>
> *When I'm with you everything inside me comes alive like a thousand butterflies waiting to fly. In your arms, I feel safe like I've never felt before. Once I am there I have a difficult time when my time is up. Although, our traditions say I should never look into your eyes, I find myself drawn into a warm abyss wondering if I will ever find my way back.*
>
> *The thought of not seeing you or talking to you is breaking my heart. I will miss everything about you. I hope that you will miss me too. Please miss me too.*

Zara closes the journal and returns it to her backpack. Though Garrett will never read it, Zara feels connected to him writing it.

Smiling to herself, she flips to the beginning of chapter three and begins her assigned reading.

Wanting to share the golden beauty of the autumn day with Garrett, but knowing she should not call him, she jots down a note in her journal once she has her coffee and is settled on the sofa in the back of the coffee shop.

> *My walk through campus was absolutely breathtaking this afternoon. The changing colors have altered the landscape and I have finally fallen in love with your college. The carpet of fallen leaves makes the best crinkly sound with every step. The girls laugh because of my excitement in seeing what is to come next.*
>
> *Midterms went very well. I have decided to take a heavier schedule next semester to challenge myself. Unfortunately, I do not know what I want to major in yet. The advisor says that it is normal and that I should continue to take basic classes.*
>
> *Eight more weeks... I miss you.*

Waiting for her study group to arrive, Zara pulls out her journal. Taken aback by the length of time since her note to Garrett, Zara quickly shares her big adventure of the morning.

> *I rode the bus by myself today. I wanted to get a Halloween costume for a party that we were invited to but the girls were busy. At the last minute, I decided to just hop on the bus alone. YAY!*
>
> *I'm excited about the party. It will be my first Halloween party. Garrett, there were so many costumes to choose from. I was going to wait and come back with the girls so they could help me. But, I decided I needed to pick one on my own. I am going to be a cowgirl. I love the outfit and it even comes with a cowboy hat.*
>
> *Can you believe I did that?*

Enjoying the sense of accomplishment, Zara remembered the last time she felt this way was this same time of year. Her parents had hosted several King Council members for dinner on Halloween. The evening was high protocol, which meant nothing for Zara as the Evans family lived every minute that way. But for her father it was on opportunity to showcase the training of his daughter, as Zara was required to serve.

Because it was intended to be a business dinner, their slaves and submissives were left at home. Zara's mother was positioned at her father's side the entire evening. Without clues or corrections, Zara navigated the meal flawlessly. She recalled falling into her bed fully clothed, completely exhausted.

Her mother walked into the room and closed the door behind her. Sitting on the bed, she spoke excitedly, "You performed beautifully. I am so proud of you. Not one misstep. Not one. Two of the councilmen complimented your father. Right there! Right in front of me!"

"Sorry, I'm late," Ollie announces jolting Zara from her thought.

She smiles up at him, still thinking about her mother.

"Can I get you a refill?" Ollie asks as he slides his bag on the chair adjacent to the sofa that Zara has claimed. "Hey, I beat Nina?"

"Umm... NO! And I already have the coffee," Nina states triumphantly.

Zara giggles as she slips her journal in her backpack and exchanges it for her notebook.

So, I went on a date last night. A guy who works at the coffee shop asked me out. The girls grilled him for an hour before he was given permission to take me out. He was very friendly and polite. He wasn't you.

I miss you more now than I did before I went out with him. Eleven more days until I get to see you. I wonder if you are missing me half as much as I am missing you.

Zara sips her coffee as she looks at the words on the page. They look almost as awkward as the date felt. Garrett wanted her to have the experiences of a normal college student.

Are first dates uncomfortable and strange for all normal college students?

Liliana had warned not go out with the coffee guy. Now, sitting in the back of the coffee shop and him in the front, the awkwardness continues.

I am not giving up my favorite place.

"Told you she would be here. Freshman, we leave tomorrow you know. One entire week without us. What are you doing here?"

"I came to get coffee and go over some notes. I need like ten minutes… promise. Please." Zara pleads with a mock frown that is quickly replaced with laughter.

"Fine. You're totally buying breakfast. Meet us at the diner. Seriously, Z… Ten minutes!"

"Ten minutes. I'm so there. Order me pancakes, please!" Zara yells after them.

Taking out her journal, Zara smiles as she opens to the page with the entry of her first night in her dorm. Flipping the pages, she realizes writing to Garrett in her journal had become her routine whenever she felt the need to connect with him. Confirming the girls are out of the shop and checking the time, Zara connects with him one more time.

I cannot believe I get to see you tomorrow. The time has flown by in some ways and dragged ever so slowly in others. It is hard to believe that Thanksgiving is tomorrow and I haven't talked to you in almost three months. I miss the sound of your voice, your laugh, and the touch of your hand on my back.

I have learned a lot about myself in the last few months and I am learning to like myself better. Before I came to school, I never gave it much thought whether to like myself or not. It just didn't cross my mind. I had a role in the Community and what I thought did not matter. Since beginning school, I have spent time with some really wonderful girls and they have helped me see that I am pretty wonderful in my own ways.

I think I understand now why you have given me the opportunity to come here and take the time to discover who I am. Knowing who I am helps me also know what I want. I have to come before you as a 'whole me' in order to have a successful relationship. Until I know who I am completely, I will not be ready to give my all to you. This separation has been very difficult. I miss seeing you. I miss talking to you. I miss sharing things with you. You said I could ask for anything I needed and you would give it me.

Your Little One

Zara grasps her pendant and rereads her entry.

Tomorrow. I cannot wait to see you.

Checking her phone, she grabs her coffee cup and makes her way to the exit of the coffee shop. She rushes, as she knows she is running late.

Walking into the diner, she knows she is in trouble.

"Fourteen minutes, Freshman!! I was just about to send Lil back to get you," Ella proclaims with a huge smile.

"Sorry. I hurried," Zara whines as she peels off all her winter layers and slides into her seat.

"Z, are you ready for your big day tomorrow?"

Zara shakes her head and mouths NO!

"Come on. We have talked about this. You know what you want–"

"Freshman!" Ella cuts Liliana off to take a firmly tone. "YOU GOT THIS!"

Zara is mournfully shaking her head when the waitress begins to place the food in front of each of them. Zara looks at the two people who have become her family in the last few months. Although the holiday break is only a week long, not seeing them is going to be painful and strange.

"See? Now you get it. That's why your little Starbucks run is out of the question on the day before breaks. New rule. Just wait until winter break, that's a full month. You are totally going to miss us," Ella tells Zara when she catches her staring.

"When do you leave again?" Zara questions in a softer voice.

"Z, don't get sad. Focus on the fact that you are finally going to see that man-hunk of yours. We leave for the airport at 5:30am. NOT A WORD, EL!!" Liliana stops Ella before she can begin whining.

"Do either of you know what Beth is doing for Thanksgiving?" Zara wonders.

"Working," Liliana and Ella say in unison.

"Does she ever not work?"

"Z, Beth is struggling to make ends meet. She picks up every shift she can. Her scholarship pays for her classes but the grants that she was getting dried up in the middle of last year. So, extras like food and clothes and everything else are considered fluff that she has to work to cover. The really sad part is she is smart as hell. Computer engineering, I think."

"She was accepted at MIT but chose to come to State because it is so close to her mom. Single-mom, only child, mom isn't well," Ella sputters.

The three finish breakfast and make their way back to the dorm. Ella immediately turns up the music as loud as possible and knocks on all the doors in their hallway. She declares another new rule. Last day before break, everyone gets up and there is a dance party while they pack. All the girls from the hall spend the day together dancing and laughing. Zara watches from the doorway of her room thinking about how different it was from move in day... how good it feels to have friends.

CHAPTER 20

Zara reads the text one more time.

"Sorry, called out of town on business. Branden will pick you up at 11am to take you to Thanksgiving at his house. Stay at my house for the weekend. If you need anything ask Branden or use your CARD!"

Resting her phone on her chest, Zara lays in bed listening to the silence. Of course, she thinks to herself, she never hears any noise from the hallway. Garrett made sure of that before she moved in, but the silence seems louder this morning.

Thanksgiving. A long weekend. No home football game. No study sessions. No friends to joke around with to help pass the time. And now, no Garrett.

Spending the weekend curled up in bed sounds like a much better idea, but Garrett did not include a phone number for Branden so canceling is not an option.

Sighing loudly, Zara checks the time once more. She still has two hours before Branden arrives to escort her to Thanksgiving dinner without Garrett. Grumpily, Zara climbs out of bed and is suddenly hit by a memory of her mother busy in the kitchen. The sadness comes fast and hard, causing Zara to buckle and sit on the floor. Thoughts of her mother were often in the context of the rules and protocols of the Community or their family. Zara had not allowed herself to spend time thinking about her family.

Without allowing herself time to change her mind, Zara picks up her phone and dials her family's number. The phone is answered after only one and a half rings.

"Hello?"

Zara is paralyzed at the sound of her mother's voice.

"Hello?" The change in the tone from the first hello to the second is clear. Zara sits frozen hundreds of miles away listening to her mother's voice for the first time in months.

"Is anyone there?"

"Mother."

"Zara Faith, are you hurt? What is wrong?"

"No mother. I am calling to say Happy Thanksgiving. And–"

"Zara Faith, you made a decision. You must live with your decision as I must live with mine. Do you understand?"

"Yes. I miss–"

"I am glad that you are not hurt and are doing well. Be safe."

The phone clicks in Zara's ear.

Zara gasps and begins choking. She drops the phone next to her and covers her mouth to suppress the scream welling up from her core. Tears pour out of her eyes making it impossible to focus on any one point in the room.

For the first time since leaving the Circle, Zara does not work to suppress her loss. She sits and allows it to consume her. Before the call, there was hope that she was still her mother's daughter, her brother's sister, even her father's daughter.

After sobbing for several minutes, Zara sits motionless, staring at nothing and everything. None of the techniques that she had been trained to use alleviate the pain of this loss. With sudden clarity, Zara realizes this is the first time she has ever allowed herself to fully express her feelings.

Lying back against the floor, Zara begins to watch her emotions drift upward. Without effort, the thought of loss and the distance in her mother's voice rise higher, slowly moving away from her still body.

One by one, the layers of emotion drift from Zara's body and float away, leaving in their place a young woman with a calm mind. As the hurt drifts out, pictures of her brother begin to appear; she recognized her favorite moments of him... watching a movie together at the library when they were both little... walking together in the park near their house. The calm that has taken hold of Zara continues as the memories of Fredrik become more vivid. His first baseball game. The Christmas that Zara picked out her own present for him. The excitement he had when he opened the skateboard. Memories lead to the sound of his laughter and Zara closes her eyes to savor the sound. His laughter as a little boy as they played a board game and she let him win.

Opening her eyes, Zara scans the room. Reaching for her

phone, Zara is surprised to find that over an hour and fifteen minutes had passed since calling and hearing her mother's voice.

Calmly, Zara stands and walks to the bathroom. Taking off her long tee shirt and panties, Zara turns to stare at her naked body in the mirror. Her eyes hone in on the necklace that is always around her neck.

Lifting both pendants, Zara examines it closely.

This is my home.

Placing the pendant back against her skin and reaching for her pink hair tie, happy memories begin to bubble up from deep inside her; the first night with Garrett on the flight to Michigan.

Blushing, Zara turns and steps into the shower. Leaning her face into the spray, she allows the lingering emotions to rinse off her like water down the drain. She rushes washing and conditioning her hair is rushed through to give her enough time to finish getting ready.

With an overnight bag over her shoulder and her phone in her hand, Zara locks her dorm room. Taking a deep breath, she makes her way down the hallway to the exit. Zara is nervous but does not push the emotions down. She wants to feel all of them, the bad, the good and the scary.

Zara opens the door and drops her overnight bag into the door, startled to find Branden standing on the other side. As she gathers herself, Branden reaches down and picks it up.

"Thank you," she smiles.

"Pleasure. You look very nice, Zara," Branden declares as he turns and leads her to his waiting car.

He opens the car door and Zara slides onto the seat. Closing the door, he opens the back door and places the overnight bag on the seat behind her, then walks around and slips into the driver's seat.

"So, you're stuck with Viv and me today. Sorry."

"Thank you for extending the invitation."

Nodding, Branden puts the car in gear and pulls away from the curb.

"Oh, before I forget, I have an extra set of keys to G's car. Don't let me forget to give them to you when I drop you off at his place."

"Thank you, Branden, but I don't know how to drive."

"Oh, I didn't know. Is that part of the whole Community thing?

G doesn't talk about that much. Shit, if you are not supposed to talk about it, I'm sorry."

Taken aback that the Community has come up so quickly, Zara does not answer right away.

"It is alright. I don't mind talking about it if you have questions."

"Seriously, because I know my sister is going to have lots of questions. She is geeked that we have you to ourselves today."

"I hope that I am able to answer them for her." Zara quickly glances from the window to Branden and back. He was a good looking man by anyone's standards. He wears his beard trimmed close to his face. And his cheekbones married nicely with his square jaw.

Branden fills out his seat as a man preparing to block a quarterback on the football field. He is in great shape and looks to be made of muscle. He and Garrett work out at a CrossFit gym several times a week and, on off days, they have a small gym in Branden's building that they use.

Branden glances toward Zara and gives her a small smile. "We are really glad you are joining us today. Garrett is truly sorry he is not here to pick you up."

Zara looks at her hands in her lap as he speaks. Her knuckles are white from squeezing her hands together tightly. This is the first time Zara has been alone with Branden.

"It will be fun. You'll see."

Nodding, Zara draws in a long slow breath. "I am looking forward to spending some time with you and Vivian."

Branden breaks into a belly laugh that puts Zara even further off balance. "Zara, you're as sweet as they come. I can see why Garrett is so into you."

His words jar her both mentally and physically. She jerks her head from watching the city passing by to the man who just dropped a bomb. Opening and closing her mouth several times, no words come out.

Branden continues to laugh. Suddenly, the music lowers and Branden's entire demeanor changes. "Jacobs."

"Do you have her?" Garrett hisses. Butterflies flutter inside Zara's stomach at the sound of Garrett's voice over the car speaker.

"Have who?" Branden asks, putting his finger to his mouth signaling for Zara to stay quiet.

"Motherfucking piece of shit assfuck. Whatever or WHOEVER you are doing, you fucking better turn your piece of shit around and go pick up my Zara. Right motherfucking now, B."

"Chill out. Damn. Do you kiss your Zara with that mouth?"

"Swear to fuck… she is all alone, B. All I asked you to do is pick her up. FUCK!"

"I am here. Branden picked me up about fifteen minutes ago. Please do not worry," Zara asserts reassuringly.

"Zara, Little One, I'm so sorry that I'm not there to spend Thanksgiving with you. I'll be back as soon as I can get this done. You're going to my house after dinner… right?"

"Yes, Sir."

Garrett sighs.

As if a mute button has been pushed, an uncomfortable silence fills the car. Zara finds her hands in her lap once again tightly gripping one another. She swallows hard and remains still.

Zar… Sir? Really? You had to say Sir?

Clearing his throat, Garrett starts to say something but Branden cuts him off. "G, we're at the house and Viv's waiting. I'll make sure your Zara is set up at your place after dinner. How's the case?"

"Shitty but you already knew that. B… take care of her."

"I got her," Branden says firmly.

With those three words, the music begins again and Zara knows he is gone.

"In case you had any doubt that Garrett is into you, that little conversation should put any questions to rest. Hell, he doesn't even like for me to go to his house."

"I…" Zara is at a loss for words.

"Good, because we're here."

Her head still spinning from calling Garrett 'Sir,' Zara looks around for a house. All she sees are large warehouses. The door of one of the warehouses slowly opens.

"When Garrett and I decided to start our business in the Lansing area, the cost for warehouse space was at rock bottom. We decided to purchase this building and the one next door. We renovated to fit our business needs."

Driving through the large opening, Branden parks in a space between an SUV and a sporty red car. The second the car is off, Zara's door is opened from the outside. With a yelp, Zara coils into herself.

"Oh FUCK ME HARD, Zara, I am so fucking sorry." Vivian steps back from the passenger side of the car to allow Zara room to exit and begin breathing again.

"Fucking A, Viv. We have to return her alive. G has already called me twice today."

Breaking into a loud laugh, Vivian wraps her arms around Branden. "I win! He called me three times."

Waving Zara to get out of the car, Vivian shuts the door once Zara has cleared the car. "He is terrified that I am going to corrupt you while he is away."

Wide-eyed, Zara tries to paste a smile on her face but she feels uneasy with their familiarity.

"I am going to do my absolute best. It's about time Garrett worries a bit. Branden, get the pies out of my car, please. Zara and I have girl talk to get under way."

Stiffening, as Vivian's arm comes around her, Zara follows her through the cars toward an elevator. Vivian hits the up button and the door opens immediately. Zara steps in behind Vivian and turns toward the cars. She can see Branden getting three pie boxes out of the backseat of the SUV.

"Hey, are you okay? Honest as fuck, I didn't mean to scare you. Sorry."

"Please do not give it another thought. I am fine. I have not spent much time in a warehouse."

For Zara, the elevator ride is over far too quickly. The momentary reprieve inside the metal box allows Zara to center herself. She takes a couple of deep breaths, and pictures the beach, the movement of the water suppressing the lingering thoughts of being alone with two people she barely knows. As the tension leaves her, the door opens. Branden steps out and Vivian grabs Zara's arm to escort her out behind her brother.

With her head down, Zara notices the flooring is a dark wood, not at all what she was expecting. She expected the living area to look like the lower level.

"We are so fucking excited that you are eating with us today.

Typically, it is just the three of us and I would much rather have you here than Garrett."

Pausing, Zara looks up at Vivian.

"Don't get me wrong. He is my other brother but when the two of them get together, it is all work all day. Please, he sucks ass at answering my questions."

"That's because he doesn't want to answer them, not because he is bad at it. We know it irritates you and is, therefore, totally entertaining for us."

Zara only half listens to the siblings going back and forth. Most of her attention is on trying to take in every nuance of Branden's house. It is breathtaking. The kitchen is huge.

Zar, STOP IT! Yes, Mother would love this kitchen. Yes, baking cakes would be amazing with her in here. Put it away.

"Zara, what's wrong? We didn't mean to upset you." Vivian stands directly in front of Zara. Almost too close. "Do you need a minute to yourself?"

Zara shakes her head and smiles.

"You have a lovely home. I don't know what I was expecting, but this is spectacular," Zara tells Branden. Vivian jumps up and down clapping her hands and Zara catches Branden rolling his eyes.

"Viv designed the entire place. I don't have a lot of visitors so she does not get the raves that she craves."

Vivian stops. Zara can see the hurt on her face from the wry wit of her brother and it becomes evident that she is not the only one that sees the change in Vivian.

Racing around the long cement-topped island, Branden wraps his sister in a bear hug and spins her off her feet. "Hey, Viv. You know I am kidding. Sister, I am your biggest fan. You are brilliant. You have a gift. I'm an idiot that should think before he shoots off hurtful things to the most important person in his life. Got it?"

Zara cannot help giggling as Branden begins tickling Vivian who does her best to continue to look angry and not smile.

"Ok. Ladies, we have some time before dinner is ready," Branden states as he hugs his sister with a final squeeze. "We have options. I'm stuck in the kitchen. You two can tour the house and talk about what a wonderful guy I am to cook Thanksgiving dinner or we can all hang out in here and ask Zara tons of questions."

He laughs as Zara's eyes widened. "Questions it is then! We will do a full tour later and convince Zara to crash here for the night in Garrett's room."

Zara remains as still as possible working to school her expression as Vivian does another happy dance.

"Zara, I do have so many questions but if you would prefer not to talk about your past, I totally understand even though I really, really want to know."

Branden makes his way to the refrigerator as Vivian motions for Zara to follow her up a transparent staircase. "We will be right back brother. Cocktail me... it's a holiday. Make one for Zara too, please. And do NOT call Garrett to ask for permission. You owe me. You almost made me cry today."

With that, Vivian starts up the stairs with Zara silently following behind. Although the staircase looks ominous, the walk up is easy. "Branden was totally against a two-story when we started. He didn't want to have to climb stairs every night. So I came up with staircases that have twice as many steps but the lift is shorter so it feels like you are walking normally."

As the pair walks across an open balcony, Zara stops and looks down at the first level.

"WOW... spectacular," she whispers. Out of nowhere, she feels two arms go around her in a squeezing hug. Feeling her tense, Vivian releases her.

"I'm sorry. No one has ever said such nice things about my work. Well, and not been related to me. Come. Let me show you."

Continuing further to the end of the balcony, Vivian opens the glass door and they enter an entryway. She opens the double door to the left of the entryway.

"Welcome to Chateau Dawson." Standing aside so Zara can enter and look around, she continues, "Branden insisted that Garrett and I both have a space here. They work constantly and it made sense to have a place to crash. My room is the other double door."

Walking into a spacious living room, Vivian takes Zara further into the suite, reminded by the design of his home and his room at the beach house. It definitely fit the Garrett that she was becoming familiar with.

"The bathroom has all your regular items and there is a section in the closet with clothes for you as well. A small section." Zara looks at her questioningly as she waves her into the bathroom.

"Oh, yes, my darling. Garrett gave specific orders where you are concerned," Vivian chuckles. "When I was organizing all of your clothes for the various locations, Branden was adamant that you would never be staying here, so why include this in the locations. Joke's on him."

The huge smile plastered on Zara's face makes Vivian laugh. "So, I am guessing you are a bath person. Me too. I blew my entire budget for my space on the huge bathtub and closet."

Zara walks over to the edge of the bathtub and runs her fingers over the different bottles of oils and bubbles. A thought pops into her mind that she knows she has no right to even ponder.

As if reading her mind, Vivian whispers in her ear, "To my knowledge, he has never brought another woman here. Even Branden entertains elsewhere. God forbid, his sister ever find out that he is not a virgin."

Laughing, Vivian walks out into the connecting room. "We have plenty of time before dinner. Why don't you take a soak in the tub? I plan to take a long bath as well. We can meet in the kitchen in an hour."

"What about Branden? He sounds as if he would enjoy company and he is preparing the meal."

"Finally, someone cares about me." Branden walks in carrying two large glasses with pineapple wedges on the sides. Handing one to Vivian, he gives the other to Zara. "I will not be offended if you do not drink this. And, please, enjoy a bath. As I remember, the dorm bathrooms are not the most relaxing. Even if G-man did make them redo it for his Zara."

Walking out, Branden waves and says he would see them both in an hour and that they had clean-up duties following dinner.

Vivian clanks Zara's glass then walks toward the door as well. "YAY... Thanksgiving bath time. Enjoy!"

CHAPTER 21

Zara stands in the middle of the spacious room. She does not know what she had expected to be doing for Thanksgiving, but standing in Garrett's home away from home was not it. Looking around, a picture on the bedside table catches her eye. Still holding the clothes that Vivian had handed her and sipping the drink that Branden brought, Zara makes her way over to the table.

Stunned, Zara sets the clothes on the bed and picks up a sleek grey frame. It contains a picture of her. Composed in black and white, it is a photo of her sitting in a park looking out at nothing. Zara recognizes the photo from a visit to one of her favorite places in Chattanooga.

Sloane had suggested that they visit the park the day before Zara's Circle Ceremony and they went knowing everything in both their lives would change the next day. The photographer had caught her in a serious moment of contemplation when she had been thinking about what her Sir would be like and whether she would find happiness with him.

Zara returns the frame to its place on the table. Collecting the change of clothes, she makes her way to the bathroom. Nothing could prepare her for how this day was turning out, but a hot bath in the middle of the day seemed like a fantastic idea at this point and she turned on the water. She plugs the tub and selects a peppermint mix to add to the water. A light knock at the door startles her.

"It's Viv. Are you still dressed?"

"Yes."

"Excellent!" The door flies open. Vivian stands in a fluffy white robe closed with a red cord. She crosses the room and places a small pitcher on a flat surface of the bathtub. "Branden makes the best cocktails even if they're virgin."

Vivian winks at Zara. "I wanted to make sure you figured out the tub and had everything you needed. Okay... Okay... Okay... I am leaving you alone now."

Before Zara can respond, Vivian turns and walks out of the bathroom.

"I'm locking the bedroom door behind me. Get your ass in that tub. We have exactly one hour," she yells from the bedroom. Zara smiles as she hears Vivian laughing to herself.

Zara checks to make sure the water temperature is just right and slowly slips into the bubbly hot bath. With a big sigh, she closes her eyes and leans back only to find she is bombarded by memories. Her mother. Ella and Liliana. School. Vivian. Branden. Garrett. The photo.

Sitting up to take a drink, Zara thinks about the photo again. The existence of the photo itself is intriguing. She could not recall a camera at the park that day.

Nothing that she contemplated on that day in the park had happened the way it was supposed to. In fact, the unthinkable had occurred and months later Zara was still trying to understand how the pieces of her life would fit together. Zara turns off the water. The tub is big enough and the water deep enough that she can fully submerge and she lies back allowing her body to fully relax.

Garrett. What is he doing right now? Where is he? What is he wearing? How did he get that picture? Did I make a mistake?

Zara lifts the pendant and studies the small 'G' as it hangs next to the large 'Z.'

Did I make a mistake choosing school? My life would have been so different if I had continued with the Ceremony. My family would still love me. Sloane would still be my best friend. I would be married to Garrett. I would be secure in my future.

Blinking, Zara fills her glass with the contents of the pitcher and takes another large sip. Setting the glass down on the edge of the tub, she focuses on the tiny bubbles clinging to the inside of the glass and tries to clear her thoughts.

Regret is unhealthy. Zara starts a mental list of what she likes about Garrett. She thinks about the time she and Garrett spent at the beach before he dropped her off at school. He always found a way to make her feel comfortable. Sitting in front of the fire, he had led the conversation in a way that put her at ease. He was fascinated with her lack of music knowledge and vowed to change that to show her how important music is to one's life.

Zara remembers how his face lights up as he talks about the things he loves, his time at MSU and, although Garrett did not talk about his work much, she knew it was a passion of his by the way his shoulders seemed broader when he commented on it.

I miss his face. I miss Garrett.

Zara sighs.

Carefully stepping from the tub, she wraps herself in a fluffy white towel and walks to the closet. Seeing Garrett's hanging clothes, she grabs a blue button down shirt and draws it to her nose hoping for a mixture of cool mint, brown sugar and lemons. She wants to smell his scent. There is nothing to smell but fresh linen.

Returning to the bathroom, Zara dries off and dresses in the soft comfy clothes she had been given. Despondently, she gathers the clothes that she had worn earlier and makes her way into Garrett's bedroom. Passing through the door, Zara freezes.

Garrett stands by the bed. "Happy Thanksgiving, Little One."

Without a word, Zara drops the clothes she is carrying and walks into his waiting arms, a sob catching in the back of her throat. She crushes him until she feels the rumble of his laughter in her chest. "Were those two that awful to you?"

In a feather-light voice, she breaths into his neck, "I have missed you."

"I missed you too." She resists as he pulls her away from his body to meet her eyes. "Please do not cry."

Hearing those words, Zara pushes herself closer into him to hug him harder. "Hey. What is it?"

Garrett scoops her into his arms and carries her to the outer room. Once seated, he takes her face in his hands and forces her chin up. "Zara, look at me."

Immediately, her eyes flickered up to confront the apprehension.

"I'm sorry. I just… I did not expect you today. I'm surprised."

"Is there anything else? Did Viv make you feel uncomfortable?" he queries with concern.

Shaking her head, she affirms how considerate Vivian has been. "No, she has been kind. Vivian let me take a bath in your massive tub. I can get off your lap." Zara begins to move but she feels Garrett tighten his grip around her. Enfolded against his chest, Zara decides to tell Garrett what she wants.

"May I ask a question?"

"Anything."

Zara likes the vibrations of his voice when she is against his chest. She takes a deep breath and leans back to look into his eyes.

"That bad?" he asks.

"Can we begin to spend more time together?" Zara blurts, surprising herself with the volume and force she uses to ask for his time. Her confidence drains away as she feels Garrett tense around her.

"Zara, what are you asking? I need you to be clear with me."

"I... I just want to be with you. I am sorry. If that is not what you want–"

"Wait... No... hey hey hey." Garrett pulls her back to his chest. "I want to be clear only because I don't want to misunderstand your intentions. You and I need to communicate very thoroughly with each another. That is the only reason I asked you to explain yourself. Does that make sense?"

"Yes, Sir."

"Zara, as much as I enjoy hearing you call me Sir, until you are ready for me to make that commitment, I need for you not to call me that. You and I both understand the significance of that title and I am not your Sir."

"I am so sorry." She swallows against the lump in her throat.

"Zara, there is nothing to be sorry about. I very much like the way my name sounds coming out of your mouth."

A knock at the door interrupts their conversation. "We need to head downstairs."

Zara nods and begins to pull herself away from the most comfortable spot she has ever been in. Garrett helps her to her feet. As he stands, he pauses to cup her face in his hands.

"We will finish this conversation after dinner, but so you don't spend the day lost in your thoughts, the answer to your question is that I would love to begin spending more time with you. If you think you're ready."

Zara cannot hide the smile or the blush that erupts over her face. "I am ready."

Zara holds her breath as Garrett lowers his face to hers to look deeply in her eyes. He brings her a little closer to look even deeper.

His gaze dips down to her smile then returns to her eyes once more, coming closer yet. Zara melts into his embrace as Garrett's lips gently brush against hers.

Unbidden, Zara's eyes close in ecstasy as he presses against her tenderly and opens his mouth to tug lightly on her bottom lip. Zara follows where he leads her and as Garrett's tongue slips between her lips, her tongue yields and meets it. Another more insistent knock issues from the door.

Garrett chastely kisses her on the lips twice and moves away.

"We need to go eat dinner before the National Guard is called out. Then we need to continue doing more of that and finish our conversation. Sound like a plan?"

Zara does not say anything. She touches her lips with her fingers and smiles.

"You liked that. I liked it too, Little One." Garrett takes her hand and draws her out of his room.

"Oh. I forgot the glass and pitcher. Garrett," she adds smiling.

Garrett kisses her lips quickly again.

"Leave it. We can get it later. And keep saying my name." One last double peck on the lips and Garrett leads her to the stairs. At the top, he steps out the way to allow Zara to descend the staircase first. Once at the bottom, she pauses. He grabs her hand again and they walk hand in hand to the kitchen.

"Well... well... well. Don't you look a wee bit happier than when you first arrived," Branden proclaims, looking up from the ham he is slicing. "And there we have the blushing to prove it. Zara, you glow when you are so happy."

Looking down, Zara focuses on her hand locked within Garrett's. "She did miss me. Maybe I should go away more often."

Zara looks up to catch Garrett staring at her with a teasing smile and sparkling eyes lighting up his face.

"No. I would prefer if you did not leave again." Satisfied by the look of surprise on Garrett's face, she giggles as he pulls her close and plants a firm kiss on her ready lips.

"If you two could stop staring at each other for five seconds, dinner is served," Vivian murmurs. Zara takes a step towards the table and Vivian motions for her to sit. As she takes her seat, Zara wonders about the difference in Vivian's demeanor.

"Vivian, is everything alright?" Zara asks in a hushed voice as

Garrett makes his way around the large island to talk to Branden.

"I'm fine. The bath and cocktails mellowed me out a bit." She gives Zara a half smile and sighs. "And I had my heart set on asking you a shit ton of questions. Garrett's ruined that plan."

Looking up, Zara shakes her head. "I am sorry, but I do not understand. How does Garrett's presence change asking me questions?"

"Because Garrett will not allow you to be pestered," Garrett answers as he places the ham on the table. He kisses the top of Zara's head and walks back into the kitchen.

"Vivian, you can still ask me whatever you want to ask. I may not answer some of the questions but you are more than welcome to ask." Zara looks down at her hands resting in her lap and smiles to herself. "I appreciate his protecting me but I would not think that you would ask to hurt me. You are one of Garrett's best friends. Please ask."

"Okay. But you have to start calling me Viv. Vivian makes me feel old." Viv's face transforms with a big smile. "Where should we begin?"

Garrett and Branden appear at the table with the last of the food, the experience entirely different for Zara than every Thanksgiving before this one. Zara's mother would have been in the kitchen for two days preparing the day's meal and Zara would also have been expected to assist at the mere request for help.

Zara finds it unsettling to see Branden in the kitchen and having the two men serve the food. She had spent her life training to serve and it takes a lot of concentration to sit and not help.

As Garrett sits down beside her, he grabs Zara's knee and gives it a quick squeeze. With the food passed and plates full, Viv asks her first question. "How does the whole thing work?"

"Viv!" Branden snaps.

"What? She said I could ask."

Clearing her throat, Zara asks her own question. "What exactly as you asking? Can you narrow the question down for me?"

"I understand the basics of BDSM. I understand that you and Garrett are from BDSM communities. But I don't understand how it works. It is my understanding that relationships of that nature take time and trust to develop. Consent and something else. Yet you're a couple that essentially knew nothing about each other when you were to marry."

"So you are asking how the Community works?" Zara restates the question in order to give herself a moment to process an answer. Viv is nodding as she is chews.

"You are correct about BDSM relationships taking time and trust. The majority of the members of the Community are individuals that made a choice to enter into the lifestyle. A very small core of members makes up the King Council. Have you discussed the Council with Garrett?"

All three shake their heads no. Garrett reaches over and lays his hand on Zara's knee. "Zara, you don't have to discuss this. You know as well as I do that this is confidential."

She pauses briefly then continues with clarity and conviction. "Garrett, I have no issue discussing this with your friends. I don't believe that either of them have plans to publish an article or are researching a book about us."

Zara turns her attention back to her waiting audience and begins to share her story. "The King Council is the core of the Community. The governing body, if you will. Let me start further back.

"In the 40's, there were a couple of major players in the world of BDSM, Ray and Seabrock. One of the founding fathers of the King Council was mentored by Seabrock. Forgive me, but some names I will not share as they hold no relevance to the explanation and, as Garrett has indicated, should be allowed to remain confidential.

"Upon settling in the United States, he was able to connect with other like-minded individuals. They were few and far between but a network formed and the group began to meet on an annual basis to share ideas, exchange instruments and, most likely, interact in demonstrations and play.

"During this time, one of the daughters of the members was beaten to death by her husband, an outsider, as you all are referred to by the Community. This event provoked communication regarding the daughters of the members and their safety.

"It is my understanding that the first match was made at the request of one of the daughters. The members saw an opportunity to strengthen already forming bonds and provide safe spouses for their daughters. The first match was held at the annual King

Council gathering. The daughter, brought to the event by her father, left with her new Dom.

"In outsider terms, they were married. It's very much like other cultures that subscribe to arranged marriages. The difference, of course, is that the daughters of our Community are trained by their mothers to be submissive for her Sir.

"As part of the deal, the young Dom would join ranks with the King Council upon the acceptance of a submissive. In this way a lasting legacy is ensured for the Council. As time evolved, certain aspects have changed. For instance, the ceremonies now occur on the eighteenth birthday of the Council member's daughter."

Pausing to take a drink of water, Zara continues. "I am the daughter of a King Council member. I was raised to become the submissive of the Dominant that my father and the Council determined would be a good match. In my family, there was never any doubt that I would walk into the Circle belonging to my father and leave it belonging to Garrett."

Taking a cleansing breath, Zara looks at her full plate feeling her hunger suddenly hit.

"That's it?" Viv squeals.

Everyone looks at her and Branden begins to laugh, "Viv, what else did you think it was? Someone being dragged into a ceremony kicking and screaming with ropes and chains?"

"The kicking and screaming is a very real part of it for some of us," Zara says softly. "However, it is our upbringing that is the ropes and chains and they are around us securely every step of the way."

The silence that surrounds Zara brings her out of her thoughts and back into the room. Realizing she has stunned her audience, Zara falters, "Forgive me. I should not have–"

"Yes, Little One, you should. I want to hear all your thoughts. However, I do think this is a conversation for you and me to have in private at a later time." Garrett nods to the siblings who are eagerly listening. "How about if we allow Zara to eat her meal and the two of you entertain her with your tales."

Viv is the first to respond and places her fork purposefully on the plate in front of her. "Our story is short and tragic. Our parents were killed and we are all that we have. I am older by birth but Branden is older by necessity. Quite a simple and short story."

"Viv... I am so sorry. I did not realize."

"No worries. They've been gone for a long time. We're fine. Right, B?" Standing up and picking up his plate, Branden moves behind his sister and hugs her with his free arm.

"We're perfect... Sister Lady." Viv's smile lights her from the inside. Returning to the table, Branden carries a pie in each hand. He carefully sets them on the table and takes his seat. "We've been on our own for years. Garrett and his family have sort of adopted us though. Hence, Thanksgiving at my house, then Christmas with the Dawson Family."

"Once we all graduated from college, my parents began traveling during the holiday so it has been the three of us every year." Garrett leans into Zara and taps her on the nose. "We're very happy to have someone new join our little Thanksgiving group."

Zara eats her dinner as the three fell into a comfortable conversation that she knows nothing about. She is content to just listen and be near Garrett. At times, he reaches out to explain a point, touching her lightly on the elbow or the knee in the process, and that is all Zara needs to feel like she belongs in the mix.

Once the dinner is over and the pies have been devoured, Zara and Viv clean up the dishes and kitchen. As Zara assists Viv with loading the dishwasher, her thoughts are on Garrett and the kisses that they have shared. "You know you are smiling while doing dishes... right? Want to talk about it?"

Zara shakes her head no but she feels her smile broaden. "Figures. Fine... change of subject. Are you glad you didn't marry or whatever Garrett that night in the circle thingy?"

The plate slips out of Zara's hand and crashes to the floor shattering.

"OH FUCK!!!" Viv shouts.

"I am so sorry. I really am sorry. It just slid right out of my hands," Zara exclaims mournfully. As she bends to pick up the pieces, Branden and Garrett rush into the kitchen.

"I see how you are," Branden says with a huge grin on his face. "I cook you a nice dinner and you break the dishes."

With broom in hand, Viv shoos Zara back and quickly sweeps the broken pieces into a pile.

Shaking, Zara turns to face Garrett and finds herself wrapped into his arms. "Hey, it is not a big deal. I just want to make sure you're okay."

"G, are we going to wait to tell her this is my dead parents' china?" Zara's hands fly to cover her mouth to hold in the gasp.

"Branden! Don't be an ass. She's upset," Viv says from crouching on the floor picking up the broken pieces.

"Z. Hey, it's okay. There's no significance to these plates. You could break all of them. Seriously. I'm just glad you're fine." Branden walks over and touches Zara's arm then bends down to help his sister.

Looking up into Garrett's eye, Zara whispers, "I am so sorry."

Garrett responds by lifting her chin and planting a soft kiss on her lips, then repeats the kiss one more time before releasing her.

The four work in relative silence to finish the last of the cleanup. Once done, Zara comments on the showplace of a kitchen, "Branden, you have a beautiful kitchen."

"Thanks, Z. It's the only room of the house that I gave a fuck about during the renovation."

"Yes, and he wasn't particularly helpful either," Viv says walking around the island, leading the way to the far end of the living space.

"I'm a chef. I want what I want."

"Okay... you're not a chef even if you do cook very well, thank you very much. But you were difficult on the kitchen," Viv declares as she plops onto the far end of the leather sofa.

"Imagine if he would have cared about the entire house," Zara says matter-of-factly.

Everyone starts to laugh. Garrett grabs her by the shoulders to prevent her from sitting on the sofa and guides her to a big leather recliner. Sitting down, he pulls her onto his lap and he squashes back into the chair to get comfortable. Branden turns on a football game and they all relax.

After the game, they put on a movie amidst pleas for mercy by the guys for food. Pizza is ordered and eaten while watching *Galaxy Quest*. Zara feels Garrett's stare as she bursts into another fit of laughter. She had never seen the movie and it quickly becomes one of her favorites. Once the movie ends, Garrett helps Zara to her feet and then stands up behind her.

"Let's talk," he says with a wicked smirk on his face. Zara

feels a blush take over her face. Her eyes center on his as he takes her hand and escorts her away, but not before she catches Branden rolling his eyes at Viv.

"Talk. That's what you kids are calling it today."

"Garrett, as excited as Zara was that you made it back today, I'm thinking 'talking' is the last thing on her mind," Viv grins at her proclamation.

"You guys stayin'?" Branden asks before they are out of sight. Garrett stops and lifts his hand to Zara's chin to draw her eyes to his.

"Are we staying here tonight? It means homemade breakfast by Chef Branden." His asking takes Zara completely by surprise. She nods, looking deep into his eyes.

I get lost every time.

"Looks like my lady wants to stay. See you both tomorrow and I am NOT working out at the crack ass of dawn so don't even ask."

Chuckling as he makes his way to the kitchen with the pizza boxes, Branden yells out, "Wasn't askin'!"

"Goodnight, Branden. Thank you again for an incredible dinner. Viv, thank you for creating the best bathtub experience ever," Zara says over her shoulder while being led up the steps.

CHAPTER 22

"Shit! Hold on!" Garrett dashes back down the stairs to disappear into the kitchen. Zara can hear Branden laugh at whatever is happening in the kitchen. Garrett reappears making his way back up the steps with bottles and glasses in hand. "Lead the way, Little One."

Zara holds the glass door open. As he passes by, Garrett drops a kiss on her unsuspecting lips. Grinning, Zara walks past Garrett to open the door to his private residence. Garrett gestures Zara to enter and kicks the door closed behind him with his foot.

Walking over to the coffee table, he begins to carefully unload the bounty stolen from the kitchen. "I didn't know what you were going to be in the mood to drink while we talked, so I brought options. I can go back down if you want something else. Branden said that you had a virgin version of Viv's favorites earlier. He volunteered to make more if you would prefer that."

"Garrett, whatever you brought up for me is perfect. Thank you." Zara makes her way to sit on the sofa. Garrett sits down next to her and hands her a bottle of water and Coke. Zara gives him a quick smile.

"Not bad for fifteen seconds." Chuckling, Garrett begins to pour himself a drink. "Which would you prefer?"

"Just water. Thank you," Zara replies softly.

Garrett untwists the cap and hands Zara one of the bottles of water he carried up. "I'd like a quick shower. Would you like me to run you another bath?"

"No, thank you. I will be fine here."

He leans in to look deeply into her eyes, as they sit silently together. Zara gazes back and after a few seconds, Garrett crosses the last few inches of spaces between them and gently presses his lips to hers. When he pulls away, he lightly tugs on Zara's lower lip.

Grabbing his drink, Garrett walks into the bedroom and out of sight. Zara sets the water bottle on the coffee table and collapses against the back of the sofa. Covering her face with her hand, she takes a deep breath and allows her mind to open to the thoughts she had been keeping at bay since the Circle Ceremony.

The lack of conversation with her mother comes crashing in like water being released from a broken dam. The joy of having freedom granted to her in every area of her life, yet being abandoned by her family because of that freedom causes a hollow space in Zara's heart. Zara realizes the only way to have the relationship she really wants with Garrett is to become the person she had never been taught to be.

I need to be me.

Sitting up, she closes her eyes and places her hands on her thighs with her palms facing upward. Taking slow deep breaths, her mind clears and her body settles. Images of the beach drift into her thoughts, how the warm sand gives way under foot with each step approaching the shore, how the temperature of the sand gradually cools as the water's edge comes closer. She can almost feel the frothy cool water as she stands ankle deep in Lake Michigan.

"Little One, did you fall asleep?" Garrett whispers as he sits down gently beside her. Opening her eyes, Zara gives him a smile. "If you are tired, we can talk tomorrow."

"Garrett, I am fine. I was just thinking."

Garrett repositions himself so that he is leaning back against the back of the sofa and places his bare feet of the coffee table. "Actually, I was thinking too, I was thinking about your first night in Michigan at the beach house. I was in the shower that night wondering how the conversation would go when I gave you the necklace.

"A lot has changed since that night, yet a lot is exactly the same. For example, you have changed quite a bit. When you talked about the Community, I sat back in awe of how comfortable and confident you were. It was fun to see you engaging with my friends during the movie. Little One, you seem to be more comfortable in your own skin. Having not spent any time with you in the last couple of months, I was blown away at the difference."

Zara picks up the bottle of water that is in front of her and takes a long drink. Slowly screwing the cap on and setting it back on the table, Zara scoots herself against the arm of the sofa and shifts her legs underneath her body. The position gives her some space between her and Garrett.

"Zara, what are you thinking about so loudly at the end of the sofa?"

Taking a deep breath, Zara knows this is a moment where she needs to be completely open and honest with him.

This is it.

"Garrett, you are right. I have changed, and hopefully, I will continue to change. But in all the changing I am doing, I am finding me. I am figuring out what I want for me and whom I want to spend my time with. I hope through all the changes I have made that you can still see me, Zara Faith."

Zara exhales. Slowly, her eyes begin to journey from her feet to Garrett's torso, his chest, shoulder, neck, and finally to his... HUGE SMILE!!! Her eyes lock onto his and she cannot help but return a smile.

"So you found yourself?" he asks.

"Probably not all of me, but I am discovering new things, and I am becoming more comfortable. I like school. I like my classes. I've selected my classes for next semester already. I have friends..." Zara's voice dwindles off at the end.

"What are you not sharing with me?" Garrett asks, reading her like a book.

Zara looks away and feels her eyes fill with tears. Tensing, she works to block the negative emotions flooding her. Every fiber of her body vibrates as again she fights eighteen years of being taught by her mother to keep her emotions hidden.

Without warning, Garrett stands. He moves to the end of the sofa, lifts Zara into his arms and sits in her spot, settling her onto his lap. "Okay... Tell me what has upset you, and this time, don't force it back down inside."

Zara's heart clenches. She knows it is now or never, time to peel away the layers of preconceived notions of a Dom and allow Garrett to be himself as much as he is asking her to be herself. Her sight blurs from the tears collecting in her eyes.

Zara snuggles deeper into Garrett's arms. "I called my house today and my mother answered the phone."

"Shit!" he said, squeezing her tighter.

"She said I made my choice. Then she hung up." Each word out of Zara's mouth becomes softer than the last.

"Little One, I'm sorry. We should have discussed this sooner," Garrett speaks quietly as he runs his hand up and down Zara's back. Some of her tears escape and form streams down her cheeks. "I'm sorry I wasn't with you when you reached out to your family. Let's make that an agreement between us… any reaching out to the Community will be done when I am with you."

Zara nods. The two sit together in silence. Zara is no longer crying but the sadness lingers deep within her.

Garrett, seeming to be in no hurry to move, is the first to speak. "Will you tell me how school is going?"

"Of course. First, El and Lil are amazing. They have been so helpful every step of the way this semester. El is even teaching me to use her camera a little. I am loving that. You should see my dorm room. The walls are covered with pictures we have taken around campus and of each other. El says it is important to document our college memories." Giggling, Zara sits up so she can look into Garrett's eyes while she is speaking.

"Most of the dorm studies together after dinner in the front rooms. Oh, Beth… she works at the front desk. She really needs a better job. She is brilliant, and studies computer science. Beth is the girl that the dorm hired to come in early to assist in getting me settled. You had her deliver my dinner. And she–" Zara stopped. Her eyes dipped down to Garrett's chin.

"She what?"

Zara's chin dips lower almost resting on her chest. "She really needs a better job. Can you give her a job?"

"Little One, I can't promise anything but I will ask around. Okay?" Garrett tilts his head to get a look into Zara'a eyes. "What else besides job placement is happening with you at State?"

"Everyone says it has been unseasonably warm and I am in for an awful winter. I have only seen snow a couple of times and it was only a dusting on the ground. I am looking forward to seeing real snow. I registered for a much tougher class load next semester." Zara stops with a gasp.

Garrett looks at Zara with a puzzled expression.

"I should have consulted you prior to registering for classes. I apologize. Ollie said that it was better to get into an advisor as soon as possible so my chances of getting into my classes were higher. I really am sorry. I used your credit card to pay for the classes."

Garrett lifts Zara's hand up to his lips and presses a kiss into the palm. "First of all, that is your credit card to use as you need to and I would only ask that you consult me if you need to make a large purchase such as a car. Not that I would tell you that you couldn't have it, but I would have you purchase the car from a different source of funding. Does that make sense?"

Zara nods.

"I'd expect you to select your own classes. I only chose the first semester's classes because of timing. Zara, this is your college experience, not mine. I am here to advise, as is Ollie, but only if and when you ask. And, yes, it has been an unseasonably warm autumn but the temperature has dropped and will drop again sharply... soon. You are going to need snow gear. How are you doing with clothes?"

Leaning forward to grab the bottle of water, Zara also picks up Garrett's glass and hands it to him. Regaining her position on his lap, she unscrews the top and takes a long drink. "Viv has managed to keep my clothes rotated for the season without me ever seeing anyone in my room. It is amazing to everyone that I have never had to do a load of laundry, not even my linens, since I have been in school. I am guessing I have you to thank for that. Garrett, I am capable of doing laundry. It seems like I should be contributing in some small way."

"Little One, I did laundry in college. You aren't missing anything. Trust me. I want this to be a special time for you. College is the only time in life when you should not have the crazy responsibilities of life. Don't worry... laundry will be waiting for you when you get out of school, but for now I can give this to you, so let me do it."

Zara moves closer to Garrett's face. Keeping her gaze averted, she eases closer until she is only inches from his face. She draws her eyes up to his and looks deep within. Zara holds her breath seeing Garrett run his tongue across his lips. Unsure what to do next, Zara leans in the last inches to press her lips to his. As soon as they meet, Garrett's hand comes up behind her head and takes control. The tension she was unaware she was holding dissolves away and she presses her body against his. Sliding his tongue into her mouth to explore the tip of her tongue, he then brings his tongue back out and lightly slips it along her bottom lip.

Please never let this end. No. No.

To Zara's disappointment, Garrett pulls away. "Okay. Tonight is for talking. As much as I would love to spend hours kissing those lips of yours, tonight we need to talk."

Zara drops her eyes and nods. She begins to pull back, but Garrett's hand behind her head does not allow it. He pulls her face back, looks in her eyes and plants a firm kiss on her lips.

Zara opens her eyes when he pulls way but he is still holding the back of her head, "Never think that I do not want to kiss you. We haven't spent time together in months and you have just said you wanted to start spending more time together. You and I, especially because of our backgrounds, need to be sure we are always on the same page. Understand?"

"Yes, Si... Garrett."

"Your discussion about school seems to be lacking in a couple of areas. Is that to save my feelings? I am curious to hear about the parties as well as the dating. To some degree, the dating."

Zara swallows. Garrett wraps his arms around her and pulls her into his chest. "What's up, Little One?"

"The two times I agreed to go out with different guys, it was awful. El said that it was a good idea to go just to verify my feelings before I 'laid my cards on the table' and she was right. The entire time, I just kept wishing I was with you," Zara says mournfully. Garrett squeezes his arms tighter around her.

"Excellent segue. You and I. My first reaction is to say yes. Let's start seeing each other. In fact, my initial reaction was to drive you home and put your collar around your neck."

Zara slides off his lap onto the sofa next to him to be able to get a better view of his face while he explains his comments.

Yes!! PLEASEEEE!!! Be my Sir.

"But I wonder if that is the best thing for you at this point." Garrett finishes his thought and Zara's heart sinks. "Little One, you are living your dream. I don't want to short-change that by throwing a relationship into the mix. College is about exploring options. Are you wanting to be with me because you are seeking a connection to your past?"

"NO! I am looking to be with you because I want you! I have missed you. Garrett, I felt something those days we were together before you dropped me off at school. It has been awful not speaking to you or seeing you all this time. I check my phone a hundred times a day hoping that you will text me. I am not asking for the entire Circle Ceremony again. I understand I missed that opportunity, but I very much want to see you and spend time with you."

"How about you focus on wrapping up your very first semester and getting through your finals, then come spend your winter break with me. We will fly down to the Caymans to spend Christmas with my parents and Branden and Viv. You and I can go off for a few days alone and really spend some quality time together."

"I would love to spend the holidays with you and your family. I was hoping you were going to ask me. Lil and El invited me to Miami over a month ago but I declined. Notices just went out that everyone has to vacate the dorms for the entire break so I didn't know where I was going to go if you had not asked." Zara's nervous giggle does nothing to mask her relief.

Scooping her back into his arms once more, Garrett lifts her chin to force her to look into his eyes. "As long as you are here, you have a home at my house. I haven't done a very good job at making you feel welcome here if you had such an uneasy feeling about the holidays. That is one thing that will change immediately."

Garrett gently leans into Zara's face and places a soft kiss on her ready lips. "In fact, next semester, we should plan for you to spend a weekend each month or so at the house so you feel more at home. There should never be a question in your beautiful head about where you can go when you need time away from school... for whatever reason."

Zara tries to hide a yawn as she nods her agreement but Garrett is on to her. "Let's go... bedtime."

Without further words, he stands with her still in his arms and walks to the bedroom. Laying her gently on the bed on the side furthest from the framed picture of her, Garrett climbs in next to her and holds her as she drifts off to sleep.

CHAPTER 23

Zara sits in her room with her bags packed for winter break. She looks out the window and sees large fluffy snowflakes falling, gently covering everything in a white blanket. Liliana and Ella had warned of a pending snow storm but Zara is in awe of the beauty it brings.

The girls had departed for the airport a couple of hours earlier and Zara is already missing their presence. All three were a bit weepy during their goodbye but Zara could tell Liliana was eager to see her family. Ella talked only of the sun and sand of Miami Beach, but Zara could sense there was more to the trip for El by her focusing so much on the sun.

A whole month without my girls. Yikes.

"Really, Zara Faith. An open door. How safe is that?" Zara turns around to find Garrett standing in her dorm room. From the tone of his voice, Zara is unsure how to proceed.

"I... I am sorry. We tend to keep the doors open so we can go back and forth. I should have closed it once the girls left." She clasps her hands together in front of her and stares at the floor directly in front of where Garrett is standing.

"Come here," Garrett replies.

Without hesitation, Zara's feet take her the four steps across her room to stand directly in front of him. She trains her gaze on the buttons of his coat.

In what feels to Zara like slow motion, Garrett takes her face in both of his hands. He looks into her eyes and slowly brings his lips to hers. Softly he brushes them together.

Zara steps in closer as Garrett parts his lips and gently nibbles her bottom lip. A soft moan escapes Zara as she feels him run his tongue along the lip he has hostage.

Garrett releases Zara's lip and pulls the hair from her face so that he is able to look into her eyes. The smile he flashes melts

Zara's heart. He pulls her in again and quickly pecks her lips a couple of times before letting her free from his hold.

Feeling awkward in the unwanted release, Zara stands in place as she has done hundreds of times before. However, this time she is doing it knowing what could be.

Kiss me again. Oh, please, kiss me again.

"So, this is your dorm. Very neat. That does not surprise me." Garrett begins to move around the small room looking at all there is to see. He picks up a small framed picture of himself and examines it with a wide smile on his face.

"I am ready. Although, I am not sure I packed enough. I have never packed for a month..." The words trail off at the end.

Being without her family has been difficult for Zara but she had been able to focus on school. Sitting around and listening to all her new friends talk about their winter breaks with their families, the traditions and special plans had left Zara feeling raw. Knowing she would be spending winter break with Garrett helped ease the sadness, but Zara still missed her family.

"I'm sorry. I'm missing them a lot these days, especially Fredrik."

Wrapping his arms around Zara from behind, Garrett whispers in her ear, "Don't apologize. I'm sorry you are going through this. I'm here if you want to talk about it. You are going to be all right."

Zara leans back into Garrett and he holds her tighter. "Thank you, Garrett."

He squeezes her one more time and moves to pick up her suitcases.

"Time to say goodbye to your lovely dorm for the next month." Grunting as he pretends he is unable to lift her bags, he mocks, "Zara, I think you've packed more than enough."

Zara puts on her coat. She picks up her backpack, purse and phone, and follows Garrett out the door. She says goodbye to everyone they pass in the lobby and stops at the front desk. Motioning to Garrett that she will be one second, Zara disappears behind the counter of the front desk to surprise Beth. Zara sets her backpack on the counter, unzips the side pocket and pulls out a card.

"Merry Christmas, Beth. This is from the both of us." Zara nods to Garrett who has since placed the suitcases on the floor to patiently wait by the exit.

"Bitch! Is there a gift card inside? You totally should not have gotten me anything. You know I am completely broke at the moment." She does a happy dance in her seat as she begins to open the envelope.

"Beth, please do not open that now. Just say goodbye. I am going to miss you. One whole month." Zara reaches down and gives her a hug.

"Okay... Okay... Okay. You are coming back. Dang. You have my number. If you feel the need, just call me." As Zara begins to release her, Beth squeezes one more time really hard making Zara's heart smile.

"Be careful out there. The roads are getting bad quickly. Get to where you are going and stay put," Beth adds as Zara makes her way back around the counter.

"Merry Christmas, Beth," Garrett says as he picks up Zara's luggage and heads for the door.

"Thank you for the present. Whatever it is," Beth says as she reaches to answer the ringing phone.

"Let's get home." Garrett heads for his car and loads Zara's luggage. The drive to his house takes longer than usual since the roads had become covered in snow and ice. With the snow falling so hard the visibility was low.

At Garrett's house, Zara finds a note left on the counter.

I know you asked me to get rid of all the food before your trip. After watching the weather report, I decided to do the exact opposite. Everything is well stocked. If they are wrong, then I will come and get all your food and donate it to charity.

"There are groceries," Zara informs Garrett as he enters the kitchen.

"What... why?" Zara hands over the note. Garrett scans it quickly and throws it on the counter. "FUCKING A!! It is not going to be that bad. We will be on a plane tomorrow at this time. Away from this cold and snow."

Garrett walks close to Zara and stares into her eyes as he slowly leans down. He places two quick kisses squarely on her lips. Without a word, he turns and walks out of the kitchen leaving

Zara standing there wanting more.

"WOW," Zara whispers as she glides her finger over her lips.

Zara picks up the note and reads it one more time. Looking out the window, she sees the snow is falling harder now, the flakes bigger and heavier. An excitement comes over her at the thought of being snowed in with Garrett.

Quickly opening the refrigerator and cabinets, Zara gets a sense of the food situation. They are indeed stocked up. At that moment, Zara decides, if they are to miss their trip, she will take over all domestic responsibilities.

Garrett has been caring for her in one way or another since she stepped out of the Circle. Zara knows that he is courting her. The time has come for Zara to begin the process of courting Garrett. Her insides tingle at the thought of taking care of his needs.

As much as Zara likes Garrett's parents, the idea of spending her winter break without them and alone with Garrett makes Zara a happy girl. Zara wanders out of the kitchen to find Garrett, feeling more comfortable now in his home. From the first day, Garrett had said that his home is her home and it was starting to feel like home.

Walking from room to room, Zara contemplates her desire to serve Garrett. She had felt an immediate attraction to him from the day of the Circle Ceremony. He was handsome and his intelligence took his sex appeal up several notches. He made every effort to make her feel cared for and safe.

Zara stops in her tracks.

I'm in love with Garrett.

Zara hears Garrett calling her from the other room and hurries toward his voice. Rounding the corner into his room, Zara freezes. Garrett is standing with his back to her completely naked and stepping into the glass shower. Zara cannot move. Her eyes wander over every inch of his naked body.

Zara's breath becomes labored watching the water cascade over Garrett's body. A glossy sheen covers his skin as the water courses down the muscles in his back and across his tight waist to his buttocks.

He reaches up to adjust the showerhead and the water spills over well-toned arms, the strength in them wholly apparent.

No wonder I cannot get enough of your hugs. Those arms.

As he put his head under the stream of water, his muscles

tighten in concert and Zara steps further into the bedroom. The steam from the hot water begins to obscure her view of him. With her next step, Zara bumps into the corner of Garrett's bed and stubs her toe.

Shaken her to her senses, Zara limps out of Garrett's bedroom and heads to the den to plop down on the sofa.

I am in love with a god!

Zara takes a throw pillow and covers her face.

Closing her eyes, Zara takes a deep breath, then another, then another and another. Just when she believes she has regained control and cleared her mind, Garrett and how the water flowed over him rushes back.

Replacing the pillow against the arm of the sofa, a set of movies on the coffee table catches her attention. Zara goes through the pile quickly... *Roman Holiday, My Fair Lady, Galaxy Quest, Breakfast at Tiffany's, Planet of the Apes, Dawn of the Planet of the Apes* and *Elf.*

Next to the DVDs is a stack of novels. Picking up the first book, *The Promise* by Kate Benson, Zara reads the back. Placing the book back on the pile and straightening it perfectly, she looks toward Garrett's bedroom to see if he is coming.

Zara picks up *Wallbanger* by Alice Clayton, the second book in the pile, and turns it over to read the blurb. Giggling, she quickly replaces the book and picks up the third and final book. A biography of Claude Monet. The giggling takes hold and Zara is now a hostage unable to stop the laughter that follows.

He even picks out books that sound amazing. What a cute butt. He has to kiss me SOON!

Zara places the books back in their original order and squares the pile. She draws her feet under her and gets comfortable on the sofa. Unable to clear his image from her mind, Zara gives up and closes her eyes. She replays every inch that she was treated to minutes ago. Garrett's amazing sexy naked sexy wet sexy body. Sexy. The view from the back is...

"Spectacular," Zara says out loud.

"What's spectacular, Zara?" Garrett whispers in Zara's right ear.

Frozen to the back of the sofa, Zara swallows hard and opens her eyes to find Garrett's lips only inches away.

"What's spectacular?"

He inches closer to her face. With one hand on the armrest and the other on the cushion next to Zara, he hovers without making contact. He waits. Zara feels the heat of a blush spreading all over her face and neck.

"Umm...."

"UMM? You don't ever 'umm.' This is going to be good!" he murmurs softly.

"Well... I was in the kitchen and I heard you calling me. I went to find you and I walked into your bedroom while you were getting into the shower. I... I kind of watched you for a couple of seconds before I came in here. That is it," Zara exhales.

Garrett waits. He doesn't say a word.

"Garrett, that is all of it," Zara pleads.

"Really. You have yet to share what's spectacular. I do believe I am going to enjoy whatever it is you are going to tell me by that lovely shade of blush you are wearing."

"You," she whispers.

Garrett leans in and places a light kiss on Zara's forehead. Shifting, he falls onto the sofa next to Zara and places his sock-covered feet on the coffee table.

"In my defense, I didn't call you. I merely said I was taking a quick shower and I would be right out." Zara hides her face behind both of her hands and Garrett laughs. "I love that you spilled your 'sneaking in and staring at me while I took a shower' experience."

Shaking her head behind her hands, Zara hears Garrett's laughter increase.

"So... request of subject change?"

"Yes, please. I will owe you big time," her muffled voice comes from behind her hands.

"I am getting hungry. How about if you take one of those hot bubble baths you enjoy so much while I make us something to eat? We can meet back in here and watch a movie."

Garrett takes her hands in his to ease them slowly away from her face but as they come away, her shoulders lift to her ears and her eyes remain tightly closed. Zara is not even trying to hide her embarrassment.

"Not a good enough change of subject?" Tugging her into his arms, Garrett holds Zara and allows her to bury her face into his chest. After a few moments in his embrace, she feels her body relax. Garrett exhales and says in her ear, "I think you're spectacular as well."

Zara begins giggling, light little giggling that she becomes unable to contain. Concerned by the sudden shivering of her body, Garrett pushes her back to look in her face. The dumbfounded look on his face when he realizes it is giggles makes Zara laugh uncontrollably.

"So... subject changed?"

"Completely."

CHAPTER 24

Waking up alone is not how Zara anticipated the first night of her winter break. Since they had slept in the same bed over Thanksgiving weekend, she had assumed they would continue in that vein from then on whenever they were together. She had loved the closeness of him holding her all night, finding their intimacy was more precious than she ever thought it would be.

Zara closes her eyes and replays the day before. It had been a perfect day filled with laughter and conversation. They had taken a walk in the snow. Garrett held a snowball-making lesson and taught Zara how to make snow angels. They had watched movies and listened to music for hours.

The smell of coffee assaults Zara's senses and she climbs out of bed. Standing at the dresser, she pauses as she is pulling out the top drawer. A pile of three smooth stones sitting on one of the many decorative boxes on the vanity catches her eye. Leaving the drawer hanging open, she walks over to pick up the stones. After rolling them around in her hand, she slowly places them back in their original spot.

Returning to the dresser, Zara grabs a pair of thick socks and closes the drawer. Dressed in the same long sleeved Michigan State tee and grey sweats she changed into after her hot shower the night before, she hears Garrett as she makes her way toward the kitchen.

"I knew if I made coffee, you would wake up." He hands her a large mug of steaming creamy coffee. Cupping it with both hands, an enormous smile spreads across Zara's face as she brings the mug to her nose to inhale. She cannot stop the moan of pleasure that escapes her lips.

"Seriously… Zara."

Zara giggles in response. "Thank you for making me coffee."

Shaking his head, he picks up his own mug of coffee. Leaning against the island, Garrett picks up his phone. It hits Zara that she had never seen his phone when they had been together.

"It appears we are in the middle of one of the worst winter storms in the history of Michigan weather." He gestures toward the window and shakes his head in utter disbelief. Zara sips her coffee and does everything possible not to give away her excitement at being stranded.

"The plane is grounded and from the weather reports, it is only going to get worse. We aren't going anywhere." He puts the phone down on the counter.

"Oh. That is disappointing."

"Come here."

She moves to stand in front of him keeping the mug in front of her mouth. Taking the coffee from her hands, he discovers her huge smile. He sets their mugs on the counter, then lifts Zara onto the island and stands between her legs. Looking up into her sparkling, happy eyes, he asks her, "Am I to understand that golden sun, hot beaches and clear water are not what you are wishing for this holiday season?"

"I love the beach!"

"Yes, I know. As do my parents, hence a holiday planned in the hot sun, on the beach, and with clear water. Why are you so happy about this development, Little One?"

Zara's eyes immediately fall. Taking a deep breath, Zara squares her shoulders.

"So… it is a deep breath and square your shoulders type of response. Should we go sit to have this conversation?"

"I just… Well, the thought of you and I being stranded in this beautiful house together alone over the holiday. It… sort of… sounds magical to me. That does not mean that I was not excited to—"

The second Garrett's lips make contact with Zara's, she opens to him and he advances. His tongue caresses hers as if exploring it for the first time. Her soft moans gave him the reassurance to continue. Releasing her face, Garrett pulls Zara to the edge of the counter. Zara's finger's wrap around his head and lock on the back of his neck. Garrett pulls away and looks into her eyes. Her lips wait, slightly open, for his to return.

"I've missed that, Little One." As he moves to close the space between them again, the phone rings and they both jump. Garrett laughs and kisses Zara's forehead.

"Dawson," he answers in a professional tone that Zara finds as seductive as his normal voice. Handing her back her coffee, Garrett positions himself back between her legs with his back to her as he listens to the person on the phone. As she sips the coffee, thoughts of the two of them spending a long day kissing and snuggling creates such a sense of happiness that a giggle sneaks out.

Garrett looks back at Zara as she slaps her hand over her mouth and begins to crack up. Taking her hand away from her mouth, he gently kisses the palm. He returns his attention to the caller.

"Mom... Mom. We're fine. Yes, we have plenty of food in the house. You were correct. I was wrong. I don't know if we are going to come down at all. We'll stay in touch. Okay. Did B and Viv get out? She is going to be pissed at him. Yes, yes. Zara, Mother says she is sorry you are missing the sun, sand and warm water and that it is all my fault. We will be fine. Tell Dad Merry Christmas."

"You know how we are completely thrilled to be stranded together during the worst winter storm in Michigan history? Guess who isn't exactly thrilled with her brother for deciding to work a couple of extra days and not flying down with my parents?"

"Oh, who?"

"Viv is so pissed off even my mom said that I should wait a day to call over there. I am not calling."

Shyly, with all the humor gone, Zara asks, "Garrett, would it be alright if I called? If she is upset, I would like to invite her to come here. Certainly it does not replace a tropical vacation, but it may beat staring at her brother. If that is okay with you."

"What about being stranded alone with me in a beautiful house?"

Zara shrugs her shoulders.

"There is always New Year's." Kissing her lips, Garrett scrolls to V and hits the call icon. Handing Zara the phone, he mouths, "Good luck."

"AND WHAT THE FUCKING HELL DO YOU WANT, ASSHOLE BEST FRIEND OF MY STUPID ASS BROTHER?"

"Viv? Hi, this is Zara. I am sorry to bother you."

"Shit... Zara. I thought you were Garrett. Are you two soaking up the sun and drinking cocktails with umbrellas already?"

"No... No. We were scheduled to take the plane down this afternoon. We are stranded here, too. I was wondering if you and Branden would like to come over and spend Christmas with us. I am planning to prepare a Christmas that Garrett will be proud to host. It would mean a lot to me if you would be here for my first Christmas away," Zara's voice drops off as the last sentence ends.

"Oh, Zara. Yes, of course, we will be there."

"Garrett said that the storm is going to get worse before it gets better. When it is safe... why not pack a bag and both of you come over and stay. We will do Christmas here like we did Thanksgiving there."

"Does G know you are inviting us to his house to stay? He is a bit funny about people in his space?"

"Mmmm... or I guess we can invite ourselves over there." Holding the phone with his hand, Garrett plants another quick kiss on Zara. "I think he is fine with you both coming here this time."

"Okay. It's a plan. B is predicting a State of Emergency will be called at any minute. So, we are here for a while. I'll text you when we are on our way. Oh... B keeps this place STOCKED with food. Email a list if you need me to go shopping in his cabinets."

"Thanks, Viv. Tell Branden we are looking forward to seeing him soon. Merry Christmas."

Clicking the *End* icon, Zara gently places the phone on the counter beside her. Viv's statement about Garrett not liking people in his space floats around in her thoughts. Never had there been a moment when she had felt uncomfortable in his space.

"You are doing it again. Talk to me, Little One."

"Are you alright with me inviting Viv and Branden over to stay? It has occurred to me that I did that without really asking your permission first." Sliding off the counter, Zara picks up both mugs and walks to the coffee maker, intentionally busying herself to avoid looking at him.

"Would I prefer to spend the next however many days alone getting to know you even better? HELL YES! Would I prefer to be alone with you on a private beach, in 85 degree weather in crystal clear water? HELL YES! Am I glad that you want to spend some alone time with me and that you like the two closest people in my life enough to invite them over? YES!"

Walking over to where Zara is refilling their cups, Garrett wraps his arms around her. She leans back into him. "In the past, I didn't have people over very often. Of course, they have been here before, but not 'here' here. I have been waiting for you."

Zara nods enjoying the warmth of his arms and the comfort of the words around her as they stand in his kitchen in the middle of the worst winter storm in history.

"I have so much to do!" Zara jumps, kissing Garrett squarely on the lips. The action is both surprising and supremely satisfying.

Well that was not very submissive of me, but it was very me.

"Just a head's up, you are not spending days in the kitchen preparing for a Christmas dinner that is going to be eaten in an hour. You and I are spending time together. That is the priority. We can all eat sandwiches. Understood?"

"Yes, Sir."

Garrett stiffens. Silence. The response stops them both in their tracks. Zara's eyes cast down to the ground in front of her. It is several seconds before either begins to move. Garrett is first to break the lingering silence between them.

"I think it is time for us to have that conversation soon. It has almost become the elephant in the room—"

"Garrett, forgive me for interrupting you. I have been thinking. You have taken excellent care of me since leaving the Circle months ago. You have provided for all of my needs. You have gone above and beyond my needs. During this break, I would like to be the one that takes care of your needs for a change.

"There will be guests but they are aware of our lifestyle. I would like to ask permission to… this made so much more sense in my head. I would like to… to take care of you."

"Okay… This is not where I thought this conversation was heading. I am getting hungry and need a shower. Let's both shower and meet back here for breakfast?"

Sinking with rejection, Zara turns to walk out of the kitchen without a word. The distance between the kitchen and her bedroom feels so much longer on this return trip. She knows Garrett is watching her walking away.

In the safety of her bedroom, tears begin to stream down her face.

I'm not the submissive he wants. The locked collar. The letter from Michigan State. The dorm room. The tuition. The new life. It is all meant to give me a new beginning so I would not accept his collar.

The kissing. The touching. That is something else. That must be a man wanting a woman. Casual. The effect of the word Sir. On the plane the first night. In the kitchen.

I am alone. No family. No Community. No collar. No Sir. No Garrett. Just me.

Training wins out over most everything. Zara wipes her tears and steps into her bathroom. Turning on the shower, she slowly removes her clothes leaving only the pedants that Garrett had given her for her birthday. Looking at them in the reflection of the mirror causes her even more confusion. "Just forget it."

"No... don't forget."

Turning, Zara sees Garrett walking toward her from inside her room. He grabs a towel and wraps it around her. Bewildered, Zara watches him step into the shower and turn it off. Walking to the bathtub, he turns on the water and adjusts the temperature. Returning to Zara, he takes his thumb and wipes away the track of tears that remain.

"I hate that I left you to think your thoughts. I know better than to allow you to get inside your head. These tears are my fault and it hurts my heart that I caused them." He presses a swimsuit into her hand. "Put this on and don't move. More importantly, don't think."

Garrett runs out of the bathroom, leaving Zara wrapped in a towel and contemplating the small royal blue two-piece Garrett handed her.

"Hold please." Garrett returns with a towel wrapped around his waist and hands Zara a tray with travel mugs and fruit. He moves a chair from the bedroom next to the tub as a stand for the tray, then reclaims it and sets up their mini breakfast. Taking something off the tray that Zara had thought to be cream, he pours it into the bath and bubbles begin to form.

"All I need is you..." Garrett extends his hand to Zara and escorts her to the tub. He drops his towel and gets into the tub, gesturing for her to join him. Zara slips in between his legs. Once they are both submerged in the hot water and thick bubbles, Garrett turns the water off.

He pulls Zara back to him and she only hesitates slightly before leaning against his bare chest. In silence, they sit and soak.

Garrett runs his fingers through the damp strands of Zara's hair, continues to stroke her shoulders lightly with his thumbs and fingertips. "I should have thought about a hair tie."

"I need to wash my hair. It is okay," Zara murmurs contentedly.

"Do you want coffee?"

"No, thank you."

"Zara, I like caring for you."

"Garrett… are you a submissive?" Zara feels Garrett's hands freeze briefly on their wayward journey from her neck to her shoulders.

"No, Little One. I'm not a submissive. Although, I don't think I'm exactly the Dom you were expecting, either. I was raised by parents that lived their lives as equals. Yes, my mother is my father's submissive but I do not know what happens in their bedroom. I know that they have a small playroom at the beach house. What they have at the main house is anyone's guess.

"I take that back. Viv would know. Being the resident decorator, she knows everyone's secrets. Anyway, I was not raised with a mother who was put in a corner if she stepped out of line. I want a wife. A partner. I would like for her to be a submissive but if that is not her thing, I am willing to walk away from the King Council."

"You will be a member of the King Council. It is your birthright. How could you think about walking away from that?"

"I want a happy wife. I want a happy life. I want happy children. I want my children to have what I had."

"But when I asked to serve you… you rejected me," Zara said in almost a whisper.

"Zara, I didn't reject you. I said we should shower and eat before we discussed it. That's miles away from a rejection. I need you to understand this. Submission is not something you practice. If you decide to submit to me, your collar is in a box in my room. I'll show you where later. And if that day ever arrives, I will proudly accept your submission. But that will be the beginning and the end for many things."

Garrett picks up a large sponge and squeezes water down Zara's neck and shoulders, the warmth relaxing her to the point of almost drifting off.

This. This is where I want to spend the rest of my life.

Startled by the sound of the water being turned back on, Zara watches Garrett reach for some fruit and hold a grape to her lips. Seeing him pop several into his own mouth with a smirk, she knew he was allowing her time to consider before continuing the conversation that could impact both of their lives.

"Beginning and end?" Zara twists around to make eye contact.

"The beginning of our life together. You were raised in the Community, so you understand what that means. We will need to make some decisions together on how we move forward from here. The collar is only the beginning of the conversation. As I said, I am a Dom – a Dom who wishes to navigate the waters with his submissive and make a happy life together. Perhaps that is why I can walk away from the King Council. I will be a Dom whether I am on the Council in the Community or not. That cannot be dictated by anyone else."

Listening intently, Zara ran her fingers through the water and the bubbles, "And the end?"

"Well… the end. That is entirely different. The end is… the end of your life as a single college student with the freedom to do as she pleases with whomever she pleases. It is also the end of me standing silently by while you deal with your family and friends. All of those issues become mine to address as I see fit. In this area, I am exactly like all other Doms."

With the change in Garrett's tone, Zara's eyes fell to her hands in the water. Garrett found her hands under the water and tugged her towards him. "Come back here, Little One."

Zara slowly moved back between Garrett's legs and leaned into his chest.

"You have changed quite a bit in the little time that you have been at school. Do you feel different?"

"Sometimes I feel I am a completely different person. When I am talking with a group of friends and we start laughing about something, or when Ella and I go to dance class and I am actually up there demonstrating how to do a new move; even singing along to a song that they have playing in their room while we are getting ready to go somewhere.

"Then there are moments, when I sit back and wonder how I

could ever fit in with these people. I am so different. The favorite pastime in the dorm is to sit around and talk about guys, who you have dated, who you have slept with, and what you did with that person. I am so out of place in that conversation. Not just because I have never had those experiences, but because of the lifestyle I was raised in."

"What do you mean by lifestyle?"

"If I were to open up about the lifestyle, they would automatically jump to whips and chains."

"You didn't seem to have an issue discussing it with Branden and Viv."

"They are your family. You trust them."

"Zara, you have to give trust to get it. I am not advocating that you make a general announcement in Yakeley Hall. You have some very close girlfriends that care for you and that mean a great deal to you. Why not start with Ella and Liliana. Give it some thought.

"You are half-way through your first year of college. You gave up a great deal to have these experiences. How are you feeling about it so far?" He stood up, leaving a coolness at her back, and wrapped his towel around his waist before stepping from the tub.

"Think on that incredibly thought provoking question. I'm going to go take a quick shower and then meet you in the kitchen. I would be honored if you would prepare us something to eat."

Zara watched Garrett pad quietly out of the bathroom.

My collar is here. There is still a chance. He will be my Sir. I can tell Ella and Liliana about the Community. Zar, not now! You get to cook for him now! Get going!

CHAPTER 25

Looking up from her book, Zara glances out the window. Surprised that she has gotten lost in the hunt for Caroline's O for so long, Zara chuckles as she puts the book down and heads to the kitchen to finish dinner. The clock on the microwave reads 4:40pm so Zara picks up her pace. Garrett will be home from the office within the hour and she wants everything just right.

As Zara reaches into the oven for the lasagna, the sound of the front door opening alerts her to Garrett's return. Carefully setting down the large dish, Zara turns to go greet Garrett and his best friends but before she makes it out of the kitchen, he walks in wearing a smile.

"Something smells delicious. I like coming home to you in the kitchen. Only four days into your winter break and I'm hooked," Garrett, says as he walks over to inspect a large pan of pasta resting on the stove.

"This looks even better than it smells." He turns and gives Zara a half smile. "Here's the deal. Branden and Viv have been over here hanging out each day almost your entire break. I wanted to spend Christmas Eve alone with you, so I asked them to wait until tomorrow to come back over. They will be here in the morning."

"Okay." Zara walks around Garrett and picks up the lasagna and takes it to the table set for four. "I hope you like lasagna."

Garrett slips up behind her and pulls her chair out for her. "I am positive that I'm going to love your lasagna as I've enjoyed all the meals you have prepared thus far. I must say I also enjoy the bit of sass in you as well."

Breathe, Zar. He is joking. See he is smiling. Tone. Breathe. It is okay.

"This is the first time I have ever had Italian on Christmas Eve," Garrett says eyeing the table. Zara sucks in air and looks at the spread of food on the table in front of her. "Little One, I happen to love Italian, as you know. We may have started a new tradition."

Relaxing, Zara begins to load Garrett's plate and then her own. The steam from the lasagna rises, adding to the heat in the room. Zara's family had lasagna many times growing up but not once did she feel the warmth she was experiencing during this dinner with Garrett.

"I didn't make a dent in it. It was great," Garrett says as he gets up with the lasagna pan in hand. "Leftovers?"

Zara nods and begins clearing the rest of the table. "I am going to take a quick shower. I'll meet you in the den."

Garrett turns and heads to his room.

The kitchen is returned to its before-dinner state in no time. Zara heads to her room to grab her book and then to the den to wait for Garrett. Stretching out on the couch, she barely gets the book open to the page she left off on before he comes walking in.

Placing a wrapped present on the coffee table in front of her, Garrett lifts her legs, sits down and places her legs across his lap. Zara stares at the large wrapped Christmas gift sitting directly in her line of sight. She slowly turns to look at him and finds him already staring at her with a big grin on his face.

"I thought you said all the gifts were down with your parents?" Zara questions in a soft clear voice.

"Most of the gifts are down with my parents. One is not. One is here. For you. To open now."

"One second, please," Zara says looking at the gift and smiling.

She lifts her legs off his and stands. Walking out of the room, Zara breaks into a jog once she clears the door. From her room, she retrieves a thin box wrapped in colorful Christmas paper. She reaches into the side pocket of her backpack and pulls out a big red bow. Peeling the adhesive, she quickly sticks it on the center of the box as she makes her way back to the den and Garrett.

She looks at Garrett as she enters the room and his dazzling smile stops her in her tracks. Slowly, she makes her way back to the sofa, but this time she curls up next to him. With gift in hand, Zara rests her head on his chest to enjoy the moment of closeness with him. Wrapping his arms around her, they sit in silence as they wait to open their Christmas gifts to each other on their first Christmas Eve together.

"Okay. Time to open your present," Garrett says, interrupting their peaceful moment of quiet.

Zara hands Garrett his present and reaches for the large box on the coffee table. Drawing it onto her lap, she begins ripping off the wrapping paper.

"I see you're not a try-to-save-the-paper kind of lady. Very cool," Garrett says chuckling.

"Save it for what? I never understood the point. Part of the pleasure of giving someone a gift is presenting the present. That means locating the best paper for the gift. It doesn't necessarily have to be wrapping paper. It could be wrapped with anything, really. But certainly not the same thing twice." Zara leans back against the sofa and stares at the package.

"No, Little One. It is not reused paper. But open it, please."

Tearing the paper off the box, Zara pauses and stares at the picture displayed on its side.

"If you don't like it, I can return it," Garrett says in a low voice.

Cautiously turning so the box stays in her lap, Zara reaches up to hug Garrett and whisper in his ear, "I love it. It's actually perfect. Thank you."

"You seemed to enjoy using Ella's camera all the time and I figured it would be easier for her to teach you if you had one of your own. You could also sign up for a photography class."

"Gifts were never a big deal growing up." Zara begins looking at each side of the box carefully. "Fredrik got me daisies for my birthday every year. We knew that I was not going to be able to take anything with me when I left, so he was careful never to get me anything that would last.

"Thank you for my camera. I am excited to begin using it." Zara places the camera gently on the coffee table and returns to her place nestled next to Garrett. "Time for you to open your gift."

With grand movements, Garrett begins the process of removing the wrapping paper from the present that Zara has given him. The plain white box gives no hint to what is inside and Garrett looks at Zara with a look of curiosity. Lifting the top, Garrett moves the tissue paper aside to reveal a frame lying face down.

He turns the frame over and discovers a picture of the two of them taken the day of the football game when Zara and her friends had joined him at The Club. Captured in the picture, Zara is in

Garrett's arms leaning against his chest, and they are looking into each other's eyes. The surroundings have been blurred and the two of them appear as if they are the only ones in existence in that moment.

Garrett leans down and places a soft kiss on Zara's lips. "Little One, this is the best gift I could have received. Thank you."

"You are welcome," Zara whispers.

"This may be my new favorite picture of you." Garrett says as he sets the frame up facing the two of them on the edge of the coffee table.

Still staring at it, he asks, "Did you keep a copy for your dorm?"

Zara nods and retrieves the camera box. Opening it, she takes out the owner's manual and puts the box back.

"Wait. What are you doing?"

"Reading about the camera you gave me."

"Aren't you going to take the camera out and play with it first?"

"I thought it better that I get an overview of what everything is prior to actually touching it."

"You could do it that way..." Garrett lifts the box to the other side of the sofa and begins to slowly open the top. "I'll just go ahead and play with the camera over here while you sit and read the manual."

Trying hard to ignore him, Zara flips to the first page with focused intent and begins scanning the page. Garrett slowly unpacks the camera from all its packaging. By page two, Zara hears the familiar click of a picture being taken.

"I know you are trying really hard to concentrate on that manual when all you really want to do it get your hands on this new camera of yours. Wait... Little One, are you trying to not smile? Are you holding back a smile? There it is!"

Click. Click. Click.

Zara tosses the manual on the coffee table next to the box and leans back against the sofa. "Garrett, may I please play with my new camera?"

"Much better," Garrett says laughing as he hands Zara her Christmas present.

With camera in hand, Zara leans forward to pick the manual

back up and returns to the page she was just looking at. Giggling, she sets the camera on her lap and examines each area of the camera with the diagram in her hand. Garrett sits next to her, speechless.

After watching her for a few minutes, Garrett picks up Zara's copy of *Wallbanger* and begins reading it. Zara notices and says, "Would you like to do something else? I can certainly play with this later."

"This is exactly how I want to spend tonight – alone with you on this sofa. Perhaps, more lasagna later, but that's it."

"Would you like me to go get one of your books or a magazine?" Zara inquires looking at her book in his hand.

"Nope. I want to see what has you laughing so hard that I can hear you from the kitchen."

Zara's eyes get big and Garrett plants a quick kiss on the tip of her nose.

Garrett starts reading again. Zara stares at the manual but does not see any of the words on the page. Her thoughts have traveled back to Christmas with her family. There was a Christmas tree decorated just so. It lacked the personal touches of a family with young children, no homemade ornaments or decorations all in a cluster. The Evans' trees were always showroom quality, as were the wrapped presents underneath, all with matching paper and bows.

By age five, Christmas had lost its shine for Zara. She knew that the perfectly wrapped presents under the tree were for display only. She had also learned that her gifts would be clothes, while Fredrik would receive a wide range of toys. Zara was expected to sit in her presentation position and watch him open his gifts one by one.

It was not long before Fredrik also noticed the incongruity and struggled to open his gifts. Zara had conversations with him for weeks before the holiday to explain to her little brother that this was how Christmas was supposed to be for all little kids. She explained that her toys were at the library. After they were dismissed Christmas morning, he would sneak one of his small trucks into her room to play and he continued to do it even up through their last Christmas together.

As they got older, both siblings began to dislike the holiday.

They went through the motions as expected but in the end, Christmas was never a happy time. Sitting quietly on the sofa next to Garrett, staring at her first real Christmas gift, Zara could not believe how much her life had changed since walking into the Circle.

This is what Christmas should feel like.

Picking up her camera, Zara points to the table she loves and snaps her very first picture. Pressing the button to review her photo, the pictures Garrett had taken of her appear. Nudging him with her elbow, Garrett looks at what she is showing him.

"Cute and studious, even reading an owner's manual." Zara cycles through the pictures; the table is the last one. Returning to the book in hand, Garrett says, "The table was your very first subject. Nope, I am not hurt in the least bit."

Zara quickly scoots off the sofa, "Hey!"

Standing in front of Garrett, she asks, "Ready for more lasagna?"

She clicks a couple of pictures right in a row. "You make a much better subject than the table."

"Pasta me, please," Garrett says smiling broadly.

Walking toward the kitchen, Zara places the camera gently on the dining table. With Garrett on her heels, she pulls the lasagna out of the warm oven.

"How did you know?"

"I make pretty good lasagna," Zara says with a proud smile on her face.

"Indeed, you do." Garrett gets silverware and heads to the table. "So many talents."

Zara's smile grows and her face is covered in a blush as she carries the plates to the table.

CHAPTER 26

"What is this again?" Branden asks as he helps himself to his third helping at brunch.

"Egg bake," Zara, Garrett and Viv all say in unison.

"Shit. B, she's told you like three times. Ask her for the recipe and get it over with," Viv exclaims. "Sucks not being the best cook in the room... doesn't it."

"Branden, the recipe is very easy. I would be happy to write down how to prepare it," Zara offers as she stands up from the table. "Can I get anyone anything while I am up? Viv, more hot water for tea?"

"I'm good. Thanks, Zara."

Garrett eats the last bite off his plate and leans back. Viv asks him, "What did we miss for dinner last night?"

"Lasagna."

"I definitely have her beat on Italian," Branden says confidently.

Garrett gets up from the table without a word and goes to the kitchen. Getting the lasagna out of the refrigerator, he shakes his head at Zara who tries to hand him a pan to warm up a small portion.

"I'm going to use the microwave."

"It will taste better if you allow me to heat it slowly in the oven," Zara replies.

"For this, it isn't even going to matter."

Returning to the table with lasagna in hand, Garrett places plates in front of Viv and Branden. He stands at the head of the table proudly watching the two of them trying Zara's dish as if he spent all day making it himself. As each of them enjoys their first bites, Garrett's smile grows wider.

"DAMN IT!"

"WOW! Sorry, brother. Zara kicked your ass in the lasagna

department," Viv says taking another bite. "Zara, this is delicious. Can you teach Branden how to make this as well?"

"Hey!" Garrett snarls. "Family secret."

"Dude, we are family. Shut up," Branden retorts.

"Oh yeah."

"I know everyone is thinking it so I am going to be the one to ask... what's for dinner, Zara?" Branden asks and all eyes turn toward Zara.

"Since there is a strict rule about how much time can be spent in the kitchen when someone is home, we are having pork tenderloin."

Branden leans toward Zara and asks, "What kind of dumbass rule is this that you speak of? Certainly not on Christmas Day!"

"My rule. Problem?" Garrett asks menacingly.

Viv hops up and picks up her dishes. "Zara, let's get this all cleaned up. Game time."

Zara is on her feet in an instant and moves quickly to begin clearing the table.

As Zara finishes wiping the table, Branden walks out to his car to get an armload of board games. Garrett walks into the kitchen and wraps his arms around Zara. She leans into him, enjoying their moment. Hearing Branden coming back into the house, Garrett kisses Zara behind the ear and walks toward the dining table. He gives Viv a one-armed hug as he passes by her standing by the entryway.

Zara, following a few steps behind Garrett, looks up at Viv. She cannot help but return the big smile being flashed to her from her friend.

Today is a good day.

The rest of the afternoon is spent playing games and laughing around the table. Zara is crowned the victor of almost every game of Jenga played. Garrett uses her new camera flash to break her concentration and everyone laughs as the pieces tumble. Finally, Branden begs for mercy declaring the smell of dinner has become unbearable and they break to eat.

After dinner, Zara busies herself as the best friends turned family bicker with each other about everything from Christmases past to the upcoming bowl game that the great Spartans are sure to win. Moving at a comfortable but steady pace, it does not take her long before the meal is put away and dessert is neatly displayed.

Though Garrett's and Branden's homes are vastly different, open floor plans with the kitchen and dining room allow whoever is preparing the meal to easily take part in the conversation. In this case, Zara is happy to be listening. Her smile stretches further across her face with each fit of laugher that comes from the table.

Garrett wanders into the kitchen as Zara gathers the last of the silverware needed for the dessert. "Little One, need some help?"

"Thank you. You can carry the cake."

With a twinkle in his eye, Garrett lifts the multi-layer round cake and walks to the table. Placing it directly in front of Branden, Garrett slowly turns the cake so both Viv and Branden can see all sides of it. Zara sets the plates, forks and napkins on the table and gives Garrett a look.

"What?" he asks innocently.

"I am positive Branden's cakes are just as good as mine."

Always one to stir the pot, Viv gleefully chimes in, "Let's cut into this work of art and see."

"Does anyone want coffee or tea with their cake?" Zara asks before handing Garrett the knife.

"G, we're staying here tonight. So we'll have drinks after the taste test," Viv declares. "Cake first."

Zara places the knife into Garrett's waiting hand. All eyes are on the cake as he makes the first cut and slides the knife through the four layers of cake and frosting. When the first piece hits the plate, she remembers the ice cream. She goes to get it and finds Garrett is gone when she returns to the table.

Once her guests have their cake and ice cream, she makes a plate for Garrett. Not big on ice cream in this weather, Zara returns the ice cream to the freezer. She smiles at Viv's comments to Branden about the cake being far superior to his last attempt.

Just as Zara takes her first bite of cake, Garrett walks back in the room.

"Guys, I need to talk to Zara." He takes Zara by the hand and leads her toward the den, away from his friends.

Zara stiffens at his strong grasp on her hand, wondering what is amiss.

Over his shoulder, Garrett says, "Branden, I need you to make a couple of calls and wake some people up now. Intel is on your phone. Viv, check your phone too."

Garrett walks past the den into his bedroom.

Something is off. Why is he not looking at me? Why is he bringing me to his room?

Zara sits on the edge of the bed as requested. She takes a deep breath when he kneels in front of her and takes both of her hands in his.

He pauses, staring at their hands woven together.

Something is wrong. What did I do? Have I displeased him?

The lack of eye contact leaves her searching the top of his head in hopes that he will look up and meet her gaze.

When Garrett finally does reward her with eye contact, she realizes the magnitude of the problem.

In a clear but quiet voice, Garrett begins to shed light on the situation.

"I have some very sad news to tell you." He paused. "This morning at about 11am, your mother passed away. I just received a call from my dad and I do not have all the details for you yet. I am sorry. I do know it was cancer."

Zara whispers in disbelief, "My mother passed away?"

My mother passed away.

"Branden is arranging a flight. I will get you down there as quickly as possible. You are in a unique situation, as you are not collared. Therefore, you have every right to return home and participate in the services without seeking permission. Zara, your father is not happy with the thought of you returning to the house. The suggestion was made for us to stay at a hotel, but he indicated that would be a further embarrassment for him. I have not spoken to him directly..."

My mother passed away.

"Little One, are you hearing me?"

Zara nods.

"How did she die?"

Garrett wipes the tears away that have started to slide down Zara's cheek. He softly answers, "It was cancer. I'm sorry, I don't have any more details at the moment."

My mother is gone. I never fixed things between us. She never knew–

"Zara Faith, your father is not going to allow Fredrik to interact with you. He has put his foot down on this. I am so sorry. You will see him at the service but that will be all."

Zara is quiet for a moment. "Garrett, would it be okay if I lay down? I know that we have guests—"

"I think they will understand. Why don't you lay in my bed for now."

My mother passed away.

CHAPTER 27

Waking in Garrett's arms, Zara feels warm and safe and does not move right away. She breathes him in and focuses on the place where their bodies meet, his arms across her shoulder, his thigh touching hers. She opens her eyes to find his are staring back with concern. In that moment, the horror of her reality comes rushing back.

"My mother," Zara whimpers, unable to get more words out.

Her eyes close as the renewed pain morphs into racking sobs muffled against Garrett's chest. He makes no attempt to move, just continues rubbing her back waiting for the pain to ease.

As the tears begin to subside, Zara pulls back but Garrett catches her face between his hands and searches her eyes. "There is my beautiful Zara Faith."

New tears begin to cascade from Zara's eyes. She does not speak and focuses on Garrett, clutching at the strength behind his eyes.

Hours later, the monotony of tires over pavement has not soothed Zara's broken heart. Tears continue to course down her cheeks as Garrett holds her close.

"I am so sorry, Zara." He holds her tighter and Zara wrap her hands around his neck. "I am right here. I am not letting you go."

Tears of exhaustion take over.

Zara awakens to familiar smells. Blinking her eyes open, Zara discovers she is in her old bedroom at her parent's house.

"Motherrrr!" Zara screams at the top of her lungs. "Motherrr. MOTHERRRRR!"

Garrett runs into the bedroom and flies onto the bed next to

Zara. He picks her up from where she lies and cradles her in his arms.

"Shhh... I have you. Little One, shhhhhh."

"Garrett, my mother is dead. I didn't get to say goodbye. I didn't tell her I loved her. I didn't tell her I was sorry for not getting collared."

He nods and places an open bottle of water to Zara's lips. He instructs her to drink and they sit together until she finishes the entire bottle. Then he tells her to go take a shower and brush her teeth.

"I will be right here when you are finished. You can climb right back in bed. I promise."

On autopilot, Zara gets off his lap and walks into her old bathroom. She turns on the shower, undresses and stands vacantly under the water. Tears mix with water and run down her face.

At some point, Zara realizes the water was turned off for her and a towel had been wrapped around her. She is guided numbly out of the shower and dried off. When a big tee shirt is slid over her head, Zara smells Garrett.

He lifts her and carries her to the bed, gently lying her down and covering her up. He does not say anything as he lies down next to her and wraps her in his arms.

The tears that had begun hours earlier continue in silence.

I cannot believe that she is gone. I cannot believe she died before I could make things right. I didn't get to tell her how important she is to me. We just never talked. I am so sorry, Mother.

Garrett says nothing, letting Zara live this horrible moment.

Zara recalls the conversation she had with her mother the day of the Ceremony. She had said that Garrett was the one and that Zara needed to trust the traditions and, more importantly, trust herself. Trust herself. At the time, the words went in one ear and out the other.

Zara had been moments from the walk up the white carpet to her new life. She had not understood what her mother was saying and did not question it either. It was the last conversation Zara had with her mother.

Zara remembered the look on her face when she stood up with Garrett's assistance. Shock had dawned in her eyes that he did not present Zara to the Community with a new collar. He had not made her his sub and she had walked from the Circle her own person.

The tears slowed again. Garrett moves to get up but Zara pulls back with a shake of her head. He just smiles gently and lies back down.

I need you. I need your strength. I need your care. I need your protection. I just don't know from what yet.

The room is dark and there is no sound but breathing. Zara wishes for music. She had gotten used to the sound of music. Music did not care when school was miles away or when the beach was not near. Music crossed all barriers.

With clear eyes, Zara looks around. This is her parents' home. This is no longer her bedroom. She realizes she hadn't looked around to see what had been changed in the months since her departure. It occurs to her that she no longer cares. Her home was miles from this place.

After some time, Garrett whispers for Zara to close her eyes. She is not looking at anything in particular so it does not matter if her eyes are open or shut. It does not feel any different with them open. It does not feel any different with them closed. Either way, Zara's mother is gone.

Zara feels Garrett stir. She opens her eyes and is surprised to find the room is light again. He is sitting next to her on the edge of the bed and in his hands is something she never thought she would see again. Garrett is holding her favorite mug, a gift she had received for Christmas years ago from Fredrik.

When Zara had opened the present, he had said she should have a bigger mug so she would not have to keep getting up to refill it. He had been twelve when he gave her the mug. It had been a proud moment for him. Later, Mother had explained that he had saved his allowance for quite some time to be able to purchase the gift. She had even offered to give him the money, but he proclaimed this was his gift to his sister so he would pay for it himself. Zara had loved it when she opened the box and loved it more after hearing the story behind it.

Zara does not want to drink any coffee. She does not want to eat any food. She wants to hold that mug in her hands again and go back to that time, a time when her mother was present.

A time when she is talking.

"Drink… please. I need for you to eat something," Zara took the mug but did not drink.

He reaches behind her and brings out package of crackers and works them open. Zara wants to shake her head no but does not have the strength. A cracker is put to her lips.

It is the worry in Garrett's eyes that parts Zara's lips and she takes the cracker he places on her tongue. The relief that shows in his eyes is worth the thump she feels in her stomach.

As the cracker dissolves in her mouth, Zara remembers the last meal she had prepared in this house with her mother. One of the aspects of her training was to learn to cook.

Two nights before the Ceremony, Zara was to make dinner for the family by herself. She was moody. Her mother came to her room twice to tell her to begin the preparations. It was unusual for anyone to not jump when told to do something in that house because there would be swift repercussions for insubordination.

The ramification for hesitation was severe. Fredrik and Zara were never abused. At least they did not think they were abused. Each of their punishments was different in nature. Zara was isolated, sent off to think about her actions. In isolation, she would have to kneel in the position that would become the norm in her future role as a submissive.

Fredrik did not speak of his punishments, but there had been occasions when Zara could hear him yell out in pain. She knew he was hit, but she had never asked him about it and he never volunteered any information.

That night Zara was to make her father's favorite, chicken parmesan with garlic sauce and lasagna. Both dishes were labor intensive and took effort for her to recall the ingredients and steps to prepare them.

When she was caught using her phone, Zara attempted to explain that she was referencing a note to make a portion of the full recipe. Her mother was furious. Zara knew just how angry she was because during her ranting of the importance of knowing how to care for your Dom and yourself, her mother's acquired southern accent slipped out, something she worked hard at hiding.

That had been the story of Zara and her mother's relationship. She was a slave. Zara was the daughter of a King Council member that would be given to a man who had been selected by a group of men, who, like her father, knew nothing about her.

Zara looks up to find Garrett is looking out the window deep in thought. She wipes her cheek on the back of her sleeve and watches him. She looks at his profile. She loves the way his hair always looks like it is two weeks after a haircut. She loves the way she can tell what he is thinking by looking deeply into his eyes. She loves the way he is always there for her, from the smallest request to getting her down to be with her family during this horrible time. She loves him.

How is it possible, in the middle of grieving for Mother, that I can decide that I am madly in love him? I am in love with you, Garrett.

As if sensing her attention, Garrett turns and looks at her. Finding sadness in his eyes, Zara cannot resist crawling onto his lap to press as close to him as she can. As he holds her tightly, Zara feels his face press into her hair.

"Thank you," Zara says in a clear voice that holds a trace of sadness but no tears. She feels him nod his head in her hair. "What is it, Garrett?"

He lifts his head and pulls away from her to stare into her eyes. A slight smile finds its way across his face. "You said my name. You never say my name. In fact, you go out of your way to avoid having to call me anything. Will you say it again... please?"

"I will say it as many times as you ask if you will tell me what is on your mind, Garrett." She says his name with a bit of a tilt of her head. Without thinking, a small smile finds its way to her lips.

The smile on Garrett's face slips away. "I was sitting here thinking it is my fault that you and your mother were not speaking. I should never have gone against the traditions of the Community and offered you a way out."

"A way out?" Zara's eyes fill with water and fresh tears slide down her face. The tears are not for the passing of her mother, but due to the realization that Garrett had intended to get out of collaring Zara. On the same day she figures out she is in love with Garrett, she finds out he does not want her as his submissive. She tries to flee his lap, but his hold stops her from going anywhere.

"No, Little One, we are not finished talking. You do not get to run off because you think you heard something that you did not. I have never given you any reason to think I do not intend to meet you in that Circle. You asked me what I was thinking and I was telling you. Please allow me to be as open with my thoughts and feelings as I hope you are with me."

Zara sits looking at him. She does not try to move. Instead she wraps her arms around his neck to remove the distance between them. She holds Garrett tight knowing she needs him, but more importantly knowing she wants him too.

There is a soft knock at the door. Garrett unwraps her from his arms and whispers that he will be right back. She shakes her head and tries to hold on.

Please. No. Nothing feels worse than when you put me down. Please. No.

"Zara. I will be right here. I am not leaving you. Let go, Little One," he says, his voice firm.

Unwrapping her arms and placing her on the bed, Garrett steps to the door and opens it. He uses his body to block whoever knocked from seeing Zara as well as to prevent them from entering their space. Zara blocks out the conversation. She lies down on the pillow and closes her eyes, not to sleep but to make sure no part of the world creeps in.

Garrett shuts the door and gets back on the bed. He stretches out beside her and gathers her into his arms.

"We weren't close." Zara's words make Garrett tense and hold her even tighter. "The night she told me that you had chosen me, I made her so angry I thought she was going to strike me. I was a disappointment to her."

"Little One, you could never be a disappointment to anyone. You were never a disappointment to her." Garrett's words were what anyone would say. Zara wishes she could believe him but the look she had seen on her mother's face at the Circle Ceremony told a different story.

"I always thought I would have time." A tear slides down Zara's cheek. Garrett does not respond. He rubs his hand in a small circle on her back. Those are the last words Zara can force out. She is no longer hysterically crying, but instead a steady flow of tears run from one eye over her nose to her other eye. Garrett does not say anything else. He just gently holds her and rubs her back.

"I didn't get to say goodbye," Zara says sadly.

"Let's go do that then." Zara wipes the tears from her face as

Garrett continues, "The service is scheduled for the day after tomorrow. There is a visitation scheduled for tomorrow. Your father has made all the arrangements. Your mother is at the funeral home. Let me take you there right now and you can say goodbye."

Zara nods feeling light-headed. Garrett stands and pulls a green pullover sweater from the closet.

"Arms up, Little One."

Raising her arms, Garrett slips the pullover over Zara's head and pulls it down. Zara takes his hands and lets him pull her to her feet. Garrett leads the way out of the bedroom and down the stairs.

Sitting in a chair next to the window is her father. He stares outside never turning to acknowledge his daughter or the man holding her up. Garrett urges Zara to step toward the door. When she looks up into his face, she sees something that she had never seen before.

Is Garrett angry?

He opens the front door and standing at the curb in front of a black SUV is the older man who had driven them to the airport the night of her failed Circle Ceremony. He stands somberly with his hands crossed in front of him. Garrett leads Zara down the front path to the vehicle where the man opens the back door.

"Thank you, Peter." It is the first time Zara hears Garrett speak to anyone in what feels like days.

As she steps into the SUV, Zara is surprised to find Mrs. Dawson inside waiting. Seeing her, Zara burst into tears all over again.

Garrett climbs in and sits beside Zara. Although they sit thigh to thigh, Zara feels like they are miles apart.

Within a few minutes, they reach their destination.

I am not prepared for this. I have disappointed her. I am not ready to say goodbye. I never fixed it. I never made it right. I failed my mother.

The door opens from the outside on Mrs. Dawson's side.

Garrett takes Zara's hand and says softly, "Little One, we can leave whenever you are ready. If you decide you don't want to go in, that's fine too. I'll be right here waiting for you."

Suddenly cold, Zara begins to shake all over.

"Hey. Hey. My mom is going to go with you."

She wraps herself around Garrett as much as possible.

"Please. Don't leave me. I cannot do this without you," she whispers hoarsely.

"Garrett, please bring her inside. She needs you right now. I will deal with them."

Garrett opens the door on his side and Zara accepts his assistance out of the car. Mrs. Dawson stands at the curb and holds out her arms as Zara approaches.

"Zara Faith, I am so, so sorry for your loss. Aubrey loved you so much. I know that this is going to be really hard on you, so lean on us. Allow Garrett and me to be your strength today."

Garrett wraps his arm around Zara and guides her into the front entrance of the funeral home.

The inside is dim. It is quiet and smells heavily of flowers. Chairs are strategically placed in mini sitting areas. The carpet is thick and absorbs the sounds of their shoes.

Zara knows when they are getting closer because both of the bodies assisting her tense. Mrs. Dawson releases her and walks through the double doors that are facing them. Garrett folds Zara into his arms.

"Okay, bring her in. Garrett, I will stay with the Community after and you may take Zara home."

With one last tight squeeze, Garrett releases Zara and leads her through the doors. Straight ahead is a casket. The top is open.

Community women dressed in dark colors sit in the pews. As the three make their way toward the casket, Zara feels the stares.

Two feet from the end of the aisle and the casket, Zara stops. She releases Garrett's hand and steps forward. Keeping her eyes focused on the floor, Zara steps up to the casket. Taking a deep breath and squaring her shoulders, she takes the last step to reach the side of the casket.

Atop a pale pink pillow lies her mother.

Mother, you look beautiful. A peach outfit. A favorite of Father's, I'm sure. It looks too big.

Looking closely, her mother appears thinner. Her hands had been crossed on her stomach.

"This is not supposed to happen," Zara repeats over and over.

Suddenly beside her, Garrett lifts her chin to meet his eyes and speaks quietly and forcefully. "No. Little One, it was not supposed to happen. You need to remember one thing: your mother was a wonderful woman and I know this because of the woman you are. You had her in your life and she spent as much time as she could getting to know you and teach you what was important to her. Take that and the fact that she loved you to get through this."

Zara processes Garrett's words looking as deeply into his eyes as she can. She was her mother's daughter.

Her mother had been a proud woman in her way. To her husband, she had been the best slave she could be. There was nothing that would make her waver in her submission to him. As a mother, she took the job of raising the future to heart every day. Every moment was a teachable one. There were no off days. There was only progress.

Garrett blurs as Zara's eyes fill with tears. Zara turns once again to look at her beautiful mother lying peacefully in her forever bed.

CHAPTER 28

Zara looks around the space that had been her living room her entire life. Nothing looks the same. Her mother is dead. Her mother. Her teacher. Her mirror. She is gone. The room would never be the same.

Standing, Zara makes her way to the bathroom to shower. She feels dirty. It may be the feelings she is experiencing or the fact that she has been in a church with her mother lying in a casket. She cannot pinpoint why she needs a shower or if it will even help.

The water pours over her head and down her body.

My body. The body that was to be owned by a chosen Dom. A future that had been chosen for me. A body that had never really belonged to me until he released me from my collared future.

Zara turns the handles of the shower to cut the water. She wraps a towel around her body and another around her gathered hair. Slipping into a tank top and yoga pants, she grasps her pendant while staring at herself in the mirror.

The light cast from the bathroom highlights Garrett's form in her bed. She flips the light off and pads lightly to the side of the bed. Climbing under the covers, she can feel the warmth of his body.

Zara stretches and moves closer to him, unable to stand the thought of space between them.

"Hey, you," he whispers. She cannot tell if his eyes are open, but she can tell he is alert. His arm comes around her and Zara nuzzles into the spoon he has created for her.

"I loved her. I wanted her to be proud of me. I thought that I would have time to make up for choosing college over the collar. I never would have stopped the Ceremony if I had known she was not going to be here.

"She taught me to be a submissive. She prepared me to serve my Dom, you, to the best of my ability. Walking away from that was like throwing everything she taught me in the garbage. It was like saying I never wanted to be who she wanted me to be.

"The worst part, I never wanted to become like her. I was ashamed when she slid to her knees at my father's command. I hated that her service to him took priority over us. I hated that she never had a thought of her own. I hated him for owning her. I did not want to be owned. I was kneeling in the Circle wishing the whole time that there was a way out.

"This is the day I am going to watch my mother buried." Zara stops. She pulls away from Garrett and turns on a lamp.

Zara stands and looks at the dress she would wear to the church. The question in her mind is not whether or not she likes what had been selected for her, but whether her mother would approve.

So many of her recent choices had been made without her thinking about whether she had the approval of her mother. Friends, music, dancing, even her feelings for Garrett that began to grow the moment he placed his hand on her shoulder inside the Circle had been made on her own. Zara's choice to walk out of the Circle and leave all of her mother's traditions had been made by Zara alone.

She considers how her choices were affecting her this day. She had been home for three days and her father had not spoken a word to her. Fredrik had not come into her room to check on her or talk about the mother they shared. Her best friend, Sloane, had turned her back on her.

As her foot hits the last step, Zara realizes there are people in the house that she had not expected. She hears whispers but is unable to identify anyone.

Every fiber of her body knows she has no right to seek Garrett's strength. There is no collar around her neck, no wedding ring on her finger and yet he holds her like he realizes he is her lifeline.

"Zara, I cannot imagine what you are going through right now. You are quieter than I can take. I know that you are working hard to come to grips with what is happening. The Council is here and your father and I need to make sure you are ready for that.

"Can you nod for me, Little One? This is part of the day's procedures. The Council is here to pay their respects to your mother. She was a highly respected member of the Community and this is an important part of the service for her.

"Zara Faith, I do not know what the reaction is going to be toward you and me. We both made a decision to walk out of the Circle without completing the Ceremony. I need to ask if you want to go in there or if you would rather I take you to the church directly.

"I will support your decision whichever it is, but it is important to me that you understand that I believe that it is your place to go in there and accept their condolences. But I also do not think you should accept any negative treatment."

Wiping Zara's tears with his fingers, he brings her face to his and places a soft kiss on each of her eyelids. "I will be by your side no matter which path you decide."

Taking a cleansing breath and squaring her shoulders, Zara takes the handkerchief Garrett offers and dabs the tears away from her eyes. She gives him a reassuring smile and his slight nod is all the communication they need as Garrett takes the first step toward the den where the guests have gathered.

With his free hand, Garrett opens the door and walks through. He says hello as he enters the room, not to any one person but to the room as a whole. Zara squeezes his hand as he gently pulls her to him. Her eyes are glued to the floor as her training rushes back instinctively.

The room becomes silent when Garrett and Zara enter. He leads her down the length of the space to the small sofa under the window and instructs her to sit. He remains standing next to her on the other side of the armrest. She looks up at him, almost hearing her mother clear her throat for taking her eyes off the floor, but today Zara needs to be able to look into Garrett's eyes. She requires his strength to get through what is ahead of her.

Zara finds his hand on her shoulder and returns her gaze to the floor in front of her.

"Legs crossed at your ankles. Back straight, Zara Faith, hands in your lap, one on top of the other. Never squeeze your hands together. Your Dom will want you relaxed at all times. Please pay attention to what I am telling you, Zara. Your actions reflect on me. I am a reflection of my Master. I will not allow you to tarnish his image."

The memory of her mother directing her sitting position floods

Zara's thoughts. Breathing as deeply as possible without making Garrett's hand move from her shoulder, Zara clears her thoughts. She begins to remember how the grass felt through her fingers while she sat in the hidden garden. The different smells of the flowers and the soil and how those smells changed as the weather changed.

Moments after calming her thoughts, Zara hears the shuffle of Council members approaching her. Her entire body tenses and Garrett removes his hand from her shoulder and walks around the sofa to sit next to her. When he lowers onto the seat, Zara releases a breath she had not realized she was holding.

Taking her hand off her lap and placing it on his knee, Zara cannot prevent her eyes from following her hand to Garrett's knee. He places his hand over hers and waits. In a matter of moments, a line of polished shoes crossed in front of Zara and are gone. Nothing could get Zara to raise her eyes high enough to scan the room.

"Time is a funny thing. When you watch a clock it seems to slow down before your eyes. And when there is no clock it seems equally slow. Are you ready to go?" Garrett asks. Zara notes that he did not lower his voice so the others in the room could not hear him.

Rising from his seat, Garrett holds Zara's upper arm to steady her as she rises. "Would you like to make a quick stop before we leave?"

Shaking her head no, Garrett wraps his arm around Zara and escorts her out of the room. As they reach the threshold, Zara turns to look back in the room to find she and Garrett are the last to leave.

Condolences had not been given to Zara on the loss of her mother by any member of the King Council. Her father had not approached her to see how see was doing. Garrett and Zara had sat in the room with the men who had paired the two of them and they had not exchanged one word with any of them.

Realizing this was the last time Zara would be in this house, her eyes fill with tears but not one tear falls. All the rest of Zara's tears today would be saved for saying goodbye to her mother.

Pulling her into his chest, Garrett holds her tightly before leading Zara out the door to the waiting car.

CHAPTER 29

Peter is wearing a black suit with a black tie. The white of his shirt is brilliant with the sun high in the sky. As they approach the car, Zara hears the older man say that he is so sorry for her loss. The thank you that comes out of her is so weak it surprises her.

Once Garrett is on the seat next to her and the door closes, Garrett lifts her up onto his lap. As he caresses her back, Zara melts into his chest and relaxes for the first time since stepping out of the shower.

Finding peace on Garrett's lap is short-lived as the door is opened from the outside. Taking a moment to settle her rattled emotions, Zara exits the car and straightens her dress.

Before Zara can turn around, a familiar set of arms wraps around her body and draw her in. Feeling her brother's hug after so long undoes Zara and her tears flow freely. Turning in his arms, she looks into his tear-filled face.

Fredrik repeats the same sentence in Zara's ear, "I am so sorry. I am so sorry. I am so sorry."

Knowing no response would sooth his guilt, Zara shakes her head and holds him tighter.

Zara's body tenses at the sound of her father's voice. He speaks to Fredrik alone, making the displeasure of the emotional outburst of the siblings clear. Zara releases her brother and steps back with her eyes on the curb.

Without raising her eyes higher than her father's hands, Zara sees they are balled into fists on either side of him. She recognizes the black suit and shoes her father is wearing. He had worn them the last time she was in his presence.

Unable to stop the sob that overtakes her, Zara places her hand over her mouth. As hard as she tries, her mother's training fails her. Continuing to sob, she realizes that her mother's training had not failed; rather, she has failed her mother.

Garrett is close enough to catch her as her knees begin to buckle. He places his arms around her to draw her close to his body. The contact gives her the strength to step forward.

As Zara takes a step forward, her father turns and walks back to the door of the building. Fredrik turns to follow, but pauses to wait for Garrett and Zara. When they get to the entrance, Fredrik holds the door open so Garrett does not need to release his sister. As she passes by, Fredrik reaches out to take Zara's hand.

Zara hears somber organ music coming from the sanctuary. Her eyes find her brother's and he gives her a half smile. It was the same smile he would give her when they were younger and he would head off to class while she stayed home to train with her mother.

It is not a smug smile. Rather, it is sympathy for things not being equal between them. Many times Zara had sat on the floor of her room and tried to explain to him that it was like that in every family. Boys were always treated differently than girls.

One night, Fredrik had snuck into her room to check on her. Zara recalled the first time she had been spanked. She had talked back to her mother at dinner because she wanted to go to a birthday party being held for one of the girls in the Community. Her father had placed his fork and knife on his plate very gently. Quietly, he said "Aubrey" in a tone that both kids knew would transform their mother.

Without a glance at her daughter who was misbehaving, their mother placed her utensils on her plate and gracefully slid from her seat at the table to kneel at her Master's feet. Verbal communication was not required between their parents and neither Fredrik nor Zara were prepared for what was coming next.

Ordered to finish their meal by their father, Zara's hands shook with every bite she had to lift to her mouth. She sat at the table with her brother and father as her mother waited at her father's side with her head lowered in perfect submission.

Once the meal was over, Fredrik was ordered to go sit in the den on the sofa by the window. Standing, her father lifted his slave's chin and they stared at one another. Walking by Zara sitting stock still in her seat, he did not look at her or say anything.

Her mother rose to her feet and came over to where Zara sat

and said, "Zara, your behavior at the table was unacceptable. When you asked if you could attend the function with Sloane, what did I tell you?"

Looking at her mother with a river of tears running down her face, "You said I could not go."

The response was a whisper. Knowing she had behaved poorly, Zara lowered her head in shame.

"Your actions are a reflection of me and you have made me look foolish. You will be punished for your actions and then you will clear the table and do the dishes. Do you understand?"

Zara responded with a slight nod.

"Good. Your father is waiting in the den for you with a paddle. You will get four swats for tonight's misbehavior. The number of swats will be increased each time you misbehave. Now go and receive your punishment."

Zara searched her mother's eyes and found sadness in them. The fact that her behavior had caused her mother to be reprimanded was a difficult concept for Zara to grasp. "Zara Faith, go now."

Sliding out of her chair, Zara lowered her eyes as she had been instructed to do when going to see her father. Walking into the den, Zara knew that Fredrik was being forced to witness her punishment. Seeing the large paddle on the sofa next to her father overrode all other thoughts.

Instructed to bend over the coffee table and hold the edge, the first swat took Zara by surprise. The intense sting was not instant. Split seconds before the second swat, the burn of the first hit took her breath away.

The intensity of the fourth swat caused Zara to release her grip on the coffee table and fall forward on it. Annoyed, her father said that her failure to comply with the instructions she was given should garner her an additional swat. Already crying hard, Zara's entire body shook at the suggestion of being hit again.

Her father did not follow through with a fifth one that night. He stood and walked out of the room without saying a word to his daughter.

Not knowing what to do once their father had left, Fredrik came to Zara's side and helped her off the table. Being the older sister, Zara instructed him to go to his room and play with his trains. He gave her a hug and ran to his room, but not before Zara saw the tears in his eyes that he tried so hard to hide from her.

After clearing the table, then washing and drying each dish, Zara had walked slowly to her bedroom. She did not change her clothes. She did not want the material to brush over her very sore behind. Lying on the bed on her stomach, Zara released the tears she had been holding in.

It was not long before Fredrik slipped in the door and sat on the floor next to her bed. He did not speak or cry. He was there to check on how his older sister was doing and to attempt to come to grips with how their family functioned.

Once Zara had stopped the crying, he asked her why their family was like that. At the time, Zara did not have an answer. She told him that it was how mother and father were raised.

Zara was seven the night that took place. Over the years, the explanations became more involved. They discussed the fact that Fredrik was going to be a Dom someday with a submissive of his own and Zara would be a submissive to her own Dom.

For Zara, stepping into the sanctuary is harder than all of those difficult conversations with Fredrik combined. The aisle Garrett had walked her down a day ago feels longer on this trip. Unlike her trip to the Circle on her birthday, Zara does not attempt to catch a glimpse of anyone as she makes her way closer to her mother's casket.

Breathing deeply, Zara uses Garrett as an anchor and takes one step after the other. Like déjà vu, Zara finds herself behind her father. So much had changed since the last time she followed him down an aisle.

Zara waits as her father and brother pay last respects to her mother. Garrett leans his cheek on Zara's head and they stand together as one until her time comes to say her final goodbye.

As Zara's only two living family members leave the side of her mother's casket, Garrett releases his hold on her. Looking up at him, the sound of a collective gasp reminds Zara they are not alone. Eyes locked on one another, no words are needed for Zara to plead with Garrett not to make her take the last two steps alone.

"I will be right behind you, Little One. I promise." Bringing his lips to her ear, he tells her she needs to do this and that she is strong enough to do it alone. He lightly brushes his lips across hers and steps back so she can proceed.

Relying on her training to carry her forward, Zara takes another deep breath and squares her shoulders. With one last glance up at Garrett, she retrieves the last bit of strength she needs to move forward.

Zara places one foot in front of the other, eyes directly ahead on the red wood casket. When she reaches her mother, she places her hand on the side. Her mother looks beautiful. Nothing had changed from the last time she had stared at her mother laying there, but this time she knows it is her last time.

Leaning in, Zara kisses her mother's cheek and whispers, "Mother, I love him. He has protected me and I think he really loves me. I am sorry I disappointed you. I am so sorry. I will make it right. I promise. I love you, Mother."

Garrett places his handkerchief into Zara's hand. She looks down at the piece of cloth and up at Garrett. Looking back down at her mother, Zara sees her tears have fallen on her mother's cheek and a choking sob bursts forth without warning.

From behind, Zara feels Garrett wrap his arms around her. Charlotte appears and together they embrace Zara and walk her to the pew.

After a few minutes, it occurs to Zara that she is surrounded by Garrett's family, while across the aisle her father and brother sit alone. On the raised dais in front of Zara, a man is talking about what a wonderful woman her mother had been. Blinking, Zara looks closer at the man to see if she recognizes him from her mother's life, but she does not.

Zara looks in her father's direction and feels Garrett squeeze her tighter. She cannot see Fredrik's face. Looking up at Garrett with pleading eyes, she whispers, "I need to make sure Fredrik is alright. He is all alone over there."

Garrett turns his head to look over to her family side. With a slight nod, he stands up and holds her hand while she gets to her feet.

The gentleman recalling the details of her mother's life pauses mid-sentence and Zara can feel all the eyes in the sanctuary watching her every move.

Silently Garrett escorts her across the aisle to where her family sits stoically before her mother's casket. She sits down next to

Fredrik and lays her hand on her brother's clenched fist. He takes a deep breath and opens his hand to accept her fingers and intertwines them with his own. Looking into her brother's eyes, she sees the deep hurt etched into his features.

As Zara's tears pour freely down her cheeks, her heart breaks watching Fredrik work to control his tears from leaking. She feels Garrett extend his arm around her back and she melts into the nook he creates. Holding hands with her brother and leaning into the man she has come to love, she begins to focus on the words being spoken in honor of her mother.

Unable to keep her mind from wandering, old memories of her mother sneak in and hijack her attention. Her thoughts drift back to the first time her mother spoke to her about her future Dom. The two of them were alone in the kitchen baking Fredrik a birthday cake for his fourth birthday.

Zara was sitting on a stool as her mother read her recipe aloud. It was not until many years later that she realized the recipe cards had been used for her benefit. When her mother cooked she never used the cards that were so neatly organized by category.

"Zara, do you know why we are making this cake for Fredrik?"

She nodded and watched her mother measure out the flour. She held the heaping cup over the canister and Zara ran the butter knife over the top to level it off.

"Cooking and baking are two of the best ways to show someone how much you love them. We could have purchased a cake, but by making it ourselves, we add our love into the mix. Someday you will be making a birthday cake for your Dom. It will be important to discover what his favorite cake is so you can bake it with love."

Staring at her mom's hand as she stirred the batter, Zara looked for the love to be added. "Zara Faith, would you like to ask me your question?"

Puzzled, Zara focused on her mother's face. She didn't understand the wide smile that covered her face but it made her smile back. "Mother, how did you know that I was thinking?"

Placing her elbow on the counter and her chin in her hand, she sat perched ready to listen to the wonders her mother would share. Her mother leaned in as close to her as she could without touching her and whispered, "You make a special face when thinking something over."

Zara mulled over this new information.

"Do you think we should practice keeping your thoughts hidden? Maybe you will get so good at it that one day I will not be able to see that you are thinking."

Zara nodded and her chin slipped from its resting spot.

"No one can hear you when you nod."

Smiling, Zara shook her head again but this time replied, "I want to be able to think without you knowing it. I want you to show me."

Zara's mother finished pouring the batter into the cake pan and set it gently in the oven. They moved to the table and the lesson of maintaining a schooled face began.

Once Zara was able to hold her facial expression steady, her mother told her about the day she would watch her walk down the aisle to the Circle and become the wife of a wonderful Dom.

"Zara, school your face again. Very, very good. Now, remember that expression. Remember how it feels and where your eyes and mouth are. That is the same expression that I want you to go to every time I tell you to school your expression. It will be a game between you and me."

Zara placed her hands on her face and felt her eyelids and lips to memorize their placement.

"Smell that?"

She nodded again and her mother's look indicated her daughter's nod was not a proper response.

"Yes, Ma'am. It smells like cake!"

Her mother stood and put on the oven mitts that were always hanging from the side of the oven. "It smells like love."

The cake pan was placed on top of the stove. "Shall we test it and make sure it is done baking?"

Zara got up from her chair and moved closer to the warm stove. She watched her mother pick up two toothpicks and hand them to her.

"School your face." Looking up at her mother, she took a deep breath and set her expression. Her hand touched her lips to ensure they were in the right place.

"Take the toothpick and push it into the center of the cake. Then pull it straight out. If the cake is finished, the toothpick will be clean. If it comes out with cake on it, back in the oven it goes. Remember, school your face, Zara."

Taking another breath, Zara extended her hand over the cake and carefully placed the toothpick all the way into the center. Before pulling out the toothpick, she looked at the cake to memorize its golden appearance into her mind. Then she pulled out the toothpick and looked to see if it was clean. Handing it to her mother, she softly said, "Mother, the cake is done."

Zara returned to the chair at the table and touched her face again. She placed her hands in her lap and looked straight ahead.

"I am so proud of you. That was remarkable. You did not change from your schooled face one time." Her mother placed her hand on her shoulder.

Zara smiled. She looked up at her mother and felt a warmth cascade through her because she had pleased her. "Now, shall we practice some more while the cake cools?"

Careful to not show any emotion, Zara whispered, "Yes, please."

Sitting down again, her mother began to tell her a story about a beautiful young lady who was married to a handsome kind man.

"One day your father will locate the perfect man for you. He will be your match in every way."

Zara watched her mother's lips as she spoke but kept the picture of the cake in her head.

"On your eighteenth birthday I will help you get into the most beautiful dress and your father will walk you down the aisle to a special circle. Once you are in the circle you will be presented to your Dom."

Zara knew the minute her facial expressions changed. She squirmed in her chair and moved closer to the table.

"School your face again, Zara Faith." Taking a deep breath and sitting up straight, she worked to push the jumbled thoughts in her head away and return to the mental cake picture. The edges were darker than the middle. The crispy edge pulled away a little bit from the sides of the pan. The yellow cake had turned a warm golden color.

Slowly, she brought her hands to her mouth and gently ran her fingers over her eyelids. She turned her head to look at her mother. There was no sign of what her mother was thinking and at that moment, she realized that this was her mother's schooled expression. It was the face that looked down at her when she did schoolwork, when she sat at the table eating dinner and even when she was being tucked into bed.

Her fingertips returned to her lips and then her hands came to rest in her lap. Her face was schooled.

"Very well done. You are very good at this, Zara. You may stop now."

Zara felt her entire body sag. The cake picture vanished and she was left thinking about what her mother had told her and the fact that her mother's face was always being schooled.

Feeling her mother looking at her, Zara turned in her chair to face her. A big smile exploded over her mother's face and she reached over to give her a big hug. "I am so proud of you, my Zara Faith."

"Mother, what if I don't have a Dom?" Her mother shook her head at her daughter. "Sorry, what if I do not have a Dom?"

Placing her hands in her lap, Zara's mother looked in her daughter's eyes and smiled broadly, "Zara, you will have a Dom. Your father will search all the land for the perfect match for his little girl."

Without thinking, Zara asked, "What if I do not want a Dom?"

Her mother's beautiful smile slipped. She stood and went to the refrigerator and retrieved a pitcher full of lemonade. Setting it on the table in front of Zara, she then pulled two cups from the cabinet and poured them both a half a cup of Zara's favorite lemonade.

With a serious expression, her mother spoke in a low but clear voice, "Having a Dom is the best part of life. Did you know when I was a young lady my father found your father especially for me?" Zara placed her cup back on the table and whispered a soft no.

"I lived in the state of Michigan. When I was little we would get snow all the way up to here." Zara's eyes got big when her mother held her hand over both of their heads. "Oh yes. The snow would get so bad that my father could not get our mail and would have to dig out his car.

"On my 18th birthday, my mother helped me put on a beautiful white dress and I walked to the center of the Circle. That is where I met your father for the very first time. And you know what?" Zara sat and hung on every word her mother was saying.

"No, Ma'am."

Her mother smoothed Zara's hair behind her ears and leaned in close. "Your father was so handsome. I was very excited to become his. From the moment I saw him, I knew I was meant to be with him. That will happen to you too.

"Your Dom will take care of you and protect you, and you will care for him. A partnership is formed in the Circle. Your life will begin when you meet your Dom."

Zara looked down at her mother's hands resting in her lap; her long slender fingers grasped the sparkly ring on her left ring finger.

Her mother began to whisper and Zara looked at her lips as she spoke. "Do you know the very best part of walking into the Circle and getting a Dom? You and Fredrik."

Beaming at her mother's words, Zara wrapped her arms around her mother's neck and received a tight squeeze.

Looking at Fredrik, Zara can see that the little boy who had eaten that cake had grown up. Though she had only been away at school for a few months, her younger brother had become a man in her absence. It would not be long before Fredrik was stepping into the Circle to collar his own submissive. Sitting there holding his hand, Zara wonders what her brother wants out of life.

Hearing her father say her name, Zara jumps. She has no idea what her father has said or when he had walked up to stand next to her mother's casket. She stares at the casket holding her mother's body and still none of the words being spoken make it through to Zara.

Garrett stands. He patiently waits as the siblings embrace. As Zara begins to stand, Garrett takes her hand.

Fredrik says in a hushed voice only his sister can hear, "Did you get the stones I sent you?"

Zara falters at his words causing Garrett to catch her by the arm. Feeling numb and confused, Zara lets Garrett lead her down the aisle and away from her mother.

CHAPTER 30

"I am planning to stay here for a while longer. I know. I miss you too. Just for a bit longer. El, I am okay. I promise. Tell Liliana I miss her, too. Okay, bye."

Setting her cell phone on the counter, Zara finishes chopping the veggies for the salad. Chicken and potatoes are in the oven, the table is set, and Zara checks the rest of the items off in her mind. Music… dashing into the den, Zara turns on the Peaceful Piano playlist on Spotify. It is one of her favorite Christmas gifts and she uses it daily. Setting the music to play throughout the house, Zara returns to the kitchen to finish dinner.

Entering the kitchen, Zara stops in her tracks. She steps closer to the counter and sees a napkin. Allowing her head to fall all the way back and exhaling, Zara feels her shoulders drop.

Zar, now you are seeing things. Really? A recipe card? Mother would be very disappointed if a card was needed for roast chicken and potatoes. Two weeks since I've been in that house and now I'm seeing recipe cards that don't exist.

Zara pulls the chicken and potatoes out of the oven when she hears Garrett's car in the driveway. Sitting down, Zara waits patiently. The smile that spreads across his face when he sees her takes her breath away. She exhales. Her nerves had gotten to her in her time alone during the day.

"I am pleasantly surprised to see you, Little One. I thought when I dropped you off at school this morning you were staying on campus tonight."

"Is this okay?"

"Is it okay… that you come to the house where you have a room and make dinner? Yes, Zara Faith, it is okay." Walking to where Zara is sitting, Garrett extends his hands and helps her to her feet. Taking her in his arms, he talks into her hair, "I was not looking forward to coming home tonight to this empty house. I missed you today."

"May I stay?"

"Yes. Smells delicious." Released, Zara slips into her seat. Garrett walks out of the dining room while Zara begins serving the meal she prepared. As if they had rehearsed their timing, he returns and grabs the chilled wine just as the last plate is placed with the evening's offerings.

"This looks amazing. Thank you. How were your classes today?" Garrett asks as he takes his first bite of chicken.

"Good. They will be a lot more challenging than last semester. Biology, Calculus, and Chemistry will be hard. I think I am going to enjoy my writing class. The professor seems very friendly."

Shaking his head, Garrett takes a sip of wine, "This is not how I envisioned you exploring your first year of college. I was completely worried about you spending all your weekend nights at frat parties and dating a different guy every weekend. Instead, you are here making me dinner, taking the heaviest class load in freshman history."

"I tried all of that. It did not hold a candle to the amazing John Garrett Dawson. There is no place I would rather be tonight than right here with you."

"Do you have a lot of studying to do?"

"Yes."

"Good. I have a shit ton of work to do for a new client and I would find it difficult to ignore you the entire night." Winking at Zara, Garrett smirked at her broad smile.

"You are in luck. We get to ignore each other in the same room."

Garrett and Zara finish dinner in a comfortable peace enjoying the soft piano dancing out of the speakers. After the dishes are cleaned and put away, the two change into comfy clothes and take up residence in the den. Garrett sits at his desk and Zara camps out on the sofa. They work in silence, but for Zara, just being in the same space as Garrett makes it well worth studying at his house.

Weeks earlier Garrett had established a new tradition by bringing Zara a special snack during their work sessions. He had walked out of the room, returned and passed Zara a small bag and returned to his seat without a word.

Zara emitted a squeal of glee when she opened the bag and

examined the contents finding blow-pops and sweet-tarts. The next day, Zara had surprised Garrett with a mix of caramel, cheese and butter popcorn. On the third day, they each had a bag for each other and each day after it turned into a contest.

There is no doubt in Zara's mind that she is taking tonight's treat competition award. Pulling chocolate chip cookie balls from their hiding place in the back of the freezer, she quickly bakes them.

Pouring milk into pre-frosted glasses and arranging the fresh homemade-out-of-the-oven cookies on the platter, Zara heads into the den to claim her victory. Walking directly to Garrett's desk, she carefully sets the platter down so it does not touch any of his documents.

"Milk and cookies?" she drawls in the sexiest voice she could muster without busting into laughter.

"You made cookies?" Garrett picks one up and examines both sides. Biting into it, he lets out a moan.

"I did," Zara says giggling.

"You know you win tonight."

"Yep."

"Thank you. These are great. I hope you made extra. I am totally taking some tomorrow to eat in front of Branden."

He reaches for the milk and takes a long drink. "You chilled the milk, too."

Zara laughs and nods.

"How much more work do you have?"

"Garrett, I am a student. Forever. What do you have in mind?"

"Let's take a drive."

"You want to take a drive tonight?"

"Yes. Bring cookies."

"Are we going over to eat cookies in front of Branden tonight?" Zara asks suspiciously.

"Or maybe we just are taking a drive with the best chocolate chip cookies I ever tasted."

"We are so going over to Branden's," Zara laughs. "I need to change first."

"What? You look adorable. Don't change. Let's go."

CHAPTER 31

Routine takes hold in short order. They enjoy breakfast together, Garrett drops Zara off on campus, and then Zara finds her way back to his house to prepare dinner. It becomes their new norm. Weekends are spent working and studying with breaks taken for a movie or dinner.

It is Friday, which means there would be a date after a long day on campus. Feeling the need to step out of her normal college wear, Zara takes extra care getting ready in the morning.

Smiling, she slips into one of her new matching bra and panties sets and picks out a pair of dark skinny jeans. Zara decides on a fitted fuzzy red sweater to complete the outfit and considers what to put on her feet. Spying the red-soled shoes she had been wanting to wear for a while, a wicked smirk comes over Zara's face.

Not yet. Soon.

Laughing at herself, she walks toward the kitchen in a different pair of 4-inch heels. As their routine dictates, Garrett would be in the kitchen preparing the coffee. Stopping in front of the window, Zara marvels at how spring had burst through winter and is taking hold. The seasons are one of Zara's favorite things about Michigan and she is already looking forward to the color tour Garrett has promised to take her on next autumn.

Hearing a loud whistle, Zara spins around to find Garrett checking her out. She slowly does a 360 to give him a complete view of her Friday outfit, and then runs across the living room to leap into his arms.

"Fuck Zara... you can run in those things." He shakes his head in amazement.

"Requirement. Mother would have it no other way. If I was to wear heels, I had to be able to really wear them."

"Sorry," Garrett says ruefully, planting a quick kiss on her puckered lips.

"It is becoming easier. I want to remember. She was amazing."

"Yes, she was, Zara."

Zara turns at hearing voices coming from the kitchen. Garrett slowly puts her down, but holds on to her to provide support.

"Mrs. Dawson... Mr. Dawson. I am so sorry. I did not realize you were here. Please forgive my rudeness this morning. I... I really." Walking around the island, Charlotte approaches Zara.

"Zara Faith, no apologies necessary. I thought we agreed that you would be calling me Charlotte. You remember Warren." Pulling Zara in for a quick hug, she holds her back to look her over. "You look positively radiant. Love does do that for some women."

Zara stands looking at Garrett's mother unable to come up with anything intelligent to say. A woman in love, she muses before being snapped out of her thoughts by Mr. Dawson's bear hug. She hugs him back with wonder that this was only the second time she could recall being hugged by a father figure.

"Zara, you do look lovely. I must say, I think Michigan agrees with you. How are you liking MSU?" Mr. Dawson asks.

"I am enjoying MSU very much, although my classes are far more challenging this semester. As for Michigan, now that spring has finally arrived, I am again a fan. Winter got to be a bit long and frigid."

Mr. Dawson lets out a booming laugh as he makes his way back around the island. "You have successfully summed up the brutality of our winter season. It is why God gave Michigan four of them."

As Garrett wraps his arms around Zara and guides her toward the kitchen island, her body becomes stiff as a board. She did not know how his parents would react to their contact.

"Relax, they are extremely happy for us," Garrett whispers in Zara's ear to prevent his parents from hearing.

With a slight nod, Zara pushes herself away from his embrace and walks to the refrigerator. "Is anyone hungry? I can make breakfast. Pancakes? Omelets? Anything?"

Zara looks as deeply into the fridge as possible to take a few seconds to gather herself. The presence of Garrett's parents has caught her completely off guard.

"Zara Faith, come and sit with us for a moment, please,"

Charlotte requests.

Closing the door to the refrigerator, Zara follows everyone to the dining table and takes a seat next to Garrett. Mr. Dawson sits in the seat directly across from her while Charlotte occupies the head of the table in the seat to the right of Zara.

"Zara, we are very sorry to show up this morning without warning. It is habit for us to pop in on Garrett, but we should have given the both of you a bit of notice. The very last thing we want to do is make you nervous in your home. We are very sorry."

"But this… this is not my…"

Garrett reaches for Zara's hand and squeezes. Giving her a smile, he looks at his mother. "Mom, I think what Zara is trying to say is that she is living in the dorm. Well, she is sort of living in the dorm."

He turns in the chair to face Zara. "Little One, you are living here. You have not spent a night in the dorm in weeks. We should move the rest of your stuff. If you want. I do not want to rush you."

"Live here with you? Permanently? Yes!"

Garrett reaches for Zara's face and draws it to him. Looking closely, he stares into her eyes for a moment. Zara has a hint of moisture building in the corners. "I love you, Little One."

"I love you too, Garrett," Zara whispers.

Zara steps out of Garrett's car in front of the dorm. It feels different. She feels different. Rewarded with a quick kiss and hug from Garrett, Zara strolls to the entrance of Yakeley. She does not need to look back to know that he is still standing there watching her. Zara can feel his eyes on her and it feels amazing.

Walking up the steps, Zara pauses to say a quick hello to Sara. The 'you're never around' comment she is hearing more frequently follows. With a quick hug and promise to catch up soon, they both head off to embark on their own day's adventure.

Standing inside the door of her first home after leaving her parents, Zara looks around and takes everything in. Nothing has changed. The furniture is still in the same position, music is still playing while a group of girls in the corner laugh, and Beth is still seated behind the desk looking like she would like to be anywhere else.

The surroundings are the same. Zara is changing. Walking toward the hallway to her room, Zara nods at Beth who returns it with a smirk.

Each of the girls Zara sees on the way to her room say hey and rave about how great she looks. "What's different about you?" "You look HOT?" "OMG… GIRL!!"

Smiling, Zara thanks them, but keeps moving.

Zara had picked this time of day to come to her room, knowing that both Liliana and Ella would be in class. It is not that she wants to avoid them exactly… well maybe that is exactly what she is trying to do. Zara closes her door and surveys her surroundings. Such a short time ago, she had spent her very first night alone in this room.

That had been such a confusing time. Leaving the Circle without a collar and having the opportunity to attend college is more than Zara had ever allowed herself to hope for. The fact it had come true was exciting, yet terrifying. Losing her family and best friend was not something that she could have been prepared for.

Waking up at the beach house and being able to spend some quality time with Garrett before being dropped off at school was a gift. Although, at the time she did not know how he felt about her, Zara had never felt abandoned. Garrett was always a call away and he made sure that she had everything she needed.

"So much has changed," Zara repeats to herself. Realizing that Garrett is outside waiting, she jumps into gear. Moving as if on a mission, she grabs a couple of the books needed for upcoming assignments and a handful of pictures.

She jots a quick note to Liliana and Ella telling them that she is sorry that she missed them and that they should do dinner next week. She locks the door to her dorm room and slides the note under their door. Making her way back down the hallway, she is out of the dorm in less than fifteen minutes.

Garrett is standing in the same spot she left him. A broad smile appears on his face when he sees her standing on the steps. In that second, Zara knows she is more than ready to make this a permanent move. Life is about changes, big and small. Today is one of those big change days.

CHAPTER 32

Telling Liliana and Ella about her decision to move in with Garrett is easier than Zara had predicted. Garrett's genius idea to invite them over for dinner and to show them the house has worked wonders.

"Zara, no wonder you don't come back to the dorm anymore. This place is to die for," Ella gushes.

Both girls seem a little taken aback when Zara takes them on a tour of her bedroom. Ella sits on the bed and forces Liliana to close the door. "Girl, explain to us why you are NOT sleeping with your man."

"It is a bit complicated." Blushing, Zara lowers her gaze and tries to find the right words to explain the situation.

"Are you waiting until marriage? That is not all that complicated. But why live together if you don't sleep together?" Liliana asks, inquiring gently.

"I love him very much. I want to spend every minute with him. I believe he feels the same about me. But there is an additional element that makes it feel 'more' right living closer." Walking over and sitting next to Ella on the bed, Zara looks at her hands that are crossed on her lap.

"Garrett and I were raised within a community where there are Dominants and submissives. Some people are familiar with that lifestyle. Well, our story is different than most. If you are interested, I'll share it with you."

Liliana and Ella sit speechless. They nod and stare at Zara when she looks up at them. Taking a deep breath and squaring her shoulders, Zara slowly tells the story of her eighteenth birthday and the Circle Ceremony. She explains the circumstances of how she came to be at MSU and in their dorm.

"Are you sorry that you didn't finish the ceremony?" Ella asks.

Zara thinks for a moment. The question is fair. In fact, she should have been prepared for it. "No, I'm not sorry. I would not have been able to get to know Garrett and discover how he really feels about me or what he wants in a relationship. I would not have met either of you. And I would not have been able to live on my own and have these experiences."

Smiling to herself, Zara is more sure of her life choices now than she has even been.

"Why the eighteenth birthday? And what about the boys? Isn't Garrett way older than eighteen?" Liliana chimes in with more questions.

"Keep in mind, the Community focuses on the Circle Ceremony as the joining of a chosen Dom to a submissive. To outsiders, it is a wedding. The age of the 'submissive' bride is the legal marrying age in the country. As for the men, the sons of King Council members select a submissive from the eligible submissives around the country. He then takes his place on the Council."

"What does the Council do?"

"That is a bigger question. The Council is the governing body for the Community. Outsiders know of the 'lifestyle' and BDSM. Some practice it in their bedrooms. There is a population that lives it – every day – in their bedrooms, at work, in the shopping malls and parks. All day... every day.

"Of course, this population interacts with outsiders, however, the interaction is kept at arm's length. All meaningful connections and bonds are made with individuals within the Community. There are no restrictions placed on whom one may speak to but the members tend to be very tight-knit.

"For example, I am the daughter of a King Councilman. I was homeschooled and the children I was allowed to interact with were very closely monitored. Regulated."

"Music!" Ella says with assertion.

"Yes, music. The entertainment I was exposed to was very limited. Coming to State was overwhelming. One of the things that made it so was that I was exposed to so many new things all at once. Music was, of course, one of them."

"Fuck... Zara. I had no idea," Ella reaches out to give Zara a hug. Liliana crawls across the bed and hugs the both of them.

"I have missed you both," Zara whispers as they break apart.

"No you haven't! Look at this place." Ella waves her arms in a

Vanna White motion.

"I still miss walking across the hall and having you guys coming in my room late at night. Just talking about nothing. It was amazing. I will miss it."

"You can always visit or better... we can visit you."

"El, I am going to hold you to that one."

"Zara, can I ask you something personal?" Liliana questions.

"Sure, Liliana."

"Are you nervous what will happen after you are collared? What he will do to you?"

"I will tell you... that is a really big fear for a submissive as we prepare for our walk to the Circle. I was raised by parents who had a high protocol Master/slave relationship."

Zara looks at the blank expressions in both girls' eyes and knows she needs to speak in outsider language for them to understand.

"My parents followed the guidelines set for being a Master and a Slave. Once I was old enough to care for my brother, there was never a time when my mother was out of the role of 'slave' if my father was present. There was a complete exchange of power between the two of them and, in his presence, her primary focus was to serve him.

"That was what I had been preparing for as I walked toward the Circle. Garrett was raised very differently. His parents have a very relaxed Dominant/submissive relationship – a completely different perspective than what I am used to.

"So to really answer your question, I am not nervous about what he will do to me once I am collared. I have had the opportunity to get to know the man that he really is and I trust him completely. Our relationship is unique in that we have been able to fall in love over time and build trust. It will make the next step a lot more exciting than it would have been originally."

"Will you wait for your rescheduled Circle Ceremony to be collared?" Ella asks excitedly.

There is a knock on the door and Garrett opens it.

"Ladies, how is it going in here?" he asks everyone, but his eyes are on only one girl. Zara gives him a smile to reassure him that she is holding her own. He returns the smile and closes the door.

"Is anyone getting hungry? Something tells me Garrett is ready to eat." Zara begins to get off the bed. Both girls follow, but Ella pauses and blocks the door.

"Zara, first answer the question."

"Collaring is a very personal and private event. I have never understood the Circle Ceremony. If it were up to me, the only two people in attendance would be my Sir and me."

Garrett asks Viv to oversee Zara's relocation. As they are tearing down decorations and moving the furniture, Zara asks if Beth could move into the room for the rest of the semester since it was already paid for. With a quick kiss on the forehead, Garrett instructs Viv to leave the room livable for the girl.

Each day Zara returns home from school, a little something has been done to make it more their home than Garrett's house. Zara's biggest surprise comes one week into the new living arrangement. Garrett suggests that they go to his office to study and work. It is the first time they would be going to his office to work.

Zara has two huge exams coming up, so wherever they were going to work she just wanted to get there and get started. The best part about Garrett's office is that it is located on the floor below Branden's loft, so she can chat with Viv during her breaks. Once they arrive, Garrett grabs Zara's backpack and his briefcase and guides her into the elevator. Lights come on as they step out of the elevator and make their way to Garrett's office.

Setting her books and laptop on a small conference room table, Zara looks around at Garrett's office. She remembered the surprise she felt the first time she walked in and saw pictures of herself. Framed pictures of her sat on his desk and on the bookcase. Ella had taken photos at several different times throughout the school year and Garrett had arranged to purchase pictures of Zara the very first time he met Ella at the MSU football game.

Shaking her head, Zara opens her laptop.

"Are you still thinking about me buying the pictures? You need to get over it. I will always find ways to obtain photos of you. I think you are the most beautiful woman in the world. Any other questions?"

"No, Garrett." Chuckling to himself, Garrett goes to work and lets Zara try to regain her focus on her schoolwork.

Turning on a classical Spotify channel, the two become engrossed in their work. Several hours later, Zara is the first to look up with a glance at Garrett. "Snacks. I did not think of snacks. I am sorry."

Garrett stands up and walks around his desk. He leans over Zara and kisses her on the forehead, "Be right back."

Zara returns to studying.

A moment later, Branden comes in and takes a seat at the table across from Zara. Saying nothing, he just stares at her.

"Hello, Branden. How are you?"

"I am well, Z. How are you?"

Zara closes her laptop.

"Fantastic. What is new with you?"

"I came in to see what you are planning for our boy's birthday. And to invite you to Viv's singing debut. Guarantee she has not mentioned it yet… little shithead."

"What? Singing? Viv?!"

"Exactly! Yes, my lovely amazingly talented designer of a sister also sings. Well, she sings secretly. I am outing her to everyone. She is performing at this exclusive function at the Henry Center next month. Black tie event. Unfortunately, it's the same day as G's birthday."

"No surprise party, man. Zara, NO PARTY!" Garrett proclaims as he strolls in and places his hands on Zara's shoulders.

"WOW… G, no one is even thinking about a party for you. Viv is performing for some black tie event the night of your birthday. I need you to come. She needs you to come. She needs you to come without you telling her that you know about it prior to the event."

"I didn't know she was performing again. When did she start? Is she dating again too?" Garrett asks, taking a seat at the table.

"She is not dating yet. Thanks… until now I had not thought about the possibility of her dating again." Branden says.

"Of course we will be there. How are you planning on getting us into the event?" Zara asks.

"Security," Garrett and Branden say at the same time. They break out in a fit of laughter as Beth walks through the door carrying two large bags of food.

Zara looks at Garrett and smiles before hopping out of her chair.

"Beth, I had no idea you were working here now," Zara says

excitedly. She gives Beth a hug and crushes the bags between their bodies. "When did you start? How do you like it? I've missed you."

Releasing her, Beth sets everything down on the table. "I've been here for almost a month. I still have a lot to learn, but it's cool. Thanks. You know… for everything," Beth says quietly.

While Garrett grabs Zara's laptop and moves it to his desk, Branden reads the tag on one of the bags and picks up the other. "Back to work, Ladies, you can catch up later. We still have a lot of work to do."

"Congratulations on the new job, Beth."

"Thanks, Zara. Let's meet for coffee soon."

Garrett empties the contents of the remaining bag out onto the table. Placing a chicken salad sandwich in front of Zara, she smiles up at him.

"Thank you," Zara says softly and he gives her a quick wink.

What the heck… Viv is a singer? Viv always seems like such an open book. Wonder why she never told me?

Zara has been open about her past and the Community. A plan is beginning to form in Zara's mind… Project Viv. Having only a few friends, it is important to Zara that she knows them and that they feel safe with her. Remembering she has only just told the girls about her past this week smarts a bit. Work needs to be done on both sides of her friendships.

"Earth to Zara." Garrett's hand is waving in front of her face.

"Sorry… So sorry. Yes?"

"It's okay. Where did you go, Little One?"

"Thinking about Viv. I guess I know her a lot less than I thought that I did."

"Z, no worries. That's Viv. That's how she operates. It's her shield," Branden explains softly as he stands and puts all the trash into bags. "You'll be around awhile. You'll get in. Just give her time. She is worth it."

Branden picked up the bags of trash and walks out.

Garrett looks at his phone. "Let's go home."

Standing up, he practically throws Zara her laptop. She can tell something is going on, so she moves quickly to pack her bag. When she is done, Garrett is already at the door waiting impatiently for her.

Garrett speeds all the way home. Sitting next to him in silence,

Zara grows more and more concerned. This is a side of Garrett she has not seen and it makes her uneasy.

The very second the tires come to a stop, Garrett is out the door and around the car to open Zara's door. Moving as quickly as possible, she jumps out of the car and hurries into the house behind him.

Zara turns to go to her bedroom. After two steps in that direction, Garrett stops her.

"Hey. Where are you going? You have studying to do."

"I thought I would study in my room."

"You never study in your room. No. Come study in the den with me. Please. Come into the den."

"Okay... okay." Zara slowly turns around. Looking at Garrett, she sees something in his face that she cannot pinpoint. He leads the way to the den.

Entering the den, Zara walks toward the sofa and places her backpack on the coffee table. She turns and looks at Garrett standing there with a goofy smile. Zara starts to giggle; that is when she sees it.

She covers her mouth with both hands, as she slowly walks toward a new desk. Somehow, in the amount of time that Garrett had taken her to his office to study, someone had come in and built connecting desks facing each other. A desktop computer with a large monitor and neatly arranged pink office supplies accent the new space, while the other desk holds Garrett's stack of files.

Walking around the new desk that had been set up for her, Zara finds a small black frame with a picture of the two of them at Christmas. Opposite her frame sits another black frame on Garrett's desk.

Bouncing out from behind her desk, Zara runs into Garrett's arms and hugs him as hard as she can.

"This is why I was in such a hurry to get home. I was excited for you to see your new study space. I'm sorry I scared you."

"I love it. Everything about it is perfect. Everything. Thank you for making me feel like I fit so perfectly here."

"You do fit perfectly."

"It's home."

CHAPTER 33

"I will be fine."

Garrett walks over to the bed and takes Zara's face in both of his hands. "How about, I don't want to leave you. How about, I'm not thrilled to be away from your beautiful face." Kissing her square on the lips, Garrett releases her to return to his packing.

"I mean... I am not jumping for joy that you are going away, either. But you did say that this was a necessary trip for an important client."

"Mhm, but I would feel better if you stayed at the loft with Viv."

"Garrett, this is my home now. Why do you want me to go to the loft?"

"Little One, of course this is your home. It will always be your home. I would like for you to be at the loft for a couple of reasons. First, Viv will be alone as well and Branden is not excited about her staying by herself while he is out of town either.

"Second, the loft has state of the art security. I want to know you are safe. As an added bonus, there is that super big bathtub that you absolutely love."

"I would be happy to stay at the loft if Viv would not mind having me as a guest. Can I use Branden's sports car to get back and forth to school?" Zara asks slyly.

Pushing her down on the bed, Garrett laughs and shakes his head. "Nope and now I am going to tell him to hide the keys. You can use my car now that you have your license to get back and forth to school."

"Thank you. Not as much fun, but very much appreciated."

"I'm going to miss you like—"

The doorbell chimes.

Garrett pouts. He is off Zara and at the door of the bedroom in a flash. "Stay in here until I come back. Understood? I am getting rid of whoever it is. I am spending the last hours before I leave alone with you."

Smiling, Zara sits silent on the bed.

"Understood?" Garrett repeats in a much more forceful tone.

"Yes."

With that, he is off to see who is at the door. In all the time that Zara has been living at the house, no one had ever rang the doorbell. In fact, there had never been surprise company. The entrance is hidden from the main road, so if someone did not know what they were looking for, they would not find the driveway.

Garrett appears in the bedroom door with a perplexed face. He holds out his hand for Zara to join him and leads her to the living room. Standing in the center of the room is her brother, Fredrik.

Zara looks at Garrett and he gives her hand a quick squeeze. Tears fill her eyes as she walks closer to her brother. He takes the last two steps to meet her, opening his arms. She hugs him so tightly he makes coughing noises.

"Little One, don't break him. He's only just arrived." Zara releases her grip on her only brother, the brother she thought she would never see again.

"Are you hungry? I can make you something to eat. You look so thin."

"I can eat. Garrett, I am sorry that I came without any notice. I hope that you will allow me to stay for a few days in spite of my poor manners," Fredrik implores.

Zara turns to look at Garrett and await his response. "Actually, Fredrik, I will be leaving on a business trip this afternoon."

Fredrik looks dejected until Garrett adds, "I'm afraid you will have to stay with Zara at the loft."

"Fredrik… how about a shower and change of clothes and then lunch?" Zara's smile grows as she watches her brother's face light up. After showing him to the guest room and giving him a few more hugs, Zara goes to find Garrett in his room where he is finishing his packing.

"Thank you for allowing him to stay."

"Zara Faith, I am not your Dom. Yes, I am your protector and I am in love with you. I know how much your brother showing up here means to you. Of course I want him to stay. Actually, the thought of him here while I am away gives me an additional level of comfort.

"I do have a few questions for him though." Closing the suitcase and lifting it off the bed, Garrett walks to the door. "The thought of your father coming here looking for him and me being away does not make me very happy. There is still a conversation that needs to happen."

Sliding her arms around Garrett's neck, Zara presses her body against his and hears the suitcase leave his grasp and thump on the ground. His hands snake around her body and she tells him, "I am going to miss you madly. Please be safe and hurry home to me."

"You have your credit card and bank card, right?" Zara nods. "If Fredrik needs anything, get it for him. He only has one small bag with him. If you are too busy with school, ask Viv to take him. In fact, I will let Viv know that she should take him, so he won't feel uncomfortable having his sister do it."

"Garrett, you have clients to take care of, you do not have time to worry about me and Fredrik."

"Little One, you will always be my focus, my priority and my greatest pleasure. This is what I do, so please let me do it."

"Thank you. I love you. You are my focus, my priority and greatest pleasure as well."

"I know." Chuckling, Garrett walks to Zara and lifts her up onto the island. He positions himself between her legs and pulls her as close to him as possible. "We should take Fredrik out to eat instead. No clean-up and I can get you both squared away at the loft before I take off."

"If that would make you happy, then it is fine with me. The fact that my brother is here and I will be spending even a couple of days with him makes me so happy. Garrett, I wish your trip could be rescheduled. I would have liked for the two of you to spend time together as well."

"Little One, we don't know the circumstances of this visit. This may be the first of many visits. Your brother will always be welcome in our home. In time, I will get to know him. But I am sorry that I will not be around for this first visit. I need for you to stay in contact with me. If your father shows up, you are to call me immediately."

"I understand and I will be careful. I am still going to miss you terribly."

As Zara lowers her lips to Garrett's, she hears the sound of Fredrik walking toward them. Changing what was going to be a very passionate kiss into a quick peck, Zara looks into Garrett's eyes and smiles. Garrett helps her off the counter.

"I can come back if you need more time," Fredrik says softly.

Garrett turns to him and smiles. "I will always need more time with your beautiful sister. If we require privacy, we will go to the bedroom. Other than that, you will have to get used to me holding her because I cannot keep my hands off her for very long."

Garrett leans down for another quick peck on the lips, and then releases her. He makes his way over to Fredrik. "We were just discussing going out for lunch. How does that sound? I would prefer to have you both settled at the loft before I leave town."

"Sure. I am good with whatever." Zara walks around the island and approaches her brother. He has grown taller in the months since the funeral. With wet hair and a change of clothes, Fredrik seems more relaxed but it still bothers Zara how thin he appears.

"I need a few minutes to throw some things in a bag. Fredrik, there are granola bars. Help yourself." Zara opens the pantry door and points a shelf loaded with snack foods.

Within the hour, the three are sitting in a restaurant placing their lunch orders. Garrett jokes with Fredrik telling him to order two entrees if he wants and to the surprise of his sister, he does. Once the waitress is away from the table, Garrett begins to ask the questions Zara has been thinking since laying eyes on her younger brother.

"Okay, Fredrik. Explain how you got to Michigan and found the house. That information is not easy to come by, so let's have it."

Eyes diverted downward, Fredrik begins to tell the story of how he walked out of their family home after months of neglect. "Once mother died, he just snapped. He didn't buy groceries and when I asked him for money for food... he would hit me."

The soft tone her brother uses intensifies the pain Zara is feeling.

"Finally, I asked him if I could spend time with some friends." Tears well up in his eyes as he struggles to get the rest of the story out. "He looked at me and said that he really did not care what I did; that all of his children were a disappointment to him."

Garrett had moved his chair closer to Zara's and wrapped his arm around her early into Fredrik's story. He hands her his handkerchief to wipe the tears away as they fall. "I am so sorry I suggested a restaurant, Little One. I would have never, had I known," he whispers to her as she turns into him for comfort.

"Fredrik, I am so sorry that this has happened to you over the last several months. Had either of us known, we would have insisted on you coming with us after the funeral," Garrett says evenly.

"He would have never allowed me to leave with Zara. He sees red when it comes to her. The fact that she showed up to the funeral at all was a slap in the face in his eyes. He trashed your room once we got home that day. On the same day that we buried mother, he destroyed everything in your room."

Reaching her hand across the table, Zara takes Fredrik's hand in hers. "Michigan is my home. The Dawsons are my family. We will do everything we can to make that happen for you too. I am going to do everything I can do to keep you safe and away from him."

She releases his hand as the waitress appears with the food.

"The sad part is, I am not even sure he is aware he is doing it. He is so lost without her. Mother was his everything."

Zara's hand slams on the table, making the plates clank and startling both men. "Then he should have treated her better."

Garrett places his hand on top of Zara's and slowly her tension eases. The three try to salvage the rest of the meal before Garrett's trip by transitioning into lighter conversation about Michigan and Zara's school life.

"Okay. This sucks."

Garrett holds Zara in his arms outside the loft while he waits for the car service to arrive. Zara can tell he feels guilty for having to leave after everything that had just come to light. Holding him tightly, she tries to reassure him she and Fredrik would be fine and that he should concentrate on work.

"I am sorry he just popped in," Zara whispers into his chest.

"Little One, we are in this together for the long haul. I am very glad that he showed up today and not tomorrow when no one would have been at the house to greet him. I am sorry that I cannot move this trip around. I have worked every angle and I am needed on-site."

"I love you so much. Thank you for giving me this last year of experiences."

"Hey... One week. I will be gone for one week. Then we will work on a solution for getting Fredrik here permanently. You will be in this spot in five days to greet me. Preferably alone so we can have a few moments of make out time. Understood?"

"Understood."

"I love you completely, Zara Faith Evans."

"And I love you completely, John Garrett Dawson."

Garrett gets in the car and Zara watches it pull off and disappear with the man she loves in the backseat. Wrapping her arms around her body, she takes a few deep breaths to get her mind under control.

She smiles and looks up at the sky.

I have not needed any of the techniques in quite a while. Ironic that the first time I hear about Father, I am pulling them out again. I miss you, Mother. I am so sorry that I let this happen to Fredrik. I am stronger now. I will fight for him.

"You have changed."

Spinning around, Zara is staring into the eyes of the only family she has left, the family she will hold onto with everything she has.

"I saw the change when you came to the funeral, but there has been even more of a change since then."

"Time and distance from that house and the Community has allowed me to grow." Zara looks at the ground and kicks some gravel around with her foot. "It is the small pebbles that create the biggest changes."

Looking down and smiling, Fredrik asks, "Do you love him? Garrett?"

"Yes. I am deeply in love with him." Zara's smile could not be suppressed. "Do you want to go back inside?"

"In a minute. Are you sorry that you did not finish your Circle Ceremony?"

Zara looks at Fredrik. "No, Fredrik, I am not. I am sorry if that seems selfish. I would not be the me that I am today had I accepted his collar that day. Garrett gave me a precious gift – the opportunity to find me before giving myself to him."

"It does not sound selfish. I am glad you chose him. Mother would have been very happy as well."

Zara stands stunned. Opening and closing her mouth, she has no luck pushing out any of the words swirling around in her mind. Grabbing the pendant that hangs around her neck, Zara closes her eyes to settle her racing thoughts.

"Zara... maybe we should go inside for this part of the conversation." Shaking her head, Zara slides down and sits on the ground. Fredrik removes a letter from his back pocket and takes a seat beside her.

"Mother knew about the letter to Michigan State University. She knew about Garrett's plan to bring you to Michigan. Did you ever wonder how the school had the documents it needed for your application? The documentation for the identification; bank account... Zar... all of that takes time to process. Mother even packed your clothes for me to sneak out to be loaded into his car."

Zara burst into tears. It is too much. First, the brother that she loved had been neglected at the hands of her father – the man that had made her childhood a living hell for all three of them. Now she finds out her Mother had risked everything to help her gain her freedom and escape the life she was forced into. Zara remembers the last time she had looked into her mother's eyes. Her mother had been trying to convey something. Zara did not understand at the time, but she had known there was something.

"Zar, I found this." With shaking hands, Fredrik slowly gives his sister an envelope with her name on it, written in her mother's handwriting.

Zara gasps.

Fredrik stands and walks into the building giving Zara space to read her letter in private.

Zara Faith,

I loved you from the moment I found out I was pregnant. You were the most beautiful baby girl I ever laid eyes on and I would spend hours staring at you. I memorized every single inch of your face. The way your eyes sparkled when you smiled, the length of your dark lashes when they would catch your crocodile tears, the way your lips would pucker when you were angry. You were mine. You were the one thing in the entire world that was truly mine and my love for you grew with every passing day.

But I also knew that I would have to give you up. I knew I had to prepare you for the day that you walked into the Circle to give yourself to another. Not knowing what kind of Dom you would submit to, I had to make it as easy for you as I possibly could.

It took incredible courage to accept Garrett's offer with your father, the Community and me watching. You have always had such strength resonating through you, so I knew that whatever decision you made in the Circle, it would be the correct one for you.

Zara Faith, I have always been proud of you, my most beautiful achievement. It has been my honor and joy to be your mother. I love you more than words can say.

Mother

Drawing her knees up to her chest, Zara sits sobbing on the ground outside of the warehouse. She realizes for the first time in almost a year that her mother had loved her so much that she gave her the greatest gift she had to give... freedom.

All of a sudden, Zara feels the strong arms of the man who always comes to her rescue wrap around her and pick her up. He carries her into the building and onto the waiting elevator. Stepping off in what Zara assumes is the loft, Garrett carries her up a flight of stairs and into his room.

Face buried in his chest, Zara begins sobbing even harder. Her safe haven has returned and she is not going to question why he is there. Garrett caresses Zara's back, allowing her to feel all the emotions going through her heart. "She knew."

"Shhhhh... I've got you, Little One." The tears cascade down her cheek again.

Looking into Garrett's eyes, Zara cannot help but smile. "You came back for me."

Garrett kisses her eyelids and then her lips. "I guess I did."

"How did you know?"

"Viv!" they say in unison.

"She came down and found you and Fredrik and texted me."

"What about your clients?"

"Okay… what did I say earlier? My focus. My priority. My greatest pleasure. Let me worry about the clients after I make sure you are taken care of to the absolute best of my ability. Today, you need your man. And I am the lucky guy who gets that lifetime role."

"Lifetime… huh?"

CHAPTER 34

During an early dinner, Viv insists Fredrik needs an evening full of classic movies that only she can expose him to. As Garrett leads Zara up to his room, Fredrik is heard laughing hysterically at the first movie Viv selects.

Zara knows that Garrett has asked Viv to entertain her brother so he can take care of her and she appreciates the time alone. Once in the room, Zara climbs into the bed fully clothed and slides her hands under the pillow. Garrett moves in behind her and presses his body as close to her as he can.

"I miss her. I never say that out loud. When I first arrived at MSU, I tried so hard not to think about her – not to think of any of them really. It hurt too much." Turning over to face Garrett, Zara caresses his face. Watching him close his eyes and lean into her touch pulls on her heart.

"Did you know she was the one that provided you the documents and clothes? Everything."

Opening his eyes slowly and focusing on Zara's eye, Garrett nods. "I suspected. I went to my parents with my plan. I explained my reasons and that I was willing to risk you choosing someone else. I wanted the choice to be yours. When I placed a collar around your neck, I wanted it to be because you wanted to be there and nowhere else. My parents are 'we will handle it' kind of people–"

"So, you come by it honestly," Zara interrupts and places a light kiss on the lips of the man that had done so much for her.

"Touché. Anyway, the ball began to roll and documents were acquired. As the Circle Ceremony approached, my father asked me only one time if I was positive that this was what I wanted. I was given your acceptance letter the day before I flew down to meet you.

"Once your clothes showed up at the ceremonial hall, I knew it had to be your mother. I never said anything to either of my parents. I felt I could not tell you if I was to keep the confidence of my parents as well as your mother."

"You did the right thing. Thank you for telling me now. Will you be able to stay tonight?"

"Little One, nothing could tear me away from you tonight. I am so sorry I was not here when Fredrik told you. Had I known... I am really sorry."

"Stop. You are with me now. Hold me." Zara turns over and Garrett spoons her as her tears silently fall onto the pillow. Zara drifts off to sleep knowing that Garrett will still be holding her when she wakes up in the morning.

Early the next morning, Zara says goodbye to Garrett for the second time. Reassuring him repeatedly that both she and Fredrik will be fine and that Viv will make sure they are well taken care of, Garrett disappears out the door.

Wide awake and refusing to miss Garrett within the first minutes of his trip, Zara invades Branden's chef kitchen and makes a breakfast that would have fed an army. Delighted to be able to wake her brother for the first time in months, Zara takes a large glass of orange juice to the room he is staying in.

After a couple of knocks with no answer, Zara enters the room to find her baby brother wrapped up in his covers the way she would find him when they were younger. Standing at the door, Zara watches him sleep for a few minutes.

"It is so creepy that my sister is watching me sleep."

Laughing, Zara walks to the nightstand and gently puts the glass down. "I made a huge breakfast. Please tell me you are hungry."

"I can eat."

"Well hurry up then." Zara turns to leave the room.

"Zar." She stops and turns to face him.

"Father said I was a disappointment to him because he found out something about me." Zara slowly walks back to the bed and sits on the edge, saddened by the slump of his shoulders. She places her hands in her lap and waits.

"Zar... I will never be a King Council member." He lowers his eyes. Although this would be difficult for her brother to tell, she had suspected since they were very small and believed she knew what was coming.

"Fredrik, you could never be a disappointment to anyone. Whatever you have to tell me, know that you are a wonderful person and I love you very much."

"I am submissive."

"What?" Zara asks, startled.

"I am submissive. What did you think I was going to tell you?"

"I… Well, I thought you were going to tell me you were gay."

"No, I am not attracted to men. I am attracted to Dommes."

"Oh, Fredrik, I am so sorry. I mean… I'm not sorry that you are submissive." Zara reaches to embrace her brother. She feels him shaking in her arms, and squeezes him tighter. Pulling away, she sees he is laughing.

"What's so funny?" she demands.

"You. You are beginning to speak like the outsiders. Are you going to bring out a southern accent next?"

"Jokes. You have jokes. I have cooked a breakfast of champions with all your favorites and you have jokes." To hide her grin, Zara stomps toward the door. Turning around, she leans against the open door with a serious expression. "Fredrik, I accept you, whatever you are, and I think you are amazing. I am so happy that you are here."

"Me too. Choosing not to complete the Circle took a lot of guts. You are the strongest woman I have ever known. Your courage helped me make my decision to leave. I am glad that you and Garrett worked out. He seems nice."

Reaching for the pendant at the mention of his name, Zara smiles. "Hurry up. I want to eat."

Garrett's trip is hard on Zara and by the end of the week it is clear it had taken its toll on him as well. Always one to be in control, he divides his time between his client meetings and calling and texting Zara. She would smile when her phone would vibrate in her pocket knowing it was him.

With finals just around the corner, Zara's time is consumed by classes and studying. Fredrik is understanding and spends his time watching movies and hanging out with Viv when her schedule allows.

Through it all, Zara misses Garrett. She misses their mornings together. She misses the time they spent at night studying and working together. She misses the crazy 'who can get the best snack of the night' game. Mostly, she misses his kisses.

Garrett is scheduled to arrive late Friday night and Viv suggests that Zara go over to the house and prep it for their return on Saturday. She could bring in the mail, check the food situation, and spruce it up. She could even start one of her delicious meals.

"Viv... I am sure the house is fine. I do not need to go check on it." Zara shrugs off the suggestion.

"Z! Seriously, your man is coming home late tonight and y'all are going home tomorrow. Don't you want to make sure there are fresh sheets on the bed and everything is neat and pretty? Maybe place a 'I missed you' note somewhere?" Viv pushes a little harder. Fredrik does not say a word and keeps his eyes on the TV.

"Are you trying to get rid of me?" she asks in an exasperated huff.

"Well... kind of. You have been a bit of a mopey downer this week. You are either studying or sad because Garrett isn't here. We could sort of use a break from that," Viv declares with a shrug of her shoulders. Fredrik pulls his eyes away from the TV long enough to glance at Zara to nod and agree with Viv.

"Fine. I'll give you both a break." Zara turns to walk toward the elevator and picks up her backpack and Garrett's keys.

"Take all the time you want. We are ordering pizza and watching all six *Star Wars* movies," Viv yells laughing.

"Later, Zar," Fredrik says.

In no time, Zara is out of the warehouse and on the streets of Lansing heading to the house that has become her home. With Halestrom's *I Get Off* screaming through the speakers at her, she sings along to the chorus.

Sitting at a stoplight, she turns her head and locks eyes with a guy in the next lane. He smiles and without realizing it, she responds with a smile of her own. He winks. Immediately her smile falls and she returns her eyes to the front of her car.

As the light changes, she continues on her way, thoughts of how her life has changed dance in her mind. A smile returns and this time it is all for her. Zara is proud of the woman that she is becoming.

The moment the key slides into the lock, Zara knows Viv's suggestion is a good one. Yes, she misses Garrett, but she also misses her home. Closing and locking the door behind her, she leans against the door and closes her eyes.

"Finally. I missed the shit out of you," Garrett says quietly as he walks toward Zara from the kitchen. She stands frozen in disbelief.

"Garrett?"

"Come here," he commands as he stops four feet from where she is leaning against the door.

Without hesitation, she walks to stand directly in front of him. Her eyes cast downward but her smile's too big to be hidden. She crosses her hands in front of her.

"Eyes." Zara looks up and finds Garrett's eyes staring down at her.

"I have missed every single thing about you, Zara Faith."

"I have missed you, too. I cannot believe you are here. I cannot believe they tricked me. I cannot believe I fell for it," she proclaims.

He takes her hands in his and leans in for a kiss. A sigh escapes her as she feels his lips lightly press against hers. Taking her hands from behind her back and stepping against his body, the kiss intensifies.

Garrett parts his lips to take Zara's lower lip gently between his. Pulling her body into his, she feels his tongue caress the lip he is tenderly sucking. Slowly his tongue moves past her lips to her tongue. Searching and dancing, they rejoice in being reunited after being apart for so long. He frees her hands and grabs her ass, pulling her tighter to him where the evidence of his excitement increases her passion.

Pulling apart, panting, looking in one another's eyes, Zara is the first to break the moment of silence, "How can it be even better than I remember?"

Laughing, Garrett scoops her up and carries her toward the bedroom. Leaning against his chest, she feels his heart vibrating.

"Not really the reaction I was expecting," she whispers under her breath, making him laugh harder.

Surprise and disappointment flash through Zara as Garrett turns into the den instead of continuing to his bedroom. While the feelings should not surprise her anymore, being intimate with him has begun to consume all of her waking thoughts.

Settling onto the sofa, he positions her on his lap so they can easily talk and he can remain holding her in his arms. He tilts his head, lifts her pendants off her chest and examines them.

"Ever wonder why I gave you these particular pendants?" He bounces his eyes back to Zara's waiting eyes.

Shaking her head no, she stares into his eyes.

"If you had to guess, what would you think the reason would be?" Garrett asks softly as he places the pendants back on her chest.

"It was your way of reminding me to explore and find out who I am while also reminding me that you are there every step of the way," she murmurs lowering her eyes to her pendant.

From the time they were placed around her neck, she had thought of them as a single pendant. It had never occurred to her that, in fact, there were two separate ones on the chain. Even as they lay together against her shirt, she had thought of them as one.

"That is the selfless reason," Garrett says staring at the pendants. "Honestly, I wanted you to think about me every time you looked at them. I didn't want you to forget I was waiting for you."

Taking his face between her hands, forcing him to look her in the eyes, Zara says, "Every day that we were apart and I was living in the dorm, I thought of you. Your plan worked. This pendant became my connection to you."

"Thank you for telling me that," he replies and mouths 'I love you'

"I love you."

"Change of subject."

"Really?"

"Please, for a few minutes. This is one of the reasons why I wanted to meet you here instead of the loft. I wanted to discuss Fredrik."

Zara releases Garrett's face, lowers her gaze and places her hands on her lap.

"Little One, eyes." She bounces her eyes back up and is met by his serious expression. "I spoke to my parents while I was away."

She nods.

"If it is alright with you, Fredrik will go to stay with them until you are finished with finals. There is a concern that he has not had any schooling since your Mother got sick, so they are going to get a tutor set up to assess where he is for the school year in the Fall. Once you're done, we will all sit down and have a discussion as to what is best for Fredrik. We can decide whether he should stay with us and go to school here or stay with my parents and go to school in Detroit. How does that sound?"

"I do not know what to say. I did not think that would even be a possibility for us. That you would allow him to live here with us." Zara stares for a moment before hugging him so tightly that he starts laughing.

"Little One, there would be a few conditions. He would have to be in school and he would have a few chores around here. There is a chance he will choose to live with my parents. I want you to be prepared for that. We are going to give him the options and Fredrik will have the opportunity to choose his own path. Either way, he will not be returning to your father."

"Thank you. Just saying it does not seem like enough, but it is all I have."

"Little One, you are quite enough."

Later, Zara steps out of the bath as Rihanna blasts through the speakers. Drying off, she could not help but dance to the music. Smiling, she chuckles at the thought of how surprised Garrett would be if he found out that this is one of the songs that she learned to striptease to with Ella.

Fredrik is safe and happy at the beach house with the Dawsons. Finals… done. First year of college… done. Tonight is all about Garrett. Tonight is the night.

The plan for the night is dinner with Garrett, Branden and the girls, then sneaking in to see Viv perform. After that, it would be home for dessert with Garret, alone.

Stepping into her bedroom, Zara does a happy dance spying a beautiful gown hanging on the back of the door. Never one to forget a thing, Garrett has also left a lovely new set of black lace lingerie on her bed.

As she shimmies into the dress, she notices the song changes to another one of the songs used in her striptease class. She finds it odd that Garrett would be listening to this song. INXS is an old band from what she understands, but then he likes tons of old music. She continues dressing and dancing around as the song plays.

The dress he has selected for tonight works well for some of her striptease moves. The dress has a form-fitted lace bodice, short tight skirt and a long see-through tulle overlay that opens in the front, giving the dress an added sexy edge. She lets out a squeal of delight when she finds the shoes and beaded purse for the night.

Checking the mirror one last time, Zara freezes when the next song blares through the house speakers even louder than the other songs. Garrett knows the entire playlist of her routine. Laughing, she looks down at her shoes. Spinning around, she goes to the closet and reaches for the red-soled shoes that should be worn, according to Ella, only 'when you go in for the kill.'

I am definitely going in for the kill.

Taking a deep breath and squaring her shoulders, she picks up her purse and makes her way toward the kitchen. Garrett is not there. She continues into the den but finds he is not there, either. She makes her way to his bedroom. Puzzled at not discovering him in his room, she walks back toward the kitchen.

"You look strikingly beautiful!" Garrett says with a smile as he walks through the front door. As he stalks closer, Zara rakes her eyes over his entire body. "I will assume from that smile on your lovely face that you like what you see."

Wrapping his arms around her waist, he pulls her to him. Instinctively, she slides her hands up the lapel of his suit and around his neck. Standing in the living room of their home, Zara and Garrett stare into each other's smiling eyes.

"Happy Birthday, John Garrett. I love you with all of my heart."

"Still the best birthday present that you can give me. I love you too, Zara Faith."

"We should get going. Poor Branden will not survive the girls for long." Despite her comment, neither of them moves an inch. Zara starts giggling and Garrett releases her.

"Way to kill the moment." He guides a laughing Zara out of the house and locks the door behind them.

Her laughing comes to an abrupt halt once the car starts and *Closer* by Nine Inch Nails begins playing. She shifts in her seat as she clicks the seat belt.

"You know," she accuses.

Smiling, he pulls the car out of the driveway and focuses on the road ahead. The song continues playing.

"I know that you know."

"Zara Faith, what are you referring to, darling?" Zara glares at Garrett. "Careful."

"Sorry," she whispers. Turning in her seat to face the front, she is confident he did not hear her apology. Hands resting in her lap, she lowers her head and listens as the song comes to an end. Halestrom's *Beautiful With You* is the next song and Garrett reaches over, takes Zara's hand and places it on his thigh. He caresses it as he drives and she knows everything is fine.

As much as she loves her friends, the idea of skipping it all to return home and give Garrett his real birthday gift seems worth missing all the evening's plans.

He lifts her hand off his thigh and kisses it. "What are you thinking about?"

"Ella and Liliana," she switches up. "I am going to miss them this summer. School will be strange without them on campus. Thank you for including them tonight."

Garrett nods. Kissing her hand one more time and returning it to his thigh, he suggests "We can fly down for a long weekend in July. Steele Security is in Miami and Branden has been trying to get me down there to meet those guys for a while. We can make it work."

Pulling into a parking spot, he turns off the car and pauses. "Zara, would it be horrible if we just turn the car around and go home? We can come up with an excuse later. I would really rather spend tonight alone at home with you and that dress. Well... and a striptease."

Slapping her hands over her face, Zara does not say anything, feeling a deep blush quickly spread up her neck and over her face. Garrett explodes into laughter and gently removes her hands from her face. "Please do not mess up that stunning makeup job."

"How... how did you find out?"

"First, hopefully, I would have found out soon anyway.

Second, you should not be upset. I would have never thought it possible to be more attracted to you. I was indeed wrong… because I am. Third, guess what I really, really want for my birthday."

"I already have your birthday present and that's not it," she taunts. She reaches for the door handle and steps out before he can rush around to assist.

CHAPTER 35

"She is amazing! Garrett, I had no idea." Zara slips into the passenger seat. Closing Garrett's suit jacket around her, she inhales. As he gets in the car, she realizes how late it is. His present is waiting for him at the house and his birthday is almost over.

Zara begins to reflect on the evening. Dinner with his best friend and hers... all outsiders. She never would have predicted she would have two friends who were outsiders and who would love her so fiercely. They had shuffled her into the bathroom upon her arrival to whip her hair into an up-do because 'the dress requires it' according to Ella.

And then there is Vivian... Viv, an outsider by her own definition to everyone. Seeing her standing on the stage in that red form-fitting dress tonight with the spotlight only on her as she sang had been amazing. Zara's eyes filled with tears again thinking how Viv sang *Beautiful With You*. Imagining where the emotions were coming from as she sang hit her deeply.

Viv has become more than a friend. Zara has come to think of her as a sister. The week she and Fredrik had stayed with Viv, their relationship had grown stronger. Zara knows she and Viv still have walls to break through, but in time they will get there. She knew, even before Branden said it, that it would be worth getting inside.

"Is everything okay? You're quiet," Garrett says once they arrive back at home. Zara removes his suit jacket and hands it back to him.

"Yes. Everything is perfect." She turns, walking toward her bedroom.

Deep breath, shoulders back, and a blank expression on her face gives her a muted sense of control. A single thought of her mother penetrated her mental walls. More than once, her mother had explained that the only true control was that of one's own mind. At the time, the words did not make sense. In the last few days they seemed hollow.

The reality is that Zara had never had control. From the first moment their eyes locked in the center of the Circle, Zara felt her control slip into his possession. Not collaring her had only removed the external proof of Garrett's ownership. When he knelt in front of her and offered her an opportunity to follow her dream, Zara had mentally submitted to her Dom. Now she is ready to complete the Circle.

Zara removes the collar from her tiny beaded bag and returns to the living room. She stands in the middle of the large open space. The soft, sweet voice of Phildel singing *Beside You* floats through the speakers. Zara smiles at the music Garrett has selected, as if he knows what is about to happen.

Garrett walks into the living room. He stops and looks at Zara in the gown that he had chosen for her to wear for the night. The slight tilt of his head and the expression on his face tells her that he is attempting to read her current state.

He moves closer to her and stares into her eyes as if searching for the answer to an unasked question. With every fiber in her body, she knows this is what she wants. This is what she needs.

Slowly, her eyes find their rightful place on the floor in front of her. Without a word, she gracefully lowers into the kneeling position to present herself to him. Extending her right hand in front of her with the palm up, she raises it above her head and opens her hand.

The collar that had been laying on the table clasped with no key at their Circle Ceremony now lies open in her hand. With only the two of them to experience this cherished moment, Garrett takes the collar from Zara's hand. He places his hand under her chin and lifts it until her eyes lock onto his. He raises the collar to his lips and kisses it.

Zara smiles. With tears in her eyes, she speaks softly but clearly, "Tonight, I freely and happily wish to grant you my submission. You have allowed me to experience my dream and all the while protecting, respecting and loving me. In my journey to figure out who I am and what I want... I discovered that before anything else, I want to be yours. I am ready to begin my next chapter."

Lowering her eyes to her lap, Zara waits. She does not have to wait long.

"Zara Faith, I loved you before I really knew you. Once I was given the honor of getting to know you, I fell even deeper in love with you. Although your time of self-discovery was difficult at times, I would do it all over again to be able to witness your inner bright light glow even stronger."

Garrett kneels in front of Zara and stares deeply into her eyes. She hopes he could detect the overwhelming love she has for him. The broad smile that slowly takes over his face makes her think he is able to see it. Garrett places the collar around Zara's neck and closes the clasp.

"Thank you, Sir."

SAUSAGE EGG BAKE
From the Kitchen of Sandy B

Preheat oven: 350 degrees

8 Eggs
1-½ Cups of Milk
Ground Sausage (cooked and crumbled)
2 Cups of your favorite Cheese
1 Bag of Seasoned Croutons
1 Small Can of Chopped Green Chiles
1 Can of Cream of Mushroom Soup
1 Teaspoon of Dry Mustard
Salt and Pepper

Spray a 9x13 casserole dish with cooking spray. Distribute the bag of croutons over the bottom of the casserole dish. Layer the cooked and crumbled sausage on top of croutons. Next, layer the green chilies over the sausage followed by shredded cheese. Mix together the eggs, milk, soup, and dry mustard seasoning. Pour the egg mixture over the casserole. Sprinkle lightly with salt and pepper. Refrigerate overnight and bake uncovered for 50-55 minutes in the oven at 350 degrees.

Acknowledgments

The writing of *Before Him Comes Me* has been a journey. Along the way I have been helped by many individuals. Some have lifted me up when I questioned my ability to finish the book. Some have pulled me away from my laptop after countless hours without a break to make me take a deep breath. Still others answered question after question about the writing, editing, pre- and post-production, marketing, and much more without ever making me feel like I was pestering or bothering them. To all of them, thank you for helping me change my life and find my passion.

I am who I am because of my parents. From my mother, I learned that a woman's place is anywhere she chooses. Work hard, have a vision and stay committed. My Dad gave me my love of sports, and taught me to be dependable and always care for others. They have supported everything I have ever wanted to do. When I told them I was writing a book, their support was tremendous.

If I had a dinner party and could invite ten people, two of them would be my brothers. Although, they both have very busy lives, there have been many occasions during the writing of this book when they have dropped everything to assist me. My sister-in-law and wickedly adorable niece were able to brighten my days during the darkness of editing. Thank you.

My friends are the family I was fortunate to find and collect around me. I am thankful for all the laughter, phone calls, dirty jokes and celebrity gossip. You all helped to keep me a little bit sane during this journey... Troy, Charlee, Katrina, Dana, Cat, Jenn, Rachel, Jason, Leigh, Sadie, Erika, Lori, Casey, Hannah, Annette, Colleen, Kate, Bryan, Melanie, Cassandra, Liz, Nicole, and Jessica.

Special thanks to Helena J., a Resident Advisor in Yakeley Hall at Michigan State University, for your time and tour of the Hall.

Special thanks to Modernjake for designing the perfect cover for *Before Him Comes Me*. I have been blown away by every graphic you have designed along the way. Thank you for all your help.

With so many books published every day, authors struggle to get their name out far and wide. I have been lucky enough to have a small group that work tirelessly to pimp me out all over Facebook. Known as Sure's Showgirls, I call them friends. Thank you.

As a reader, I heard that the author community had cliques and was competitive. Fortunately, I have discovered the opposite of that to be true. From the moment that I mentioned I wanted to write, I found every author, blogger and personal assistant to be supportive, encouraging and helpful. From the beginning, Rachel Rae, A.D. Justice, Anie Michaels, Ella Dominguez and Melanie Harlow encouraged me to write my story.

When I typed 'THE END' in March of 2014, I had tears and I called my very dear friend Kasidy Blake to celebrate this milestone. After a few moments of woohoos, she said, "Now the real work begins." At the time, I had no idea what she meant. Well, eight months later, I get it. The individuals that got me through the darkest period, also known as 'editing,' are Kasidy Blake, Al Daltrey, Elias Raven, Kate Benson, JL Sins (umbrella), and Noelle Bodhaine.

Thank you to the grammar queens, Ali Reynolds and Angie Wieber, for the commas, tenses and all the other issues you caught. So many track changes!!

This book would have been a rambling 109 thousand words without Richelle McFate. She had no idea that agreeing to read a single section of my book would lead to editing and so much more. Working with Richelle was an amazing experience and I am looking forward to tackling the next book with her as my editor.

Before Him Comes Me began with a conversation in my living room with Shayne McClendon and me. Working with her taught me a great deal and I will always cherish that period in my life.

To the readers, thank you for taking a chance on me.